ROGUE WHALER

ROGUE WHALER

by Rita Ritchie

W · W · NORTON & CO · INC ·

New York

This book is for
Michael J. Kondos
with thanks.

Contents

Contents

Author's Note

THE HARPOON, the principal weapon used in the capture of a whale, was originally known as a harping iron, and in the language of the old-time whalers, the man who used the harping iron was the harponier. Several authorities with experience aboard the old sailing whale ships have emphasized the point that whalemen did not use the term "harpooner" which has come into current usage. I have therefore employed the older word, "harponier," throughout this story.

 one

Buzzard's Bay

THERE SHE WAS! Yards slanting across the wind and sails drawing full, the whaling bark sped in toward Buzzard's Bay.

Toby Clayton, breathing hard from his climb up the steep hill, dropped his bundle at the side of the cart-rutted road and stood watching the vessel reaching for the distant harbor, glittering under a bright June sun.

Before him, New Bedford gently sloped down to Buzzard's Bay, the shaded streets laid out as plumb as the oaken keels which spined the town's famous whaling vessels. Wharves, long and broad, neatly squared the waterfront into docks and slipways. A forest of masts reached for the sky, and their yards perched cockbilled or hung aback with sails clewed up, drying, or furled smartly. Here and there showed the gaunt ribs of vessels a-building, or broad encrusted hulls hove down for breaming.

And far out the bark *Rogue* drew a creamy line upon the intense blue of the ocean. She was Toby Clayton's vessel, coming home to fetch him out to sea.

Blunt-bowed and beamy as a good whaler should be, the bark stepped three masts, the first two crossed by yards squaring sails between them, while the sternmost mast spread a fore-and-aft spanker from gaff to boom. Certain details, such as the jaunty rake of her jibboom and the slant of her counter, identified her as surely as the painted name which was too far away to read.

Toby knew the *Rogue* well from the carefully labeled drawing sent to him by Captain Noah Clayton, her owner and Toby's uncle. That was two years ago, in 1833, just before another of his uncle's Pacific whaling voyages. Captain Noah had agreed to sign Toby on as cabin boy when he returned from that cruise, his first as master of his newly purchased *Rogue*.

Now the *Rogue* was coming home, and Toby had a new reason to be glad of her arrival. With her return he could begin supporting himself. While he knew he was welcome as part of the family, he did not want to become a burden to Captain Noah and Aunt Prudence. He would stand on his own two feet, though he stood alone. For Toby Clayton had neither parents nor home.

His loss had come suddenly. One day he had been walking behind the ox-drawn plow on his father's farm, helping to fit the fields for the spring planting, impatient for the end of grammar school and the start of his journey to New Bedford, there to stay with his aunt and await the return of the *Rogue*. Yet the next day, or so it seemed, Toby had stood at the graveside of both parents who had died of the smallpox which had whipped through the little farming community. He had gone back to the home which was soon to be taken from him to satisfy his father's debts, to sort and pack the memory-laden possessions. Neighbors had taken him in while he finished his schooling, and both the blacksmith and the miller had offered apprenticeships.

But Toby's mind had been filled with visions of the distant sea and the lift of a ship's deck as canvas boomed over the roar of waves. And so he had determined to carry out his original plans, drawn both by the whaling bark *Rogue* and the secret of the paper he had found among his father's belongings.

This paper he had placed in the pouch of small coins strapped to his belt beneath his coat for the journey to New Bedford.

For the next five days Toby Clayton had trudged the rutted roads, fording rivers, eating the johnnycake he carried in his bundle of possessions, and chopping wood at farms in exchange for a night's lodging in barn or stable. When the chance offered, he had helped load a wagon, earning a ride for several miles, or found an inn where a few pennies bought a sturdy meal.

Now he stood on the last hill, New Bedford descending before him and, like a miracle, the *Rogue* herself winging in toward Buzzard's Bay.

Shouldering his bundle, Toby started down the sloping road that soon turned into a shaded cobbled street. He marveled at the large houses set well back among trees, at the many shops and stores, and at the numbers of people, horses, and wagons moving about purposefully. Nearing the harbor he passed buildings bearing the signs of rope-walks, sail lofts, chandler's shops, smithies, and boatbuild-ers. Rounding the corner of a huge brick warehouse, Toby came out on the great open wharves.

Hulls loomed vast and dark against the sun-struck water, their spars pointing skyward. Toby was pleased to find that from the descriptions his uncle had written he could identify the rigging of ship, bark, brig, and other vessels. The harbor rang with the thudding caulker's mallet, the rasping cooper's saw, squealing blocks and tackles, and the trundling of whale-oil casks unloading from a nearby ship. The air was charged with the richness of raw wood, the pungence of hot tar, the sourness of new manila line, and the tang of wet seaweed covering the acres of full oil casks against shrinking.

This was the world of the sea's edge, and Toby Clayton walked through it in wonder and joy. He saw riggers swarming over a brigantine, and, close by, masons bricked in trypots on the deck of a newly built sloop. At an open shed two longshoremen were weighing long staves of whalebone. Horse-drawn carts piled high with ship's stores and whalecraft rumbled urgently among the moored vessels. A blacksmith's boy paused on his errand to speak with a spar-turner's assistant. Sailors bearing sea chests strode to a waiting vessel. Here and there idled well-dressed men, keel backed, their faces leathered and white bearded, probably retired masters come to taste again the realm of ships and the sea.

As Toby passed two such strollers, he heard one of them mention the *Rogue*.

The two old men were holding a newspaper between them as one ran his finger down a column. "Here she be! Bark *Rogue*, spoke off Hatteras by fishing schooner. Estimated arrival June 12." He looked in triumph at his friend. "That's her coming in now, right on schedule. Told ye I couldn't mistake the *Rogue*."

"Aye," his companion acknowledged. "*Rogue* she's named and rogue she be. Scarcely a Captain owns his own vessel. And this particular bark—why, she's well-founded, her keel straight as an arrow, and scarce twenty-five year old. Noah Clayton fell into good luck when the Zephyr Company changed from whalers to packets."

" 'Tis greasy luck he'll be needing now to keep her out of bankers' hands," replied the first man. "Though they do say Captain Clayton can fetch up spouts in the midst of a desert. 'Tis a man like that should sail a vessel of his own, 'stead of hiring out to a company."

By the time Toby reached the end of the wharf the whaling bark *Rogue* had passed the islands that marked the entrance of Buzzard's Bay. Her broad bows lifted from the sea as she drove into the harbor under taut-bellied canvas. Toby's heart swelled with pride.

It was not long before he could make out the men working on deck, and he pictured Captain Noah calling orders from his station beside the helmsman. Now the bark was shortening sail, slowing toward her mooring. At last, backing her yards, she swung into the wind, halting, and let go the anchors.

Almost immediately one of the whaleboats lowered, and under expert hands it rapidly pulled toward shore. The boat carried two passengers in the reefers and billed caps of officers. Toby waited by the landing ladder, wondering if he could recognize his uncle from a resemblance to his father.

The boat came in smartly. The oarsmen fended off, then steadied the craft as the two officers climbed up the ladder.

Toby studied the side whiskers and mustache framing the wide-boned face of one and the lean-cheeked bearded features of the other, then voiced his uncertainty. "Captain Noah?"

The man with the wide-boned whiskered face glanced at him coldly. "Don't bother us, boy."

But the other with his lean bearded cheeks paused in front of Toby, forcing his companion to an impatient halt. "I'm Mr. Hughs, the First Mate. Do you have a message for Captain Noah?"

"He's my uncle," Toby said. Then, half afraid that the Mate's rude companion would prove to be his relative, he added hopefully, "Is he still aboard the *Rogue?*"

The Mate said, "So you're Captain Noah's nephew! Did your aunt send you to meet him, Toby? I have sad news for you. Your uncle died three weeks ago at sea."

Toby took a step backward. Captain Noah dead? Sunshine winked hotly from the harbor, gulls creaked as they wheeled in the sky, the white triangle of a sail moved out from a dock. The sharp smell of new paint and the zest of the sea mingled over the wharves. The *Rogue* of Toby's dreams rode her anchors. How could Captain Noah be dead?

The First Mate added, "There's another thing—"

"Why tell him?" interrupted the man with the whisker-framed face. "He has nothing to do with it. Our business is with Clayton's widow."

The First Mate's mouth tightened, but he spoke gently to Toby. "Come with us, then, while we break the news to your aunt."

"None of that!" exclaimed the other. "We'll go direct to the Marine Traders Bank. Mrs. Clayton can meet us there. Come along, Hughs!" The insolent fellow began striding up the wharf.

With an apologetic shrug to Toby, First Mate Hughs followed, and where street met quay, Toby saw him hail a carriage. The two men got in and trotted off. Glancing seaward, Toby watched the whaleboat which had brought the officers hauling back to the *Rogue* where the crew was busily putting a harbor stow on the sails.

The whaling bark looked as trim and disciplined as if her Captain-owner still held the quarter-deck. That would be the product of First Mate Hughs's authority, Toby realized, for as the highest ranking officer aboard he would have assumed command upon Captain Noah's death. But then all the more puzzling was the behavior of the other man who had been brought ashore in the whaleboat.

That man had to be a junior officer, yet he had spoken and acted insultingly to his superior. And while First Mate Hughs had plainly disliked the man's conduct, still he had tolerated his junior's insubordination.

And now other questions crowded into Toby's mind. How had Captain Noah died? What would happen to the *Rogue?* Did the "other thing" the First Mate mentioned have anything to do with the whaling bark?

The paper in the pouch on his belt made this very much Toby's business. He strode off the wharf, walking beside piles of ship's gear and whalecraft, and stacks of raw yards near the spar shops. He went past the warehouses and marine stores, the oil refineries, the candle factories, the whalebone trimmers.

He found the main street, wide, shaded and cobbled, and thick with traffic. He walked up one side, carefully reading the signs on the buildings. Then, dodging a fast

carriage and a heavy freight wagon, he crossed the street
and went down the other side. At last he saw the words
"Marine Traders Bank" in gilt on a very dignified-looking
brick building. Mounting the wooden steps, Toby pulled
open the heavy ironbound door and stepped into the
lobby.

It was dark and cool after the warm sun outside, and
smelled heavily of polish. A wooden counter ran around
three sides of the room, fenced in with brass rails. It en-
closed three or four desks over which clerks were bent,
studying papers or scribbling in huge ledgers. Two doors
were in the wall behind them. A cramped staircase led to
floors above and below.

A voice floated out from behind the counter. "Yes?" A
man rose from one of the desks and opening a section of
the counter came out to Toby. He was tall and spare, balding and pinch-faced, and he spoke with an elaborate for-
mality. "Whom did you wish to see?"

Suddenly conscious of his homespun garments and
country shoes, dusty from a week of travel, and the grimy
bundle he carried, Toby flushed. But he thought of the
paper in his pouch and remembered that he had every
right to be here. "I want to see—" Who, indeed? He looked
fruitlessly for a sign or notice. "I have to see the banker."

A smile quirked the man's mouth. But just then one of
the inner doors opened, and a man in sea clothes stepped
out. It was First Mate Hughs, his face set grimly. Before

the door closed behind him, Toby had a glimpse of people in a paneled office, among them the other officer.

Toby started to speak to the First Mate, but the bank clerk stepped in front of him, screening his view as he escorted the officer to the door.

Swiftly Toby went through the counter opening. One of the seated clerks began to rise, but Toby quickly opened the inner door from which the First Mate had come, and stepped inside.

Three people grouped about a walnut desk looked up with an air of interruption. The insolent officer gazed at Toby directly. The broad face, framed by his whiskers, seemed impassive, and his eyes, instead of reflecting his thoughts, were but twin masks for his mind.

Next to him sat a woman who was apparently serene from her close-fitting bonnet to the hem of her rather plain skirt. This must be Prudence Clayton, Toby's aunt. By now she would know of her husband's death. For a moment Toby felt her pain in remembering his own loss.

Behind the desk sat a stout clean-shaven man with a kindly face and a heavy gold chain across his vest. There was a worried furrow in his brow, but seeing Toby, he quickly smoothed it and spoke benignly. "I think you have the wrong door, young man."

"No, sir. I'm Toby Clayton."

Surprise lighted the banker's face and he stood up. "Well, well, Master Toby Clayton! Captain Noah spoke of you often." He shook Toby's hand. "I'm Giles Thaxter, a close friend of the family. And this is your Aunt Prudence."

Aunt Prudence inclined her head toward him. "You are welcome, Toby, though I did not expect you so early in the summer. Did your journey go well?"

"Yes, ma'am," he said, and because of her drawn face and pale color he decided to postpone increasing her sorrow with news of his parents' death.

Banker Thaxter gestured to the officer who sat holding his sea cap on his knee. "Toby, this is Mr. Peter Flick. He was Third Mate on the *Rogue*'s voyage. The bark arrived not an hour ago."

"Yes, sir. I saw her sail into Buzzard's Bay." He turned to his aunt. "Mrs. Clayton—I mean, Aunt Prudence, ma'am—I was sorry to hear about Captain Noah. The First Mate, Mr. Hughs, told me."

Third Mate Peter Flick glanced distastefully at Toby as he spoke to Giles Thaxter. "Let's get on with our business. I have to pay off the crew and begin unloading."

The banker returned to his chair behind the desk. "Yes, of course. Er, Toby, will you wait outside?"

Aunt Prudence spoke up. "He is part of the family, Giles, and this affair concerns him also as he was to have sailed with Noah." She faced her nephew. "The *Rogue* is lost, Toby. Mr. Flick owns her now."

"She's lost, ma'am? How can Mr. Flick—" Toby was bewildered. "I mean, you're Captain Noah's wife. . . ."

"True, but I do not inherit the *Rogue*. Before Noah died, his vessel had already passed out of his hands." She glanced at the banker. "Explain it to him, Giles. And I myself would like to hear it again."

Mr. Thaxter unhappily shuffled through some papers on his desk. "Toby, your uncle sold the bark to Mr. Flick shortly before losing his life in a storm."

"That can't be!" Toby protested. "He'd just bought her. And he wouldn't sell the deck from under his feet. Besides—"

"Here is the sales agreement." Mr. Thaxter handed Toby a sheet. "This was written out by Mr. Flick and signed by him and Captain Noah." He sighed heavily. "The paper is properly drawn up, and you can see where the witness put his name."

Toby read the paper. It stated very simply that Captain Noah transferred his ownership of the whaling bark *Rogue* and all her outfit to Peter Flick in exchange for a group of six matched pearls estimated to be worth about $10,000.

Glancing at the banker's desk, Toby saw a half dozen pearls gleaming on the square of canvas in which they had been wrapped. It seemed a fortune for six lustrous baubles, but Toby knew the worth of the whaling vessel. "The *Rogue* is worth four times that much! And Captain Noah couldn't sell her—"

Aunt Prudence interrupted. "Hard indeed is it to believe he would do such a thing, although Mr. Flick keeps stressing that Noah felt it was a mistake to assume complete responsibility for a whaling venture."

Peter Flick spoke stiffly. "Ma'am, your speculations force me to tell what I had hoped to keep concealed. Captain Noah Clayton was a gambler."

"Noah—a gambler? Impossible!" exclaimed Aunt Prudence.

"True enough." Mr. Flick went on relentlessly. "His losses were never heavy, but one night I won every hand. Finally, in a burst of anger, Captain Clayton put up the chance to buy the *Rogue* cheap. I won that, too." He fingered the bill of his sea cap. "Life at sea is harsh, Mrs. Clayton. It changes men, often for the worse. Some take to drinking, and others to gambling. A master has crushing responsibilities. Why, the last time I commanded a vessel—" He broke off and gestured vaguely. "I must see about disposing of the cargo."

While he and Mr. Thaxter spoke of insurance, the current prices for various grades of whale oil, and other matters, Toby studied the sales agreement still in his hand. Beneath the signatures of Captain Noah and his Third Mate was an inked impression showing a tiny silhouette of a boat with a harponier standing in the bow, hefting his iron. Beside this was neatly penned, "Witnessed by Alexander White, Boatsteerer."

Perhaps the paper was final as far as Captain Noah was

concerned, whatever reasons he may have had for entering the agreement. But the *Rogue* could not be disposed of so easily. There was something else to be considered. "Excuse me, Mr. Thaxter!"

The men glanced up, and even the banker seemed annoyed at the interruption. Toby plunged on. "Captain Noah couldn't sell the *Rogue* because he didn't own her outright."

Peter Flick, suddenly aware that Toby still held the sales agreement, took it out of his hand as Giles Thaxter began a patient explanation. "It is very unusual for a vessel of this tonnage to have a single owner," the banker said. "It costs a large sum to supply and equip a whaler for a voyage of two to four years. And mind, young man, it could all be for nothing if the vessel fails to fetch in enough oil, or if there is serious damage to her at sea. Perhaps the vessel herself be lost." He gazed thoughtfully out the window at the blue-green patch of Buzzard's Bay gleaming distantly between buildings. "Usually several people own a whaler in partnership and hire a Captain. Then, too, one man may own shares in many different vessels. And a person can always invest any amount of money in any whaler without actually buying a part of her."

"Yes, sir," said Toby, curbing his impatience. "I reckon I can understand that. But the *Rogue* still—"

The banker continued speaking. "But your uncle, Captain Noah, wanted to be in complete charge of his vessel in port as well as at sea. He put up half the money to buy the *Rogue,* and this bank lent him the other half. But it was a personal loan, Toby, and the vessel was never mortgaged. The bank has no claim at all on the *Rogue.* Mr. Flick does indeed own her outright, even though the money Noah borrowed from us—twenty thousand dollars—must still be repaid."

Aunt Prudence added, "He means, Toby, that I must repay Noah's bank debt out of all he left to me, and not have a vessel to show for it."

Puzzled, Toby turned to the banker. "But, Mr. Thaxter, why can't the bank be paid back out of the *Rogue*'s cargo?"

Peter Flick scowled. "You're uncommonly curious!"

Giles Thaxter rearranged some papers in a folder. "Mr. Flick owns the cargo now, Toby, as well as the *Rogue* herself. Noah's debt will have to be paid out of his estate." Gently, Mr. Thaxter touched the pearls gleaming on the square of rough cloth. "These will cover just half his debt. I will keep them for a few months, however, and with luck the price may rise and they'll fetch a thousand or so more." He glanced up. "I'm sorry, Prudence."

"Nonsense, Giles," she said crisply. "The house will bring a goodly sum. Then there's the Captain's share of bone and oil—" She glanced sharply at Peter Flick. "Surely Mr. Flick will not deprive me of that?"

Peter Flick's eyes darted like terns. "Why, ma'am, that might run as high as five thousand dollars!" His knuckles showed white as his grip on his cap tightened. "Besides, Mrs. Clayton, I don't recollect that your husband signed ship's articles as is proper to merit a Captain's lay."

Mr. Thaxter spoke out with surprising firmness. "Nevertheless, Mr. Flick, the Captain shall have his wages. I doubt if any court would fault him on that."

Toby could almost feel the surge of Peter Flick's resentment, though the officer covered it with hasty capitulation. "Of course, I shall see his widow get a generous share as she stands in need," he said. "But I like it understood that I consider it entirely a matter of honor to offer her this benefit."

Aunt Prudence's mouth tightened. Giles Thaxter turned his face away, plainly distressed by the insult of Mr. Flick's pretended charity.

Toby's temper flared. "Mr. Flick, we don't need any of your bone and oil! I'll make up Captain Noah's debt myself!"

Aunt Prudence stretched out a cautioning hand, and Giles Thaxter exclaimed, "Toby!"

Peter Flick laughed mirthlessly. "Make it good indeed! And out of what, pray?"

Toby took the paper from the pouch on his belt. "I'll pay it out of my share of the cargo." Unfolding the document, he held it up before Peter Flick. "You see, I own half the *Rogue*."

 two

A Riddle and a Warning

PETER FLICK STARED as if he had been turned to stone. His voice grated harshly. "Impossible!" Then mounting anger spurred him to life. "How dare you jest with me?" His hand darted toward the paper.

As Toby swiftly stepped out of reach, he saw Mr. Flick's hand square into a fist.

Giles Thaxter cried out. "Mr. Flick, you forget yourself, sir!"

Peter Flick spoke through clenched teeth. "Quite so, Mr. Thaxter. As does the boy himself."

Aunt Prudence's face was troubled. "Toby, I must ask you to wait outside while we finish our business."

But Toby was determined to stay. "Ma'am, I walked a hundred miles on account of this paper." He held it out to the banker. "Read it, sir. You'll see I'm telling the truth."

As Giles Thaxter examined the document, Toby broached to his aunt as gently as he could the news of his parents' death. When her face reflected surprise, then grief, at his words, he quickly added, "Then I found the paper, and as well as I can reckon by it, ma'am, I inherit my father's half of the *Rogue* just as it says there in Uncle Noah's own handwriting."

Aunt Prudence's voice held a note of relief. "I am glad, Toby, that the *Rogue* does not pass entirely out of the family."

Peter Flick said fiercely, "I don't care what your father's arrangements were! The *Rogue*'s mine from jibboom to rudder post. I bought her fair and square!"

Giles Thaxter looked up from examining the paper, and gestured for attention. "Prudence, I can see that Noah never informed you of his business affairs. According to this document, which is legally drawn up, Toby's father put up half the money to purchase the *Rogue,* but had nothing to say about the operation of the vessel. He was to be a silent partner so that Noah could manage everything with a free hand. But the profits from each voyage were to be divided evenly between the brothers."

Peter Flick broke in angrily. "What about the sales agreement Captain Noah Clayton signed?" He faced Aunt Prudence. "Share the pearls with your nephew, ma'am, if you will. But no one takes the *Rogue* from me!"

The banker shook his head. "Nor is she to be taken from Toby, sir, for as his father's heir he now owns one half the vessel. Noah could sell only his half, not his brother's. And I might add, sir, that under these circumstances the price

Noah accepted from you for his share of the *Rogue* appears more reasonable." Mr. Thaxter allowed himself the trace of a smile. "You and the boy are partners now, Mr. Flick. It'll be share and share alike for every voyage."

The officer protested bitterly. "He didn't mention that in the sales agreement, Captain Clayton didn't, sir! How was I ever to know?"

Aunt Prudence spoke, tart with impatience. "Doubtless Noah would have informed you before reaching port, Mr. Flick, had he not died so suddenly. Perhaps at the time of signing the agreement he had other matters on his mind."

Peter Flick's face drained white. Words seemed at last to be reaching him, touching some cord deep within, forcing him to accept the facts. He muttered, "What of the cargo, Mr. Thaxter—what of that?"

The banker's face was bland. "Why, half to Toby, of course." He turned to Mr. Flick's youthful partner. "Young man, shall I act for you in business affairs? Someone must, as you are under age."

"Yes, sir, I'd be obliged if you would," Toby replied. "And I meant what I said before. I want to pay Captain Noah's debt out of my half of the cargo."

"Wait!" exclaimed Peter Flick. "When a partner dies, the other partner inherits the business, not his kin. What of that, Mr. Thaxter?"

The banker raised his eyebrows. "Did I fail to read that part aloud? In the ordinary way, you would be right, Mr.

Flick, and the surviving partner would assume full owner-ship of the *Rogue*. But the way this partnership paper is drawn up, an heir is named for each of the brothers: Toby for his father, and Prudence Clayton for Captain Noah. Prudence, of course, does not inherit Noah's half of the *Rogue* because he sold it to you."

"Excuse me, Mr. Thaxter," Toby said. "Could I name Aunt Prudence to inherit my share of the *Rogue?*"

Giles Thaxter slowly shook his head. "That isn't in the partnership paper, Toby. You and Mr. Flick might draw up a new agreement between you, naming heirs, but as of now the ordinary rules are in effect. That means that if something should happen to either one of you the surviv-ing partner assumes full ownership of the *Rogue*. Of course, you may sell your share of the bark any time you wish."

Peter Flick leaned toward Toby, speaking swiftly. "I'll buy your half of the vessel with my share of the cargo. That'll come to some twenty thousand dollars after the crew and outfit's been paid for. You'll have close on forty thousand dollars in your kit, boy. Think of it!"

Toby felt shaken. Forty thousand dollars! Ought he to accept? He glanced at Aunt Prudence and Giles Thaxter in a mute plea for instruction. But neither face expressed advice. Toby was on his own.

He recalled how his vision of the *Rogue* shouldering aside the big waves had carried him through grammar school and the rounds of farm chores, tasks from which he derived little joy. Like his uncle, Captain Noah, Toby longed to slip the hawser binding him to the immobile land. Had his father sensed this in him? Perhaps that was why he had put up the farm to borrow the money to buy the *Rogue,* and why he had it written down that Toby was to own half of her.

He faced his partner. "I reckon I'll keep her, Mr. Flick."

The officer's eyes looked like coiled serpents. "You may come to change your mind later." The words sounded very nearly like a threat. He spoke more briskly to Giles Thaxter. "About that advance, sir, I must pay off the men at once."

The banker rose. "Yes, we'll carry on with the vessel's business as we decided, Mr. Flick. And I will act for Toby. Meanwhile let's put that sales agreement between you and Captain Noah in a good secure place."

"It'll lie snug in the *Rogue*'s safe," Peter Flick said.

But Mr. Thaxter was already at the door, speaking to one of his clerks. Turning back, he explained apologetically. "I am afraid you must humor a banker, Mr. Flick. A vessel can be lost, but if this paper is safe on dry land, you can the more readily prove your ownership and thereby collect the insurance handily. Otherwise you might be put through a great deal of inconvenience. Ah, here are the deposit boxes. We'll put Toby's paper in the other one."

The thin, balding chief clerk set two metal boxes on the

desk and handed keys to Mr. Thaxter. The banker held
out his hand for the sales agreement, and grudgingly Peter
Flick gave it up. Toby saw the dark smudge of the boatsteerer's seal folded outward as Mr. Thaxter put the paper
into a box and locked it, keeping one key and giving the
other to Mr. Flick. Then the banker locked up the partnership paper Toby had brought with him, but he kept
both keys. The clerk took the boxes away to some unreach-
able part of the bank.

Mr. Thaxter went to the safe in the corner, speaking
over his shoulder as he unlocked the heavy iron door. "You
may both have access to your own deposit boxes any time
you wish. Just apply to my chief clerk. Let's see—thirty,
forty. . . ." He rapidly counted out a pack of various bills
he had taken from the safe, then slipped them into a large
envelope.

Peter Flick signed for the money and Mr. Thaxter escorted him to the door. "Good day, Mr. Flick."

The officer looked affronted. "*Captain.* It's Captain
Flick now, isn't it, Mr. Thaxter?"

"Why—uh—by all means, Captain Flick."

"Another thing," the officer said. "That partnership
paper between Captain Noah and his brother named heirs,
and you're holding me to that. Now the ship's articles
don't say anything about a Captain's share for Noah Clayton, and I'm holding you to that."

Mr. Thaxter looked troubled, but Toby agreed at once.

"Aunt Prudence, you can have the Captain's share out of my cargo money."

Captain Flick barked a laugh. "You're so freehanded with your riches, boy, you'll soon find you've nothing to live on."

"I'll be earning my way," Toby answered. "I'm signing on for the *Rogue*'s next voyage."

Aunt Prudence whispered, "No, Toby!"

Captain Flick's face hardened. "Better find out what sea life is like first!" Then he closed the door behind him.

Aunt Prudence's face was grim. "Toby, I fear to have you aboard the vessel with that man."

Giles Thaxter carefully wrapped up the six pearls in their cloth. "Perhaps Toby will reconsider—"

"No, sir. The *Rogue*'s my vessel and I'll sail in her till I work up to be her Captain myself. I don't fear hard work. I've done plenty of it."

The banker smiled wistfully. "Very few boys can start out in life the way you can with all this money, Toby. Stay ashore. Let me invest your share of the cargo. You could go on with your schooling, travel like a young gentleman, or set up in some trade."

"He must learn a profession," Aunt Prudence said thoughtfully. "Law, or perhaps medicine."

Toby shook his head stubbornly. "The money's to go for Captain Noah's debt and if anything's left over 'tis for Aunt Prudence. After all, ma'am, I'll need some kind of home between voyages. For I do mean to go to sea."

They both argued, but Toby was unshakable. At last they had to let him have his way, "for the time being," said Aunt Prudence, rising to go.

Mr. Thaxter said, "I'll see the vessel's papers are sent over when Captain Flick is done with them, Prudence. They belong to you, along with all of Captain Noah's personal effects."

Riding homeward in the carriage Mr. Thaxter had called for them, Toby asked, "Aunt Prudence, is Mr.—I mean, Captain—Flick a New Bedford man?"

She shook her head firmly. "He comes from farther down the coast, Toby. Connecticut, it may be. He'd lost two whaling vessels under his command, and had trouble finding a berth. Noah met him shortly before the *Rogue* sailed. He felt sorry for the man, and thought to train him to be a better officer. Peter Flick signed on as Third Mate."

The Clayton house, Toby saw when they reached it, was more modest than its neighbors, but like them it was painted a sparkling white and set in a neat lawn with a flourishing garden behind. Aunt Prudence prepared a late lunch, and by the time Toby finished helping her with the washing up, a messenger from the bank had left the bundle of the bark's papers and Captain Noah's sea chest. Aunt Prudence, excusing herself with a headache, retired to her room.

Toby idled around the parlor, looking at the curious objects Captain Noah had brought home from distant lands. Bamboo chairs stood on brightly dyed coconut mats. The mantelpiece boasted a huge polished turtle carapace and a dozen large and wonderful shells from the coral seas. In one corner stood a cabinet containing many items carved from whale ivory—wheels for crimping pie crust, knitting needles, thread reels, inkstands. There were paper knives of mahogany, a jewel box of teak, and a model ship whittled from pine. Aunt Prudence had called this handiwork "scrimshaw," explaining that Captain Noah had carved it all himself during his voyages.

The parlor walls were hung with pictures of many kinds of vessels, but the *Rogue* was not there. That drawing had been sent to Toby, with all the lines and sails neatly labeled by Captain Noah, and the margins filled with sketches of knots to practice. The picture lay, rolled, in Toby's unopened pack. He must give it back to Aunt Prudence before he himself set sail in the whaler that was now half his own.

What kind of vessel was the *Rogue?* Was she sea-kindly? What sort of voyage did she make? Had something gone wrong with her so that Captain Noah sold her his first chance?

On the table beside the lamp lay the books and papers of the *Rogue's* last voyage. Toby began turning them over, then took them up and went out into the kitchen garden where he could feel and smell the sea breeze under the hot

June sun.

Wedging his back comfortably against an apple tree, he began with the ship's articles. This was a printed paragraph setting forth the object of the voyage, which was the getting of whales and such work as to render the catch into oil. The long white space below and an additional sheet bore each crewman's signature, his rating aboard the bark *Rogue,* and his lay, or share of bone and oil for which he agreed to work ship.

Among the thirty-three Yankee names scrawled on the articles were many devices: a clever drawing of a whale spouting, several X's with "His mark" followed by the man's name written in for him, the sketch of a sailor's knot known as a carrick bend, and the stamped silhouette of a boatsteerer with harpoon in hand which Toby remembered from the sales agreement he had seen in the bank. This impression showed details more clearly, and beneath it, as beneath the other, was written the name of Alexander White, Boatsteerer.

A boatsteerer's lay was $\frac{1}{70}$. Out of every seventy barrels of whale oil stowed down, Boatsteerer White owned one, plus a proportionate share of bone. These goods he was obliged to sell back to the vessel when they made home port. Indeed, by now he had received his money, if he had not squandered it during the voyage.

Toby turned to the account book, kept by Third Mate Peter Flick. Here were listed the changes in the ratings and lays of various men throughout the two-year voyage. Some had risen in rank, two had been disrated for disobedience, and one had been paid off and set ashore in New Zealand at his own request. There was a page for each crewman, and on this was an undated list of every item and its price bought from the vessel's store. There was occasionally a note of money borrowed for shoreside spending. Finding Alexander White's name, Toby shook his head over the man's extravagance. The boatsteerer had borrowed heavily against his future earnings, and bought freely from the *Rogue*'s slop chest. Charged against him were chewing tobacco, razors, soap, and many articles of clothing. Alexander White must have been the cleanest and best-dressed sailor afloat, and by now the poorest ashore.

Toby turned to the logbook. It was an ordinary ledger with the inked title: "Voyage of the bark *Rogue*, 1833 to ———" The second date had not yet been filled in. Riffling through pages spidered with Captain Noah's writing, he noticed here and there inked silhouettes of whales. Next to each stamp was written the number of barrels of oil the animal had yielded, or sometimes there was a comment like "Drawed iron," and "Gallied, made off with line." Toby paged past a gale in October, 1833, a record cut of five whales in the Off the River Grounds, a leak of 1,500 strokes a day on the Line (they put into Ponape to repair a sprung strake), and the recruiting of some Maoris in New Zealand, followed by names of exotic islands as the

Rogue humpbacked through the South Pacific. A boat was stove one Saturday last February, but for many days throughout the logbook little was recorded but the bark's position. Nothing seemed to foreshadow Captain Noah's abrupt sale of his share of the *Rogue*. And then, near the end of the book, Captain Noah's handwriting stopped and a new pen took over. Toby read:

"Wednesday, May 20, 1835. Begins with ESE wind freshening. About 11 AM reefed topgallants, took in staysails. Half-gale at 2 PM. Reefed topsails, took in flying and outer jibs. Whales raised but let go. Captain Clayton killed on deck by shifting casks, and committed to the sea. Full gale by 7 PM. Hove to. Lat. 24° 14′ N., Long. 66 27′ E. First Mate Hughs writing this and assuming command of the vessel. So ends this day."

Toby read the rest of the log closely, but learned only that the First Mate had pressed on for New Bedford. The last entry reported raising Buzzard's Bay, but should have included coming to anchor and the paying off of the crew. Perhaps it was at this point that Third Mate Peter Flick revealed his ownership of the vessel to Mr. Hughs and the logbook remained incomplete.

That afternoon friends and neighbors came to call. They brought condolences and, often, a dish or a cake. Feeling awkward and useless in the house, Toby spent the time hoeing and weeding the kitchen garden. His only contacts with Captain Noah were a long letter, much of it sailor's instruction, and the annotated drawing of the *Rogue*. He wished he could really have known his uncle, and could have shipped out under him to learn of life at sea.

Toby and Aunt Prudence ate supper alone, and afterwards they sat in the parlor, talking of Captain Noah and of Toby's parents and their farm. When the doorbell rang, Toby jumped up to answer it.

He swung back the heavy door. "Mr. Hughs!" He stepped aside. "Come in, sir. Aunt Prudence is in the parlor."

The bearded First Mate, still in his sea clothes, hesitated, then recognized him. "Of course, we met at the wharf. You're Captain Noah's nephew—you're Toby." He shifted a canvas bag he carried to his other hand while he took off his cap and followed Toby into the parlor.

Mr. Hughs made a short bow in front of Aunt Prudence. "Ma'am, we are sadly met. I can't tell you how I feel about your loss, and mine too. Captain Noah was as fine a master as ever wet a keel. I should have said this when we met in the bank today, but the business in hand took it clean out of my mind."

Toby remembered Mr. Hughs's silent anger as he left the bank. Plainly, the officer felt the injustice of Captain Noah's widow losing the *Rogue*.

Thanking him, Aunt Prudence gestured him to a chair. "Tell me this, Mr. Hughs. Did Noah ever gamble?"

Toby could see that the words astonished the First Mate. "Why, no, ma'am! And I've sailed with him two voyages —in the *Benjamin Franklin,* and then his own *Rogue.*"

She waved an impatient hand. "Mr. Hughs, I pray you not to be kind. It is important for me to understand why Noah sold his vessel. Mr. Flick claims it was to settle a gambling loss."

The First Mate shook his head decisively. " 'Tis hard to keep secrets aboard a vessel, ma'am. We're all jammed in together with hardly room to swing a mackerel. I take my oath that Captain Noah never gambled, neither cards nor dice."

Something tugged at Toby's memory. "Mr. Hughs, did you know Alexander White?"

"Alex? He was Captain Noah's boatsteerer."

"He couldn't read, could he? I mean, sir, on the articles he signed his name with a stamp instead of really writing it out."

Mr. Hughs nodded. "That's right. I supervised those articles. We always read them out to the sailors before they sign because so many of them can't read, having gone to sea before they had their schooling. Is anything wrong?"

"If Alex White couldn't read what it was that Captain Noah and Mr. Flick were signing, I reckon Captain Noah meant to keep the sale of his vessel quiet."

Aunt Prudence leaned forward. "Toby means that Noah could keep a secret when he wanted to, Mr. Hughs, even supposing he did gamble."

Mr. Hughs looked thoughtful a moment, then shrugged. "Well, ma'am, Captain Noah did not confide such in me, and I did not hear any scuttlebutt about gambling. As for selling his vessel in mid-ocean, it came as a shock for me when Peter Flick stepped up to call her his own just after we raised Buzzard's Bay."

Toby asked, "Mr. Hughs, exactly how did Captain Noah —I mean—" He broke off, remembering Aunt Prudence.

But the First Mate understood his question. "It happened in the midafternoon watch. A gale was in the making and the *Rogue* was pitching lively. We had some full oil casks lashed on deck. Just then whales were raised and Captain Noah came up on deck. He was passing abeam the oil casks when the lashings parted and the casks tumbled over on him. We were quick to get them off, but 'twas too late. He just had time to pass a message to me before he died." He fumbled with the bill of his cap. "I'm sorry, ma'am. I'd like to tell you kinder, but that is the truth of it."

Aunt Prudence, her face ashen and lips tight, nodded. "Thank you, Mr. Hughs." Her voice was a strained whisper.

Toby could see that First Mate Hughs had not meant to hurt his Captain's widow. Life at sea had shaped him to face squarely the harshest reality.

Aunt Prudence cleared her throat. "And the message?"

A puzzled look came into the First Mate's eyes. "It was for Toby. Captain Noah said, 'Mr. Hughs, tell Toby to look through the devil's eye.' "

"What does that mean?" Toby asked. "What's the devil's eye?" He could not remember any sailing term like that.

Mr. Hughs shook his head slowly. "All I can say is perhaps he was too near the end for making any sense. He wasn't even looking at me when he said it, though he called me by name." He sighed, then pulled open the canvas sea bag. "I brought some of his things from the *Rogue,* ma'am, whatever wasn't in his sea chest, seeing as Mr. Flick didn't take many pains. If there's anything I forgot, I'll gladly go back aboard after it." He laid the bag's contents out on the parlor table. There were spare sea boots, writing case, letters, some books, a penknife, sheath knife, pipe, tobacco, flint and steel, a small oil painting of Prudence Clayton, and many other personal items. "I would have brought his charts, ma'am, but I figured they belonged with the vessel, and seeing as he sold—"

"Quite right, Mr. Hughs."

Among Captain Noah's things were four or five pegs whittled from whale ivory, each about the size and shape of a man's thumb. Toby picked one up. An ink-smeared silhouette of a whale was carved in one end. "Is this scrimshaw, Mr. Hughs?"

"Those are whale stamps, Toby. They make it handier to keep the log. Captain Noah scrimshawed them himself when he became a master."

Mr. Hughs and Aunt Prudence talked about Captain Noah for a while, and then the First Mate took his leave. As Toby went to let him out, Mr. Hughs paused at the door. "Toby, you were meant to sail with Captain Noah, weren't you? He spoke of it now and again. If you still want to go to sea, I'll gladly find you a vessel."

"I have a berth already, sir. In the *Rogue.*"

Mr. Hughs studied him a moment. "She won't be the same with Captain Noah gone. Peter Flick's her master now." He glanced down the hall to the parlor door, then lowered his voice. "I don't like the way Peter Flick suddenly got to be owner of the *Rogue,* nor his highhanded manner once he claimed his vessel. None of this business sits well with me, and to tell the truth I mean to ship out in the first berth I can find before anyone can draw me into some unpleasantness."

"You reckon someone might accuse you of—"

"—of anything that would suit Mr. Flick's purposes, whatever they might be." Mr. Hughs looked as grim as when he had left the bank that morning. "Likely everything's legal and proper, but I don't care for Peter Flick. He's a bad sailor and a mean fellow, and looks out only for his own advantage. He'll ride his crew hard and hungry."

Toby felt some of his resolve weakening. But surely Captain Flick would not be foolish enough to ill-use the men who pulled his riches out of the sea. "How did he treat the crew on the *Rogue*'s last voyage?"

"Well enough, but he was only Third Mate then. There was a master and two mates above to help him keep his bad temper. Any of the same crew signing on again will get the surprise of their lives once land drops astern. Toby, take my advice. Don't sail in the *Rogue*."

"The *Rogue* was my uncle's vessel, sir. And now she's mine."

Mr. Hughs shook his head in dismay. "You'll earn every penny six times over, and before the voyage is out you'll wish a hundred times you'd never left New Bedford."

 three

Rainy Night

IT WAS A CHILL and gloomy September morning when Toby Clayton joined the line of seamen standing outside a chandler's shop at the foot of the wharf where the *Rogue* was secured. Like the sailors, Toby was dressed in jersey shirt, canvas sea jacket, dark-blue denim pants, and knitted watch cap. And like them he was waiting to sign articles inside the shop for the *Rogue*'s whaling voyage. In four days the bark would put out to sea.

He shivered in the wind whipping up fretful harbor whitecaps. The windows of the shops and forges along the wharves were cheerful with fire and lantern light. But no one lingered outside if he could help it, for the sky promised a long slow rain.

In the past weeks Toby had watched the *Rogue* being brought into dock and hove down. He had seen her hull scraped, repaired, and caulked. Then riggers and carpenters had swarmed over her, replacing and repairing. On Captain Flick's orders a door had been cut between steerage and the officers' dining saloon to provide a second exit from the boatsteerers' quarters in case of emergency. Toby reluctantly admitted to himself that so far Peter Flick was proving a suitable master for the *Rogue*, though it was only because Mr. Thaxter encouraged him to visit his office that Toby knew the business of the vessel.

Now the whaler was taut and ready, wagonload after wagonload of boxes and barrels crammed into her holds, hull glistening with new paint, black with a broad white stripe. The white band had black squares resembling a frigate's gun ports painted on to frighten away possible pirates and warlike Pacific Islanders.

The line of sailors moved up, and Toby squeezed inside the warm stuffy chandler's shop. Bright with its whale-oil lamp, the store was crowded with noisy whalemen. Many, after signing the articles at the wooden counter, left the line to mill among the goods for sale.

At one end of the counter the chandler and Captain Flick were talking. The line, moving, brought Toby close enough to hear the shopkeeper say, "I have here a remarkable new invention for the getting of whales, Captain. No longer will your irons draw and let your prize escape."

Captain Flick spoke coldly. "I doubt not it costs more than an ordinary hand iron."

"Nothing to you, sir," replied the chandler. "Only try it out, and perhaps you can recommend it to other Captains." He drew from beneath the counter what looked to

Toby like an ordinary percussion rifle, except that it was shorter and heavier. The chandler said, "A harpoon gun, sir, working exactly like a musket, and invented by New Bedford's own Mr. Tenpenny. Just load, aim, and fire— and your whale's as good as in casks."

Captain Flick drew his head back. "Explosive, sir? I won't have weapons in my vessel. Can't have the crew getting wild ideas. Don't trust the men with gunpowder, sir!"

"This is quite safe, Captain," the chandler said. "When you set this lever here, the gun cannot be shot accidentally."

The Captain picked up the harpoon gun, examining it carefully while the chandler explained its various details. It seemed the gun was loaded exactly like a regular musket, only instead of a ball being rammed down the barrel, the shaft of a harpoon was inserted, the four-flued head remaining outside the muzzle. To this was fastened the whaleline. Extra darts came with the gun.

Captain Flick swung the gun to his shoulder several times. "It'll be unhandy in a seaway."

"You needn't aim careful, as the iron drives deep," said the chandler. "Mr. Tenpenny has split three-inch oaken planks with it." His voice softened with persuasion, and Captain Flick's eyes became thoughtful.

Suddenly those eyes focused sharply on Toby, the brows lifting in surprise. "Come here," Captain Flick ordered him, setting the harpoon gun back on the counter.

Toby followed the Captain to a deserted corner. Captain Flick said, "So you're determined to go. I warn you, lad, there'll be no nursemaiding on this voyage."

"I know that, sir."

"And I won't have you for cabin boy or galley mate or any other kind of idler. You'll turn to with the men or stay ashore."

Toby spoke up. "You'll find I'm willing enough to work hard for my own vessel. Never fear, sir."

Captain Flick's jaw was set like a sprung trap in the framework of his whiskers. "You don't sign up here. Come to the bank the day before we sail, sometime after noon. There'll be a particular paper waiting. Meanwhile, keep your tongue belayed about our business." Dismissing Toby with a nod, he went back to the chandler. "All right, I'll take along Mr. Tenpenny's harpoon gun. But, mind, I don't promise to use it!"

As Toby pushed his way through the crowd toward the door, a seaman called out to him, "What's the matter, little feller, the Cap'n toss back the undersize ones?"

The sailors guffawed, and the catcalls sprang up. Toby's ears burned, and he was glad to slam the shop door behind him. Cramming his hands in his jacket pockets, he began walking off the wharf.

A voice behind called, "Hey, you, there!"

He glanced back at a young seaman hurrying up to him. He was a freckled and red-haired youth of about Toby's own age, and he bore the faint swagger of an experienced whaleman. Gray eyes studied Toby with friendliness. "My name is Ben Valentine, and I signed on as able seaman. I saw the Captain turn you down. Don't feel bad about—"

"He didn't turn me down!" Toby said heatedly. "He can't keep me out of the vessel. Why, I own half of the *Rogue!*"

Ben Valentine paused, startled. Then laughing, he cuffed Toby on the shoulder. "Oh, come off being sore-headed! You're new on the wharf, ain't you? I'll help you find a berth if you like."

Toby's lips framed a retort, but it dissolved under Ben Valentine's cheerfulness and obvious good will. "Thanks, Ben, but I really am sailing in the *Rogue*. Captain Flick is going to get up a special paper for me to sign."

"Are you going to be an apprentice?"

That meant that besides learning the seaman's trade Toby would also receive officer's training from the Captain and Mates. "I—I reckon so."

Ben looked thoughtful. "Can't say as I heard of but two or three apprentices in the whaling trade, and they were owners' sons." He grinned suddenly. "Say, are you really half owner of the *Rogue?* That makes you and Captain Flick partners, don't it?"

Toby caught the implication. He said determinedly, "I'll work my way, you'll see."

The young seaman glanced at the ground. "I wasn't saying you was an idler." He looked up. "If you mean to really work, all you got to do is pass the word to Mr. Barksdale. He's to be First Mate. What's your name?"

Toby told him, and shook Ben's calloused hand with his plow-hardened one. Ben looked so surprised that Toby laughed. The red-haired youth clapped him on the shoulder. "You're all right, Toby Clayton! I'll help you learn the ropes aboard, if you like. See you in four days."

They went in opposite directions, Ben Valentine heading for Johnnycake Hill where most of the sailors' boardinghouses were located. Toby went home feeling that he would have at least one friend in the *Rogue*.

The afternoon before the *Rogue* was to trip her anchor, Toby was preparing to go to the bank when the doorbell rang. He hurried to the front hall.

A man in faded canvas sea clothes stood awkwardly on the stoop. Wind and sea had aged him as it aged driftwood, stripping away the outer softness, leaving sinew stark against the bone like the gaunt grain of a waterworn branch. He was carelessly shaved, wiry whiskers spiking his seamed leathery face. But the knotty hand which swept his cloth-billed cap from his gray head could have crushed an oar. His voice—gale-roughened, Toby thought—declared, "I'm a-looking for the Missus. Who be ye, young feller? Oh, g'afternoon, ma'am!"

Aunt Prudence had joined Toby in the hall. "Won't you come in? Toby has to keep an appointment." To

Toby she added, "You must not keep them waiting at the bank."

But it was Toby who was kept waiting outside Mr. Thaxter's office. Captain Peter Flick had to be sent for, and he did not hurry his late dinner for his junior partner's convenience. Then Mr. Thaxter was called out on some town business, as he was a selectman of New Bedford. But at last they were all met in the walnut-paneled office.

It was not an apprenticeship paper Toby had to sign, but an agreement that had been especially drawn up for this occasion. Giles Thaxter explained it to him while Captain Flick gazed out the window toward Buzzard's Bay. Toby Clayton was not to infringe upon Captain Flick's authority in any way during the voyage. To make certain of this, he was to keep his half-ownership of the *Rogue* a secret from everyone in the vessel. While at voyage's end he would divide the profits with his partner, on board Toby was not entitled to any special treatment, but had to place himself under the regular maritime laws and his Captain's orders.

Captain Flick pulled his gaze back into the room. "Do you understand everything, Clayton? Any breach of this agreement means I may put you off the vessel to be shipped home under discipline."

"I reckon I understand it, sir."

The master pushed the *Rogue*'s articles toward him, and Toby, scrawling his name with a goose quill, found himself a green hand standing before the mast at 1/150 lay.

Clouds had gathered during the long wait at the bank, making a gray end to the afternoon. It began to drizzle as Toby pushed open the front gate of the Clayton house.

He found supper simmering on the back of the stove, and Aunt Prudence in his room packing his sea chest. He began rolling his blankets, stopping them down with line, as he told her he had just signed a paper making him a fo'c'sle hand with no voice in the vessel's affairs.

She shook her head. "I don't trust Captain Flick, Toby. But at least Alex White will be aboard, and perhaps he can keep a weather eye out for you."

"That's the man who witnessed the sales agreement, ma'am?"

She nodded. "He came to pay his respects. You met him at this door today. He has much the same temper as Noah—" She cleared her throat and went on more briskly. "Alex was hardly more than a boy when he made boat-steerer, and he's spent forty years all told following whales. The last ten years he always shipped out under Noah. Not many Captains lower after whales, Toby, but Noah and Alex never missed a chase. I came to know Alex between voyages—sometimes he couldn't stretch his pay. Noah would lecture him severely, but there was always some work I needed done in the garden, or the cellar—"

"Or an extra pie going begging," Toby added with a grin.

"He was partial to gooseberry." She became serious again. "After paying his respects today, he said he was glad the *Rogue* was still in the family. I do feel, Toby, that you might practice keeping your business affairs to yourself. It isn't wise to—"

"Aunt Prudence! How did he know about me being part owner? If you didn't tell him, who—"

"No, Toby, I'd not make gossip out of anyone's business arrangements. Alex said he'd heard it from a sailor. Are you certain you—"

" 'Tis to be kept secret!" Toby felt hollow with alarm. "That was in the paper I signed, too. I can't sail in the *Rogue* if the crew hears I'm one of the owners. How many know about it?" Swiftly Toby dumped his remaining gear into his sea chest. "Maybe 'tisn't too late. I'm going down to the vessel. Back soon!"

He crammed into his jacket and slung his sea chest up on his shoulders. He was out of the house despite Aunt Prudence's protests of rain and no supper.

Toby headed toward the wharves, staggering under a chest suddenly heavier in the gloomy cold drizzle. The bitter thought arose that perhaps Captain Flick had put the news abroad in order to prevent his young partner from sailing with him.

Panting, Toby arrived at the deserted wharves. The few lighted shop windows only made the dusk seem deeper. The *Rogue* looked derelict in her rain-stained timbers.

Toby climbed up the slanting gangway.

A voice came out of the dark. "Bunks aplenty in the fo'c'sle—take your pick! Hey, you're Toby Clayton, ain't you?" Ben Valentine came forward from the web of shadows spun by masts, cordage, and superstructure.

"Ben!" Toby could see the red hair like a glow against the darkening day. "I'm looking for Alex White. Is he here?"

Ben shrugged. "I can't say, Toby. I just brought my sea chest aboard. But let's go look in steerage."

Toby left his sea chest near the gangplank, and turning his collar up against the light rain, went with Ben around masts and under superstructure. The young seaman bent to a hatch and slid the cover open. "Boatsteerers live here. C'mon." Toby followed him down the ladder and waited in the dark while Ben scrabbled with a match. A lantern sprang into flame and Ben moved it throughout the small room lined with double-decker bunks. Each berth was empty, though three or four sea chests stood on the floor. "Asleep or awake, no one's here," Ben declared, lowering the lantern. "Look there! Alex White's been and gone. That's his sea chest. I know it by the beckets."

Ben pointed to the rope handles, one on each end of the sea chest. They were knotted in a very complex and decorative way. "Once you see beckets like that, you don't forget. Now let's go put your own sea chest in the fo'c'sle."

"Ben, I must talk to Alex right away! Did he say where

he was going tonight?"

"No reason for him to tell me his plans, Toby. I only met Alex this morning. I was heaving an iron off the wharf near the whalecraft shop, practicing. Alex White come along and give me some advice on how to dart. That's when I found he's shipping with us as boatsteerer. He said he'd help me with the harpoon, did the Mate give me leave to practice during the voyage."

"But you recognized his sea chest!"

"He had it with him. 'Twas empty then, and he was taking it to the whalecraft shop to have a broken iron band mended." Ben swung the lantern. "Here 'tis, on the lid. You can see where they welded the break. But I know his sea chest by the beckets. You need see them only once to know them every time." He glanced at Toby's face. "Don't fret. You'll see Alex aboard tomorrow."

Toby swallowed hard. "Likely I won't be aboard tomorrow, Ben. 'Twill be too late then." He sat down on a sea chest and sighed. "You see, Alex heard something about me—" He stopped in sudden memory. " 'Tis my own fault, Ben Valentine! Recollect three days ago when I told you I owned half the *Rogue?*"

Ben nodded solemnly, though one corner of his mouth quirked in a suppressed grin.

"True enough," Toby assured him. "But I'm not to tell anyone, though I didn't know then 'twas to be kept secret." He explained about the paper Captain Flick had him sign only that afternoon. "It hardly matters how the crew comes to know of it, Ben. If Captain Flick hears any talk of it among the men, he'll take me out of my own vessel!"

Ben Valentine whistled. "So you're going before the mast! You must really want to sail." Then he glanced down and studied the deck planking. " 'Tis my doing your secret got spread, Toby. I told it to Alex this morning, kind of making a joke of it. I didn't reckon to see you aboard as a working hand."

"You told—? I reckoned someone had overheard me that day." Toby managed a grin. "The blame's not yours, Ben, for you didn't know. Besides, there's a good chance Alex hasn't told it to anyone else yet. All I need do is wait here for him to come aboard."

Ben shook his head. "He won't be back aboard tonight, Toby. Captain Flick ain't paying anyone to keep ship, though we're allowed to put our sea chests aboard and pick our bunks."

Toby stood up. "Then let's go to Alex's boardinghouse. Do you know which one he stays at?"

"Alex is an old sailor, Toby. And this is his last night in home port for two or three years to come. Likely he's running his easting down to every tavern on the waterfront."

Toby's heart dropped. "Likely he's wagging his tongue lively, too." He recalled the wind-bent and wave-scoured man at his aunt's door. Staunch and sober, Alex White did not seem a man who would make scuttlebutt out of his dead Captain's nephew. But what of an Alex White brought to half seas over by a sailor's farewell?

Ben's voice was cheerful. "We'll make the best of a bad tide yet, Toby. If you like, we can ask for Alex at the sailors' boardinghouses. But it'd save time to wear ship through the harbor taverns. D'you know the Kedge Anchor?" Ben named some more places, describing their locations. "I'll search the others, and we'll meet back aboard here. We can kindle a fire in the galley and dry out while we figure out the next step."

Ben blew out the lantern, and they left the dry stuffy steerage for chill twilight and a deck slippery from the rain. At the gangplank Ben stumbled over Toby's sea chest. "Here, I'll put that down in the fo'c'sle for you." Ben swung the sea chest to his shoulder and vanished into the darkness. Toby waited under a nearby shelter covering part of the deck. Ben came back, tugging his watch cap down against the drizzle. "Got you a good bunk, Toby. You ought to ride snug and dry in anything short of a Cape Horn gale."

They parted where wharf met cobbled street. Ben went off whistling. Toby pulled up his collar, jammed his cold hands into his jacket pockets, and hunching his shoulders against the penetrating drizzle, followed Ben's directions to the first tavern.

The cobblestones glistened where lamplight from an occasional shop window or the living quarters above shone into the street. Toby passed the painted and pictured signs of a candlemaker, an umbrella and buggy whip factory, a pharmacist, and other users of the whale's products. He came to the Kedge Anchor, its sign creaking like a hungry gull in the wind. Toby went inside.

This was not the sort of tavern Toby knew, offering meals for families and haven for travelers. The long tables of the Kedge Anchor were scarred as from battle, and stained with the mug rings of beer, rum, and port whose stale odors came reeling toward him. The air was thick with pipe smoke and loud talk from men in brightly striped jersey shirts, worn canvas jackets, and faded denims. They were arguing, boasting, playing cards, singing, or sleeping with heads on the rough tables. No one paid any attention to Toby as he went through the crowded place. When he had seen every face, he left, glad for the tang of seaweed in the rain.

The sign of the Top Hamper, true to its name, showed only the rigging of a ship, her hull down behind the horizon. Toby searched carefully among the sailors and was again disappointed. Then just as he was leaving, someone came dashing in out of the rain and they collided, falling down hard outside the tavern.

The sailor began chuckling, then suddenly broke off. "'Vast, 'tis young Toby Clayton!" A hard hand pulled him upward. "Far from home, lad, be'ent ye?"

Light from the tavern window showed a weathered face dewed with raindrops. Toby's heart leaped. "Alex White! I've been looking for you."

"No, have ye?" Alex exclaimed, and his voice was thickened with rum. "He sent ye to find me, did he? Last night's my own, tell 'im that!"

"Nobody sent me, Alex. 'Tis about—" Tony broke off as a pair of sailors reeled out of the tavern, brushing past them. "I've got to talk to you, Alex. Come on home with me." He could go later to meet Ben in the *Rogue.*

But Alex drew away from Toby, lurching a little. "I'll be aboard when we shove off. Alex White still knows martingale from maintop, blast his eyes!"

"Who are you talking about?" Toby began to feel he had found Alex too late in the day.

"Mr. Flick." Alex stood in the patch of light from the tavern, rain soaking the shoulders of his jacket and dripping from the bill of his cloth cap. Suddenly his features quirked in a foolish smile. "Oh, *pardon*—" He swept off his cap and made a clumsy bow. "I mean *Captain* Flick!" He shouted with laughter, face upturned to lantern light and streaming rain.

A coach rattled down the narrow street, wheels spraying water as it went through a large puddle before turning the corner. Likely some merchant heading for home in a better part of the town, Toby thought.

Alex tugged his cap on over wet hair. "Going to toss a

few combers under the hatch, mate. Le'see, been here, so th' Twin Flukes're next." He trudged down the street, clearly forgetting he had not yet been inside the Top Hamper.

Toby hurried after him, matching Alex's big loose stride, and caught up with the boatsteerer as he veered around the corner. "Alex, you got to help me keep a secret—"

"Tell ye one o' mine," Alex confided, slowing his steps and bringing his head close to Toby's. "Ye couldn't get me in the *Rogue* this trip 'cause they's many a master as likes Alex White for their boatsteerer. Aye, and better men they be than *him!*"

He thumbed derisively toward the docks where, hidden behind warehouses, the *Rogue* awaited the morrow and the master Alex White scorned. Toby's head followed the boatsteerer's gesture, and suddenly he blinked.

For one startled moment Toby thought a nearby shadow moved as if it had a life of its own. He stood still and listened to the drill of rain, the distant soughing of the surf, the groan of swaying signboards.

He heard Alex coughing, and realizing his companion had ambled ahead while he paused, Toby quickly joined him. The boatsteerer stopped and began searching through his pockets.

Toby remembered the sea chest. "If you're not sailing, how is it your sea chest is aboard?"

"Aye, aye, 'tis aboard, and so be I come mornin', with a

belly as green as bilges. Ah, here 'tis!" Alex produced a leather bottle from some inside pocket and took a long pull, gasping when he finished. " 'Tis *him* as made me sign f'r this trip b'fore he discharges me from th' las' voyage, Cap'n Flick did. Says I borrowed 'n' bought so much I owe from a voyage I ain't even been on yet!" He took a long, indignant pull from his bottle. "Can't set a foot on dry land, says he, less'n I sign f'r the nex' voyage. A boardin'-house crimp, tha's all our brave Cap'n Flick is."

Toby remembered the heavy sums listed against Alex's name in the account book for that voyage. It was only fair that Alex should pay back the money advanced or work it off. But it was mean of Peter Flick to force a man into a three-year voyage on the strength of a few dollars' debt.

Alex slumped against the shop where they had stopped. It was a marine supply store, closed and dark but for a lantern placed in its window as a charity against the street's darkness. Toby watched the boatsteerer dolefully shake the leather bottle near his ear. "Alex, how do you get money for rum?"

"Sign f'r it, mate! Cap'n Flick'll pay 'em all, an' th' boardin'house, too. Then he takes it out o' my lay f'r the next voyage. Lookee here!" Clumsily he dug into his various pockets, then held out an ivory cylinder twice as thick as his thumb. He waggled one flat end in the lantern light, and Toby caught a glimpse of incised lines and smears of black.

Alex, thick-tongued, explained it was his signature seal that he himself had carved out of whale ivory. "Tha's me, 'bout to toss th' dart, see? Ain't landlord nor potboy in all New England 'n' half the Pacific what don't know my seal." He returned the carved ivory cylinder to his pocket, patting it protectively. "Why, I even stamped her down on some important paper what Cap'n Noah has me sign that there last voyage!"

That was likely the sales agreement which transferred ownership of the *Rogue* from Captain Noah to Peter Flick. "Did Captain Noah explain why he drew up the paper?"

"No, he di'n't say." Alex scratched his head. "Someth'n there strikes me 'bout it, though."

Toby, thoroughly soaked and cold, waited for Alex to remember. The rain dashed down like a charge of silver spears breaking their points on the cobblestones. Across the street a shadow flitted, but when Toby glanced there he saw by lighted upstairs windows that a loose shutter was slowly swinging.

Alex said loudly, "I recollect now!" He swayed and steadied himself against the shop wall. "Ye had a secr't ye wanted t'tell me. Tol' ye mine, now tell me yers."

Toby saw how deeply the rum had worked into the boatsteerer. "Come along home, Alex, where 'tis warm and dry." He put his hand out as a guide, but Alex pulled away, reeling and flailing his arm for balance. "I knows the way, blast them shoals!"

Alex began lurching down the street over the slippery cobbles tiled here and there with patches of light falling from the living quarters above the dark and silent shops. The rain beat a steady tattoo as Toby hurried after him.

Suddenly Alex stumbled and sprawled in a puddle. As Toby ran to him, he thought he saw from across the street a shadow start, then retreat.

The boatsteerer muttered, "Rig th' lifelines. Deck's awash!" But his eyes were closed.

Kneeling beside him, Toby shook the man's shoulder. "Can you get up?"

Alex's eyes flew open and he spoke clearly above the rain spatter, as if he were a dying man summoning all his ebbing strength. "—loose casks. I'm a goner, Mr. Hughs. Tell Toby . . . to look through the devil's eye."

"Alex, what are you saying?" Those were the words Mr. Hughs had passed on from the *Rogue*'s dying master! And suddenly Toby understood that Alex had just relived Captain Noah's last moments.

The boatsteerer's brow wrinkled as he hovered between past and present. "Cap'n Noah spoke to Mr. Hughs." There was a long silence filled with the drumming of rain. Then Alex's head rolled sideways. "But he was lookin' at—" He broke off, staring.

Toby followed his gaze across the rounded gleams of rainswept cobble, into the deep shadows at the side of the street, to the shine of wet boots.

Up against a pharmacist's shop, faintly outlined by reflected glow from the quarters above, stood Peter Flick.

Alex began snoring loudly, and Toby crouched beside him as with measured tread Captain Flick came toward them and stood looking down at the boatsteerer. "I'll take him home." His boot jabbed into the unconscious form. "Get up!"

Toby cried, "Don't!" adding lamely, "—bother, sir. I'll get him over to my house."

"I've been watching the drunkard. I know his kind," Captain Flick said bluntly. "He owes from his last voyage. He's signed on and we sail tomorrow. I won't have him jumping ship."

"I'll see he gets aboard, sir."

"Best you stay clear of him. This sort can get you into trouble. Now you get along home. I'll tend to him."

Toby sensed a hint of danger in the voice, and wished Peter Flick's eyes were not shadowed by his hat brim. "Alex White and I are going to be shipmates, sir, so I reckon I'd best start by helping him when he's down." He looked boldly at the shaded, unreadable face.

Captain Flick jerked his head in irritation, spinning drops from his hat brim. After a moment he spoke. "I hope you know what you are doing."

Then Peter Flick turned on his heel and strode down the dark and rainy street.

 four

Cast Out to Sea

WHEN TOBY CLAYTON heard the first order, "Heave short!" he dropped his knife and the half-peeled potato. Ignoring the cook's shout, he stepped out on deck and went around to the cooper's tool chest lashed forward of the galley in the stern. Here he could sit safely out of the way, a green and so far useless hand, as the *Rogue* cast out to sea.

Ben Valentine was among the sailors grouping around various belayed lines, readying for orders. Looking far forward to the windlass just behind the heel of the bowsprit, Toby saw Alex White among other men toiling with the handspikes, heaving in the anchor chain.

After Captain Flick had left them last night, Toby had heard the quick tattoo of footsteps, and out of the rain-swept shadows had come Ben Valentine. Worried over Toby's tardiness, he had searched until he saw him in the patch of lamplighted street. Together they had managed to rouse Alex enough to get him to the Clayton house where Aunt Prudence had firmly set about readying hot food and snug beds. Ben had soon gone off to spend his last night ashore with friends of his Nantucket family.

The next morning, quantities of hot coffee had cleared Alex White's head, enabling him to eat a hearty breakfast. Toby at last had had a chance to ask if he had told anyone of his part ownership of the *Rogue*. Alex had shaken his head decisively. "I don't bandy a man's business about, drunk 'r sober, Toby." And when Toby had explained the need for secrecy, the boatsteerer had been quick with his promise not to tell.

At the harbor they had found that the *Rogue* already had been hauled out to anchorage. But one of her boats, stationed for that purpose, had fetched them out to the bark. They had no sooner stepped aboard than Mr. Barksdale, the First Mate, had rounded up Alex with some other experienced men to brace the yards for casting off.

Toby had stood at the gangway, marveling at the confusion of shouting and scurrying men, the squealing of penned pigs, the squawking of cooped chickens. Two sailors had come thundering around the skylight, hard after a nanny goat which had jumped skittishly over the booby hatch. Other men had been stuffing cabbages and boxes of salt cod under the spare boats, and stringing dried onions to the skids, while a group of hands had struggled with loaded barrels under the eye of a harassed officer.

Then a man with a dirty apron over his faded dungarees had laid hold of Toby. "You a greenie, huh? See can you bear a hand with them potatoes. Thirty-three mouths to feed and me still having to stow provisions!" And so the cook had marched Toby aft along the deck to the galley in the stern, just forward and to starboard of the helm. But determined to see the *Rogue* making sail, Toby had fled at the first shouted command.

Now, sitting on the cooper's chest lashed securely in front of the galley, he watched the anchor chain being hove in. At last the Mate had the brake set and glanced aft. From behind Toby came the order: "Set the tops'ls!"

Glancing back around the corner of the galley, Toby saw Peter Flick standing at the Captain's post beside the helm, a position from which he could best see the rigging and still direct the man at the wheel. Turning to look forward, Toby saw men at each of the three masts, hauling on lines. These were sheets, he knew from his uncle's labeling on the *Rogue*'s picture, and they led to the corners of the sails. He watched the topsails, square on fore- and main-masts, and triangular on the fore-and-aft rigged mizzen-mast, stretch out along the yards. The *Rogue*, lying head to wind, began lifting against her anchor.

Once more the windlass was manned until the Mate, peering over the bow, shouted back, "Up and down!"

"Break her out!" Captain Flick ordered. And to the man on the wheel, "Port your helm."

Toby knew the moment the anchor broke free of the bottom, for the *Rogue* suddenly began canting her head to starboard, falling off the wind. The topsails swelled as the breeze hauled aft and filled them.

"Meet her!"

The helmsman checked his wheel, and the bark leaned eagerly out to sea on the port tack.

"Set all sails!"

Four triangular jibs blossomed out along the bowsprit; on fore- and mainmasts more sails were squared between the yards; on the mizzen the fore-and-aft spanker was sheeted home along its boom which reached aft beyond the taffrail, jutting out over the sea. The wind sharpened on Toby's cheek as the *Rogue* ran down Buzzard's Bay with a bone in her teeth.

But there was no rest for the working crew. First Mate Barksdale set men aloft and alow to the thousand particular refinements of coiling, stopping, bracing, and paying out necessary after each maneuver at sea.

A head came around the corner of the galley. "Hey, you there!"

It was not the cook, but an officer. Toby jumped up. "Yes, sir."

"Landsman, eh? You'll say 'aye' soon enough. I'm the Second Mate." He was the harassed man Toby had seen directing the stowage of barrels. "Captain Flick sends for Mr. Barksdale. That's him for'ard."

"Aye, aye, sir!" Toby said smartly. Though he had seen the *Rogue* often while she was lying in port being refitted, and had actually been aboard her only the night before, this was the first time Toby had really been able to examine the vessel of which he owned half. Like all whalers, she was flush-decked from bowsprit to taffrail. Leaving his place before the afterhouse in the stern, Toby walked forward down the starboard side of the vessel, passing on his left the waist-high angle-roof skylight, then the mizzenmast with its fore-and-aft boom reaching back over the sheltered helm.

He went under the skids, an open roof stretching from bulwark to bulwark, upon which were lashed two spare whaleboats, keel up. Set into the deck beneath this housing was the booby hatch, a sliding cover leading down to the boatsteerers' quarters where he had gone with Ben to look for Alex the night before. Temporary vegetable bins and a pen for the goat had been put up under the skids, and from overhead beams dangled strings of onions.

Forward of the boat skids was the mainmast, surrounded, as were the other masts, by a maze of rigging pegged to an encircling fife rail. Here also were the bilge pumps and the fresh-water cask. Toby went on between the main hatch amidships and the gangway on his right, the opening now blocked by a movable section of the bulwarks.

Then came the large square brick tryworks in which the crew would boil the blubber of the whales. Twin chimneys led up through a housing similar to the boat skids. Beneath the workbench on the after side of the tryworks chickens were cooped. Toby passed the forward hatch, the foremast, and the fo'c'sle companion which was a separate structure with double swinging doors leading to the seamen's quarters below. Toby's sea chest rested beside one of the fo'c'sle bunks, though he had yet to see it.

Forward of the fo'c'sle companion, the windlass reached nearly from bulwark to bulwark in the broad blunt bow of the bark. Just ahead of the windlass the heel of the bowsprit was covered by a short low fo'c'sle deck, part of which was now fenced off to contain the pigs. Standing on the starboard side, Mr. Barksdale was supervising the catting of the anchor.

"Captain Flick sent for you, sir," Toby said.

"Watch that fluke!" the Mate said sharply to one of the men hauling on the fishing tackle.

The man was gaping out over the harbor. "Mr. Mate, sir, there's a boat yonder!"

Mr. Barksdale took one startled glance at a fishing sloop which had suddenly loomed up from around a point. "Belay that tackle!" Then he cupped his hands and yelled aft. "Boat reaching broad on port bow—closing fast!"

One of the hands muttered, "Boat's gotta give way, seeing's we're in the right. But lookee at 'im!"

There was a moment of waiting silence. But the fishing sloop kept running free and the *Rogue* stood on as if her track had been made of iron.

Once more the Mate bellowed. "Collision course on the port bow!"

Still the *Rogue* rushed on.

"Whyn't that durn sloop git out'n the way?" demanded another hand.

Mr. Barksdale narrowed his eyes against the shine of the harbor. "Looks to be caught in a current." Now when he cupped his hands he yelled a warning toward the sloop. "Ahoy the sloop! We're standing on!"

They could see the crew of three fishermen scrambling among the gear tumbled on deck. Mr. Barksdale muttered helplessly as the 311-ton bark bore down on the sloop. But suddenly the fishing craft shipped a great steering oar and the three men threw their weight on it again and again. Finally, mere yards from the bow wave of the *Rogue,* the sloop turned, and the men sculled madly out of the way. A cheer broke out among the *Rogue's* crew.

Mr. Barksdale turned back to the anchor. "Here, get that hook catted. You, there, Captain wants me, you say? Come along." He stepped off the fo'c'sle deck and led the way aft. They went along the larboard, or port, side where the *Rogue* carried three whaleboats, one after the other from foremast to sternboard. Each boat hung outboard of the bulwarks in a pair of davits, right side up and hoisted well above the rail. The fourth boat, Toby knew, was on the starboard side, outside the stern quarter.

When they reached the Captain's post beside the helm

under the sheltering afterhouse, Peter Flick and Mr. Barksdale began discussing the setting of the vessel's routine. The helmsman stood to one side of the wheel, now and then glancing through the skylight on the deck before him to the compass suspended below the glass panes, or looking up through an open hatchway in the afterhouse roof to see how the sails were drawing. Two large compartments were built into each side of the afterhouse. The starboard structure housed the galley forward where Cook was banging his pots, and the bosun's locker aft. On the larboard side, the companion to the main cabin was abaft a storeroom.

Captain Flick nodded a dismissal to Mr. Barksdale, but the Mate lingered. "I reckon the wind was against me, Captain, and you didn't hear me warn you of that fishing sloop."

"I heard you, Mr. Barksdale," Captain Flick replied evenly. "If you recollect, we had the right of way."

"Aye, sir, we did. But the sloop looked to be caught in a current, and her crew couldn't fight her free till the last moment. We might've given her a little more leeway."

"Not without straining our canvas," Captain Flick said sharply. "We're setting out on a three-year voyage, Mr. Barksdale. Where am I to find good cotton sails at reasonable prices if we ruin all our canvas through charitable acts?"

Toby watched the Mate's face tighten. Mr. Barksdale

said, "Aye, aye, sir."

Captain Flick's voice eased a bit. "You did your duty by passing me the word, Mr. Barksdale. And I did mine by making the best decision for the vessel." Once more he nodded dismissal, and this time he left the helm to pace toward the bow.

Mr. Barksdale turned to Toby. "Fetch down that sea chest into my stateroom." He pointed to a chest just forward of the storeroom. Toby shouldered it and followed as the Mate went past the helmsman and opened the main companion door. They climbed down the iron ladder which curved directly into the after larboard corner of the main cabin.

Toby paused at the bottom of the ladder, resting the Mate's sea chest on the railing as he looked about with lively interest, even though all his uncle's belongings had been removed and the cabin housed someone else. The room reached across the vessel's stern perhaps twelve paces wide and half as deep. But there were no ports cut in the bulwarks. Instead, sunlight shafted through the overhead skylight, making a darting shadow of the compass hanging directly beneath and throwing on the carpet and scant furniture below a pattern of the brass bars that protected the glass topside.

The Captain's desk was against the forward bulkhead, a straight-backed chair bolted through the carpet to the deck. Another chair stood nearby. The cabin's mahogany panel-

ing bore navigational instruments, chronometer, and two
or three framed charts. A horsehair sofa was placed before
the stern bulkhead. Above it a square outline and small
brass lock showed that the vessel's safe had been built into
the *Rogue*'s transom. On either side of the locked cuddy
hung a telescope. One of the glasses was bound in plain
leather and smooth brass rings. The tooled casing of the
other telescope was fitted with elaborate brass decorations.

Mr. Barksdale broke into Toby's absorption. "First voyage, eh? I don't recollect signing you on."

"I—I signed on later, sir."

"Well, look around. You might be sent below on errands." The Mate gestured forward. "In here."

Hoisting up the sea chest, Toby followed him through a
doorway in the forward bulkhead. The Mate said, "Dining
saloon."

The skylight extended partway over the dining saloon.
The mizzenmast came right down through the small com-
partment. Built up against it was the table with benches.
There was just enough room left to reach the various door-
ways. Mr. Barksdale said, "This is my stateroom." He held
the curtain aside so Toby could step into the cramped
space and set down his sea chest next to the bunk. A
hinged panel swung down from the bulkhead to make a
tiny worktable. Mr. Barksdale grinned at Toby's surprise.
"You lads for'ard get more space than the afterguard. Second and Third officers are over here."

Their room was even smaller than the Mate's, barely containing double bunks and sea chests. A closet on the other side of the saloon was for the Fourth Mate, though it would stand empty this voyage. The lion's share of the space to starboard was taken up by the Captain's stateroom. It had a real bed hung in swivels so it always stayed level no matter how the vessel pitched.

There were two doors in the forward bulkhead of the dining saloon. "This leads to the pantry," the Mate explained. "The other goes into steerage. It's kept locked."

Toby saw the hook and eye, and nodded.

Three double strokes of the ship's bell clanged from overhead, muffled by the planking. The Mate said, "Six bells. Time to choose up watches. Come along."

Land had dropped far astern when Toby went forward to join the crew gathering amidships. Captain Flick stood up on the cooper's chest, his Mates grouped nearby. The Captain gave what Alex White later said was the customary speech on setting out; he'd treat the men square if they did their work and no slacking. Respect the authority of Captain and Mates. Don't waste time or food. Any damage to the vessel's property would be punished. Soonest the casks were filled with oil, the soonest they'd be homeward bound. Any questions? If not, they'd pick the watches.

The Captain and the Mate took turns choosing, gesturing men to either starboard or port. Mr. Barksdale thumbed both Alex White and Ben Valentine to his side of the vessel. When the crowd in front of Toby thinned, the Mate caught his eye. "You, there, to port."

Pleased, Toby stepped out smartly. But as he joined his friends he felt the probe of eyes. Turning, he found Captain Flick staring at him. With a chill, Toby hoped he only imagined the menace in his partner's expression.

When the crew had been divided, the Mate shouted, "Fetch your whack and eat hearty. Then it'll be port watch above, starb'd below!"

Ben tugged at Toby's sleeve. "Let's get our kit." They moved forward with the others and tumbled below into the fo'c'sle. "Your bunk's here, Toby!" Ben called out.

Toby stood beside the ladder, blinking in the gloom as sailors shoved past him to their sea chests. This was the first time he had been in the fo'c'sle, which was up in the bow of the vessel, making the same blunt point with two of its three sides. Daylight shafting through a bull's-eye set in each of the forward bulkheads and the burning whale-oil lamp hanging between overhead beams only emphasized the intervening pillars of darkness. Double-bunk berths lined all three sides, and before them stood the sea chests. Oilskins and spare gear hung on nails beside the bunks or on the massive upright timbers running through upper and lower decks. There was a door under the ladder and directly behind Toby, which he guessed gave access to the rest of the between decks cargo and working spaces.

Ben was sitting in a lower bunk to starboard, digging

into his sea chest. He pointed to the berth forward of his. "I got you a lower one, too. That's your sea chest."

"Ben, why do we say 'port' for some things and 'larboard' for others? I reckon they mean the same side of the vessel."

"Aye, they're the same, and only whalers use 'em both. 'Port' is mainly for sailing, and 'larboard' mostly for whaling. Now fetch your pannikin and let's get above!"

Together they tumbled up and joined the long line passing before the galley door. With full pannikins and cups, they went forward. The best places were already occupied, so they had to content themselves with sitting on the low fo'c'sle deck, right next to the pigpen. Soon Alex White joined them and they shoved over to make room.

"Why, Alex," said Ben. "I reckoned you boatsteerers were too grand to do but eat at your own table in steerage!"

Alex set his coffee mug on the deck, bracing it between his feet. "'Tain't all glory down below. Stuffy, too, now and again. Even the idlers is eatin' above today."

Toby shook his head. "I don't see how anybody dares idle in front of Captain Flick."

Ben laughed. "Idlers is the ones with all night in, Toby. The blacksmith, cooper, cook, and sailmaker—and cabin boy if there's one aboard—don't stand watches. They work all day and sleep all night. But you 'n' me have got to turn to every four hours, night and day."

Alex added, " 'Cept for the dogwatches. They's two hours each at evening. That makes a kind of hitch, see, like the sogers take a half step when they march so's to change their pace."

Nodding, Ben said, "That way, nobody has to work the same hours all the time, but trade their hours about. Eight bells is always the change of the watch, 'cept when watches are dogged every night. The watch hours are rung two bells, four bells (that's the middle of the watch), six bells, and eight when you go below."

"What do we do when we're off watch?" Toby wondered.

"Sleep!" Ben and Alex exclaimed together, and the boatsteerer explained: "Sleep is something ye won't get 'nough of. Sometimes, though, ye want to stay up and maybe scrimshaw or yarn a bit. Ye can do pretty near what ye want, provided ye don't get in the way of the duty watch."

Ben drained his coffee cup. "You always got to tumble out at All Hands. Many times you just go off watch when the Old Man decides to go about or spread another sail and you got to turn to right away again. Why, I've worked a whole off-watch that way and then had to stand my regular trick!"

Alex White squinted at his young shipmate. "How many vessels you been on yer whole lifetime?"

"This'n's my third," Ben said, coloring faintly. "I didn't

relish schooling much, so I shipped as boy in the *Nancy and John,* Nantucket. Better'n a year later, while we were in Guam, the *Philadelphia,* out of Martha's Vineyard, was recruiting. The Old Man let me go over to her as a green hand. Now I'm a seaman, and I aim to work up to boat-steerer this voyage."

Four double strokes clanged brassily against the keen of the wind and mewing of gulls spiraling above the vessel. The Mate called out, "Watch and watch about."

Ben wiped his plate with a scrap of biscuit. "Turn to, boys."

Toby stood up uncertainly. "What should I do?"

Alex handed him his pannikin and cup. "First, ye can wash my kit and stow it under the boat skids, handy to the booby hatch. Then ask the Mate for a job."

Toby did as he was asked, taking Ben's kit too, and swishing the tin dishes in a barrel of sea water set out before the galley for that purpose. Stowing the pannikins and cups, he reported to the Mate. Mr. Barksdale looked him over. "You look strong, young fella, but sailing needs brains, too. I'm not sending you up aloft for a few weeks. Meanwhile you can get an experienced hand to show you how to splice an eye, then keep all the tub beckets in good repair. That'll be your regular job now, aside from whatever scrubbing and hauling I give you."

Alex White and the Mate must have already had it worked out, for as Mr. Barksdale turned to supervise the foretop gang, the boatsteerer came up with a couple of marlinspikes and a length of line. Settling on the forehatch cover just forward of the brick tryworks, Alex showed Toby how to unlay the strands and tuck them in again.

As he practiced with the line, Toby was conscious of the *Rogue*'s gentle roll, the chuckling of sea water under the bow, and the sun warming his back. This was pleasantly different from Mr. Hughs's grim forecast the night he gave Toby his uncle's dying message. "Alex, last night you told me Captain Noah's last words, and before that Mr. Hughs said the same thing. But what is the 'devil's eye,' and how can I look through it?"

Alex gazed beyond the railing, though his fingers never ceased manipulating the strands of rope. "I been giving that a deal of cogitatin', Toby. Reckon Captain Noah might've meant the Evil Eye. That's a set of rocks in the Azores. Most ships know of it, for they got to steer clear if they go around that end of that particular island to stand on for Europe."

"Did Captain Noah take the *Rogue* that way? What does the Evil Eye look like, Alex? How does that fit in with my uncle selling the *Rogue* near the end of the voyage?"

The old boatsteerer waved a gnarled hand impatiently. "Here, now, I don't know nothing 'bout it! I never been near the Evil Eye, nor I reckon was yer uncle. Leastways, he didn't take the *Rogue* that way, and we only touched the Azores outward bound, not coming home two years later—'sides, he were dead when we come up in them latitudes last June."

Toby sank back on his heels. "First you say he meant the Evil Eye; then you tell me that's got nothing to do with Captain Noah at all."

"I says 'tis the best I can think of, young feller! I don't know of no 'devil eye' at all, and might be with the wind howling half a gale that Mr. Hughs and me both heard his dying words wrong. Anyways, we're heading for the Azores now and we'll be having a run ashore. Won't do no harm to spend our time looking at some scenery, eh? Could be they's a clue 'r something else that'll end up explaining everything."

Toby dropped his line. "Will you do it, Alex—will you help me look through the Evil Eye?"

"I says I will, ain't ye listening? Now, lookee, ye got that splice loose enough to drive a whale through."

During the fine autumn days that followed, the whaling bark *Rogue* coursed through the North Atlantic, sails drawing full with the wind coming over the quarter, now port, now starboard, but the vessel always bearing east by a half south, running down to the Azores.

Watch and watch about, the men worked ship, keeping the clews snug to the yardarms, hauling braces around to catch the best wind, coiling, stopping, and overhauling. Besides his ropework, Toby helped as they scrubbed and polished, chipped rust and painted, and each day sounded the bilge pumps. Soon it was time to go over the whaleboats. They pulled them in from their davits, repairing and painting. The hands drew the line out of tubs, coiling it down again. They sanded, painted, and thrummed the oars.

The idlers were the busiest of all during the long days. Besides his regular work of cutting new sails and repairing the old, Sails went over the boat canvases, too. Smitty tempered the harpoons and occasionally hammered out a new point. Cooper sweated at his grindstone, putting an edge on each lance, iron, and cutting spade, when he was not working with his adz and plane. Alex White and the other three boatsteerers mounted irons and lances on rough-barked poles six feet long and stopped down with line, and, under supervision of the Mates, oversaw the work done by the fo'c'sle hands.

The work was hard and continuous, and Toby, new to the sea, struggled through it with little thought of complaint. But the other fo'c'sle hands began to grumble, saying they were being pushed and given no rest.

"And we're on Cape Horn rations already," one of the men added indignantly to Mr. Barksdale. He and Toby and two or three others had just finished taking the winch apart for cleaning. "They's still good cabbages and onions under the boat skids," Zachary went on. "Live pigs and chickens. But the crew's on biscuit and old leather and say thankee for it, too!"

"It's still food and you won't go hungry as long as you do your work," the Mate said. "Even if Captain Flick runs a tight ship—"

"—and a hungry one, too, blast his eyes!"

Captain Flick's voice cut sharply across the sea wind. "I heard that!"

Toby and the winch gang froze into terrible silence as the Captain stepped around the fo'c'sle companion and came forward. He stopped in front of the man who had spoken so recklessly. "Insubordination and mutiny! Disrespect to an officer! Mr. Barksdale, put this man on biscuit and water for three days. Another rebellious word out of him and he's to get the rope's end."

"Aye, aye, sir." The Mate's face was nearly as chalky as the offender's.

And then, as Captain Flick turned, another man said loud enough for him to hear, "Too bad ye had to open yer mouth, Zachary. Now ye can't have any o' my fresh fried chicken tonight."

But, both incredibly and luckily, the Captain apparently did not hear. The Mate said in a low, tense voice, "You watch that jaw, Jake Underhill, or he'll have you seized up in the rigging."

Jake lounged against the bulwark. "I'm gettin' tired of all this work, Mr. Mate. Mind if I take the rest of the watch off?"

Mr. Barksdale's face suffused with anger. "I'll fetch you

a clout in your saucy mouth, Jake Underhill. Turn to!"

Toby went to fetch rags for the winch gang, and as they cleaned and greased he studied Jake Underhill. A mite short, he was, thin, with a scrawny face that was neither shaved nor growing a beard. He had a knowing look in his eyes and an insolent quirk to his mouth. He had been slow to obey orders, but he had never shown any sauce until now. Toby had thought the man a little dull, as was Zachary who had complained about the food. But Zachary, muscular and good-natured, always turned to smartly when there was work to be done.

It was Zachary who sat down on the forehatch cover next to Toby and Ben during the port watch suppertime at the end of the first dogwatch. He munched dry biscuit and sipped from his cup of water. "That Jake Underhill. Dunno what got into him, sassin' like that."

Ben nudged Zachary. "My pannikin's right next to you. Reckon I ain't too hungry now."

Zachary shook his head. "You don't go fetching me any more trouble, Ben Valentine! The Ol' Man's maybe watching for this, and then 'tis a dozen from the rope's end for you 'n' me both! A little biscuit for a while don't hurt nobody."

Ben shrugged and went on eating.

Zachary thoughtfully chewed his biscuit until it was soft enough to swallow. "Me 'n' Jake was shipmates in the *Rogue* last voyage, and he sure wasn't nothing like sassy then. Just can't figure it."

Alex White came by and stopped, looking down at Zachary and his slender meal. "Well, now," said the boatsteerer. "Too bad yer such a strong feller, Zach, and not sickly like that Jake Underhill."

Toby and his two companions stared at Alex, waiting. The boatsteerer cocked his head and squinted aft. " 'Cause that pore sickly feller is back there in the galley, a-stuffing hisself with fresh fried chicken."

Zachary said flatly, "They'll keelhaul him for that."

Alex shook his head. "He's sick. Needs good food. Captain's orders."

 five

Through the Eye

TOBY HAD NEARLY finished scrubbing the quarter-deck one morning when he straightened up to stand respectfully near the wheel and wait for Captain Flick and the helmsman to move aside so he could finish the job. Suddenly from aloft came a long wail. "Blo-o-ws! He blows and flukes!"

Whales!

Heart thundering, Toby strained forward to catch a glimpse beyond the men in front of him. Perhaps the Mate would let him go in a boat!

Feet drummed as the off-watch tumbled up, and men shouted excitedly until Mr. Barksdale yelled for them to belay their jaws. Captain Flick cupped his hands and called aloft, "Where away?" In the interval between question and answer, the Captain glanced over his shoulder. "You, there! Fetch up the glass—quick!"

"Aye, sir!" Toby opened the main companion door and tumbled down the curving iron ladder. Weeks had gone by since the time he had brought the Mate's sea chest below. Toby dimly remembered telescopes. They should be in the main cabin. He looked around the paneled walls, cloaked in dimness beyond the reach of day from the skylight.

There they were, above the horsehair sofa across the stern. Toby crossed the cabin in a few paces and reached up for the one whose intricate brass ornaments and polished tooled leather had first caught his eye.

A voice rang through the cabin. "Not that one!" Captain Flick, openly chafing at the delay, had come partway down the companion ladder. "That one's broken. No one ever uses it. Fetch the other, lively now!" He sprinted back up the ladder and slammed the door behind him.

Seizing the plain black leatherbound glass, Toby tumbled up on deck.

Men were clinging in the weather rigging, muttering in suppressed excitement and gesturing two points forward of the starboard beam. Captain Flick stood at the rail, intently staring seaward. Toby hastened under the boat skids and handed him the glass.

The Captain braced the telescope against a backstay and studied the horizon. "About seven miles to windward. A loner. Have a look, Mr. Barksdale."

"It'll be an old bull. Mean devils they can be." But the Mate obediently used the glass. "Sperm, Captain. One lone mean old sperm."

"Close to the end, he is," Captain Flick said. "His

spout's weak and he doesn't sound for long. He won't put up much of a fight."

Mr. Barksdale looked at him in amazement. "You don't figure to lower, do you, sir? Why, we've not mustered our boat crews yet!"

"One boat will do," the Captain answered. "There's experienced whalemen aboard, Mr. Barksdale. Pick six of the best. They should have no trouble putting a boat on a dying whale."

The Mate's voice was so low that Toby, nearest of the crew, could barely catch the words. "Sir, sending an undrilled crew is condemning good men to certain peril!"

Captain Flick's features froze into an ugly contortion. He said harshly, "Mr. Barksdale, you will lower a boat. You're to head, and—" He glanced around. "Alex White can steer." A humorless smile thinned his lips. "Take Jake Underhill—"

Jake must have been listening all this time, for now he stepped out from behind one of the vegetable bins under the boats skids. "Captain, sir, I ain't feeling so good, and I reckon I better stay aboard."

They stared at each other, the Captain and the fo'c'sle hand. Behind him, Toby heard Zachary mutter, "Now he's done it up proper!"

Captain Flick turned back to the Mate, and his voice had resumed its normal brusqueness. "You and Alex White, Mr. Barksdale, and four others of your choosing.

The *Rogue* will run you in five miles. You can sail the rest of the way. Carry on." He stepped close to the Second, who bent his head for orders and then passed them on to the crew. Toby soon found himself paying out a weather brace as the *Rogue* hauled her wind to run down to the lone sperm. By the time Captain Flick backed the foreyards, Mr. Barksdale had the larboard boat cleared for running. His boat crew lowered with a spank into seas still creaming from the bark's way. Fending off, the men spread their tiny canvas.

Ben and Toby settled themselves in the weather fore-shrouds, luckier than those left at the railing who would see almost nothing of the chase. Tops and trucks had long been filled with the quickest of the watching crew. Toby saw the whaleboat's gaffsail and jib alternately thrusting skyward and disappearing into a trough as the Atlantic rose and fell. He could not distinguish the distant sperm, except the two or three times Ben pointed out a roil of white water. "How does the Mate know where to steer?" Toby wondered aloud.

"Likely the Captain's posted a lookout and a signal-man," Ben answered. "Even if the signal board ain't up for the crew yet, the Mate and the Old Man would've had it all worked out by now. Look, flukes! Ripples now, he ain't far down. Coming up again, see his spout?" There was a cry from the masthead. Ben glanced aloft. "The wind pennant's been hauled to half stay. Look, the boat's heading a point to starb'd. They's using signals, all right."

Far off Toby saw the silver flash of the whale's spout, and sometimes a darker patch on the gray water. Now and then he could follow the progress of the white canvas until it was furled. Ben whispered with excitement. "They'll be going in under paddles, I reckon. Wood to blackskin. Flukes, flukes!" he yelled. "They hooked him!"

The men began cheering. Captain Flick shouted, " 'Vast that racket. Next man who opens his mouth gets a belaying pin in it."

The crew grumbled into complaining silence, but soon the tension of the distant chase dispelled resentment.

For Toby, the whale hunt was marked out in a series of vague blurs and splashes of white and silver against the gray of rolling seas. At times the commotion moved along the horizon. Sometimes it stalled and backed. Then, finally, becoming more furious and foamy, it frothed to an end.

The Second Mate shouted the order. "Haul round the foreyards!"

They jumped to their places. The *Rogue* began stepping through the waves. Soon they dropped down to the whale and the boat standing off, her crew of six strangely grim in their victory.

All attention was on the dead sperm. The Second cracked with the Captain's orders. The men threw down lines and made the whale fast along the starboard side of the vessel. Almost unnoticed, Mr. Barksdale's boat rowed around the stern to its davits.

Toby and Ben tailed on to the lines along with the other men. The fluke and fin chains were hauled and slacked so that finally the whale lay belly up, waves washing over the dark-gray skin. The officers talked among themselves and the men waited for orders.

Ben put his head over the gunwale, then nudged Toby. "Lookee here, that's why the Captain's been so anxious," he muttered.

Toby, leaning over the railing, saw the whale's long wrinkles and lean flanks. It meant nothing to him. Ben whispered an explanation. "He's a dryskin. No oil. Weak and sick."

Captain Flick's voice sounded hearty. "Come along, Mr. Barksdale, we're waiting for you. This is a welcome prize."

Toby, still puzzled, turned to watch the Mate's bulky figure coming across amidships toward the Captain. His face was locked with suppressed anger. "Captain, sir, one of my men was seriously injured. That sperm took his arm and a chaw out of the gunwale 'fore I could get a set at him."

"Gave you a good fight, did he? Something must've been bothering to make him that mean." The Captain sounded jubilant. "Fetch the spades, Mr. Barksdale, and we'll dig out our treasure."

Toby could sense the wave of excited agreement that

ran through the crew. Everyone seemed to understand ex-cept him. What treasure from this oilless, nonwhalebone, diseased dryskin?

Ben explained in one whispered word. "Ambergris!"

Ambergris—this was fortune indeed! Who had not heard of that gray waxy substance said to be a product of a sperm's illness? The base for the costliest perfumes, and, in the East, a potent medicine, ambergris was recovered so rarely during whaling voyages that Toby had long ago ceased to dream of finding the precious material. Now here were riches for all, since the crew shared in everything got in a whale chase, whether the luck be good, bad, or, as here, fantastic.

But Mr. Barksdale stood stiffly in his anger. "Sir, the in-jured man needs immediate care."

Merchant vessels seldom carried surgeons and whalers never. Toby knew it was the Captain's duty to care for all injuries personally. Captain Flick gazed hungrily at the sperm overside. "Well, send down a man to stay with him. This is a pressing business, Mr. Barksdale, and I'll need you."

"Aye, aye, sir." The Mate turned, sweeping his glance over the men. Alex White caught his eye and with gestures volunteered his services, then made his way to the fo'c'sle. The rest of the crew moved forward eagerly, crowding against the railing, but leaving a space for the officers be-fore the opened gangway.

Captain Flick and his Mates tied on safety lines, then lowered down onto the whale. They received the pikes and spades handed down to them, not the 22-foot instruments manipulated from the cutting stages but the shorter ones carried in the whaleboats. Captain Flick had thought to save time by not rigging the stages.

The Second and Third stationed themselves at either end of the whale, pikes ready to deal with the sharks whose triangular fins were beginning to appear among the gray razor-edged waves breaking over the dead sperm. Captain Flick and the Mate began chopping a line down the whale's belly. Then with pikes they peeled back the blubber. Captain Flick knelt down in the slime and salt water and plunged his arms into the whale, wrestling something up out of the cut.

The odor broke over Toby and sickened him. He turned away, but the others hung over the railing, grinning their encouragement.

Toby went and sat on the forehatch cover. He thought of the man below, bloody and maimed from his contact with the sperm. He did not think he would be able to give that man any kind of cheer. And so he sat, unnoticed, until the daylight began to fade and the officers came back on deck.

Their clothes were soaked with blood and sea water. Failure of the whale's intestines to yield up treasure was stamped on their faces.

Captain Flick stared around at the mute faces of his crew. "Nothing. Nothing! He was clean, through and through. But by all rights he should've been chock-a-block with ambergris!"

Mr. Barksdale said testily, "Likely cast it off a day or two ago to wash up on some beach a thousand miles from here."

Captain Flick gripped a backstay until his knuckles went white. "If I knew where—I swear to you, Mr. Barksdale, if I knew *where*. . . ." His eyes, catching the reflection of the setting sun, glowed like coals, and his breathing was heavy on the clean sea air and the quiet sigh of moving ocean.

And then another sound broke over them, a single snickering which made mock of the silent men. Jake Underhill let the chuckling rattle out of him, his thin shoulders shaking with the strength of it.

Toby, glancing sharply at the man, saw at once that this was no reaction to a shattered dream.

Jake Underhill was laughing his scorn of Captain Flick.

Mr. Barksdale gave an order without consulting his superior. "Cast off that carcass!"

The crew stirred at last, as if awakening from a dream. But Captain Flick, moving more quickly, shouldered his way through the men, making his way aft.

And all the while Jake Underhill's laughter rose and fell like the hollow coughing of waves slapping together in the vessel's wake.

Just after the port watch's breakfast two days later, Captain Flick laid the foresails to the mast and Mr. Barksdale formed the men in two lines along the weather bulwark. As the *Rogue* lay abox with only a hand to watch the wheel, the four officers huddled in conference.

"Picking boat crews," Ben whispered to Toby. "Boatsteerers first."

Finally each officer pointed to one of the boatsteerers, the Mate selecting Alex White as his harponier. Now the Captain and his Mates began striding up and down between the lines of men, sometimes pausing to ask about previous whaling experience. Each officer in his turn selected one of the additional four crewmen his boat needed, thumbing the man to stand beside his boatsteerer.

The Mate stood before Ben Valentine. "You're a sight young, but a good seaman. You rowed for the *Philadelphia,* didn't you?"

Ben spoke up smartly. "Aye, sir. Worked up to Tub Oar in the Mate's boat."

"That'd be Mr. Eversaw. He'll turn out a good one now and again. Start you out on Tub Oar." He thumbed Ben toward Alex White, then turned to Toby. "Sit out for shipkeeper." He pointed to the bench abaft the tryworks.

But as Toby fell out of line, Captain Flick called out. "Just a minute, Mr. Barksdale! That boy is to go in a boat."

The Mate raised his eyebrows. "He's not even a seaman,

sir!"

"He'll learn to pull an oar sooner than reef a sail," the Captain countered. "We're one hand light, Mr. Barksdale, so stay him in the line, I say."

The Third Mate sighed unhappily. I reckon the lad'll be landed on me."

Alex White coughed, and a glance passed between him and Mr. Barksdale. The Mate nodded to Toby. "All right. Reckon you can be Midship Oar for me."

As Midship, Toby's duty in a boat would be only to row and bail, while the rest of the Oars had additional responsibilities. He did not know whether his luck was good or bad, but Alex and Ben winked encouragingly as he joined them.

Finally all the men were divided among the four boats, but for a half dozen extra hands told off for shipkeepers. Captain Flick called, "Hoist and swing!"

The Mate put his fists on his hips. "Men, we'll walk this time. But, after this, when you hear that order I want you to jump! Come along."

Each header led his crew to his own boat to begin the first practice drill, Mr. Barksdale taking his men to the larboard boat davits in the stern quarter. Alex White and another man stayed by the forward davit while the Mate took the rest up the ladder to the top of the afterhouse. "Clear for running," he ordered.

The men sprang to their tasks, snatching off the canvas

tub covers and lifting the coiled whaleline into the boat. Toby felt useless as he watched them cast off the gripes. When the boat was free of these lashings, the two outboard cranes upon which the keel rested were swung in, and the weight fell on the davit tackles.

"Lower away!"

Ben turned to Toby. "In you go!" He gave him a push, and Toby tumbled into the boat, sprawling among thwarts, oars, and gear as the craft rode down the falls to meet the waves with a hearty slap.

"Look out below!"

Toby scrambled to the middle thwart as the men slid down the falls. They unhooked the bow and stern blocks and pushed away from the bark with oars. As the craft fell astern the whaler, Toby clung to the gunwale, conscious of the broad sweep of the sea.

The others, balancing on thwarts and gunwales, were busy unfurling the sails, stepping and staying the mast, and shipping the boom, unmindful of the ocean's swell which was so much more noticeable than in the *Rogue*. Mr. Barksdale, standing in the stern sheets, had shipped the long steering sweep to the larboard gunwale of the pointed stern. Now gaffsail and jib were run up. The Mate shifted the sweep, ducked the swinging boom, and the boat fell off the wind until they were running free.

The sea was frisky and Toby was soon wet from spray. Shaking the water from his eyes, he saw the other boats under sail, spreading out on the ocean until the scending waters hid them from one another. Mr. Barksdale's boat heeled under a smart breeze, and the men grinned at one another, enjoying the sport.

The Mate soon set them to work. Heaving a harness cask overboard to represent a whale, they practiced coming up to their quarry under sail and with paddles.

Finally they shipped their oars, each man thrusting the loom through the tholepins on the gunwale opposite to where he sat in order to get the greatest amount of leverage. Toby looked at the stern before him where Mr. Barksdale leaned on the great steering sweep, waiting for the men to settle themselves. Before the Mate, Zachary sat on Stroke, then Ben Valentine as Tub, and after him Toby as Midship. Behind Toby sat Bow Oar, and in the very bow itself was Alex White rowing the Harponier Oar. Stroke, Toby as Midship, and Harponier, sitting on the larboard side of their thwarts, rowed Starboard Oars, and from Ben's tales of his experiences Toby knew the header would sometimes address them as "Three!" Tub and Bow, Larboard Oars, would be called "Two!"

Mr. Barksdale put them through maneuvers. "Back, Three! Watch that crab, Midship. Now, for'ard, Two! Lively, now. For'ard, All! Lay me on, wood to blackskin!"

After several clashes with neighboring oar blades, and catching crabs or losing hold, Toby eventually began rowing in something resembling proper order.

They spent above an hour running up to the hapless harness cask and going through the motions of harpooning a whale, the header and harponier exchanging places, and finally getting a set for the kill.

Toby's muscles were hot with strain and he groaned aloud with relief when Mr. Barksdale ordered them back to the *Rogue*. Steering with the big sweep, the Mate said, "I don't want any whaling for glory, boys, but there'll be no hanging back either. Later on we'll have drill in our regular duty watch, and when I say, 'Row!' I want you to spring your backs out, hear?"

And spring their backs out they did. Now it became a regular thing to be interrupted in the middle of some shipboard task with the cry, "Larboard boat, hoist and swing!" They jumped for their boat, cleared away and lowered, often into a running sea with the *Rogue* full under way, driving until the oars bent under their hands. The Captain, Second, and Third likewise drilled the crews of their own Starboard, Waist, and Bow boats.

Toby went through several stages of weariness and sore muscles until finally he became so used to the work that he began to enjoy the drills. But he was still glad the day the posted lookout hailed the Azores.

The land grew from a purple smudge on the horizon one day into a palm-fringed shore the next. By noon the *Rogue* swooped into Ponta Delgada, capital of the island São Miguel. She came on the run, dropping one anchor and laying out cable, then putting topsails to the mast and letting go the other hook, winching in the slack chain.

Toby was impressed with the maneuver, and told Alex White so. The boatsteerer glared at him. " 'Tis called a flying moor, and them makes it what wants to show off."

Captain Flick was rowed toward the colorful stone houses of town, and soon a stream of provisions came out in bumboats to be hoisted aboard and stowed by the crew. Then they had to clean and clear and scrub and polish, but the Mate gave them an all night in, except for an anchor watch. More supplies were ferried out the next day, but by noon the work was done. The Mate announced a run in town for all hands.

Mr. Barksdale had to wait until the cheering died down before he could add the warning to be back at the boats by sundown. "The Captain sends word you can have another all night in."

"Aye," said Jake Underhill. "Gives the Portugee authorities all night to hunt up the deserters."

"Another word out of you, Jake Underhill," warned the Mate, "and you can spend your free time slushing down the masts."

With a dollar advance on wages in his pocket, each man swarmed down the falls and rowed madly for the stone landing. As they tumbled out of the boats, the Mate cried, "Back by sundown, men!"

In the last week before raising land, both Ben and Alex

had learned from Toby all the circumstances of the *Rogue*'s complete change of ownership, as well as Toby's hope that in the Azores he could discover the meaning of Captain Noah's mysterious last words.

Together the three entered the town under white stone arches and walked up the brick-paved street.

Toby's senses spun as he turned his head in every direction, overwhelmed with the warmth and brightness of the sun. The arched and balconied houses of pink, yellow, blue, and white were hung about with flowers and shaded by swaying palms. Birds sang from everywhere. Bullock carts squeaked past with the pleasing fragrance of the sun-ripened fruits and vegetables they bore. Women went shrouded in vast dark hooded cloaks, strange for such a bright warm land, Toby thought. But he listened with joy to their speech—Portuguese it would be, of course—as merry and colorful as the land around them.

Alex was speaking, too, scraping up fragments of what sailors called Portugee to bargain for provisions at outdoor stalls. He had exchanged some of their money for the local coin, and now he loaded Toby and Ben's arms with string bags of food. Then, leaving them while he went to seek out a stable, Alex presently came back leading three saddled horses. " 'Bout an hour's ride up to the north coast," he said. "Feller reckons we can rent us a boat from the fishermen there."

Soon the three were trotting on a road which cut across

the island. They passed long high stone walls sheltering orange and lemon groves, rode through mountain valleys patched with tea plantations and vineyards, and watched windmills churning their trysailed arms. After an hour's steady ride, the long gray Atlantic breakers came into sight, rolling up against the forbidding rocks of the north coast.

Alex found a fisherman's cottage and bargained energetically in his few local words. Soon he, Ben, and Toby were rowing along the rugged coast, heading for the Evil Eye.

" 'Tis called that from all the shipwrecks seen there," Alex explained. "A tempting spot it be, for masters what don't know better take it for a good short cut. By the time they pile up on the rocks 'tis too late to mend a bad guess."

They pulled around a bend of the shore, and the Evil Eye reared before them. Toby rested on his oars, staring.

A narrow strait opened in front of them, both sides walled in by great black cliffs falling sheer into the water, as if the rock had been cloven with an ax. The farther end of the cliffs on the ocean side of the strait tumbled down into a long low reef running far out to where the sullen Atlantic rollers foamed over it. Toby could see why an impatient master might decide to risk the strait rather than tack around the reef, especially as there seemed to be a strong onshore current near the rocks. Toby said, "Give me a stern wind and I'd try for the Evil Eye myself."

Alex snorted. "Then down ye go to Davy Jones's locker!" His gnarled finger jabbed here and there along the foot of the cliffs. "There, and over thataway. These cliffs're like icebergs—they's got feet sticking out in the strait, only underwater, and likely ye don't see 'em till ye open up the hull of yer vessel. Now let's shake an oar and keep a weather eye out for Cap'n Noah's clue."

Ben made an offer. "I'll row and you two keep your eyes peeled. Alex, that message to Toby might've really been a secret for you to figure out."

The boatsteerer ducked his head in assent. "Aye. Toby, ye be lookout to larboard, and sing out when ye raise something what 'pears to fit."

Under the sweep of Ben's oars they entered the Evil Eye. The cliffs to starboard took the force of the Atlantic so that the narrow waterway was fairly calm. Toby could see a black rock curving out underwater, like the roots of a tree. A vessel charging through under a stern wind, as she would have to, could easily rip her keel. Besides the underwater gougers, there were great angular boulders like a child's building blocks tumbled into the sea. He asked Alex about them.

The boatsteerer scratched his head. "Reckon them earthquakes shoved them down from them cliffs up there."

Ben paused in his rowing to study the high black cliffs overwhelming their tiny rowboat. "Likely any more earthquakes today, Alex?"

"Never can tell," answered the boatsteerer. "Something's a-shaking every day somewheres 'mongst the islands. They got volcanoes, too. Mountains what of a sudden blasts their heads off, or maybe a stream of fire shooting up in the sea. Now what d'ye think of the fine tropic land?"

Toby shook his head. "Reckon I'd rather have a New England winter."

Ben Valentine bent to the oars, and Toby and Alex keenly studied their sides of the Evil Eye. But in all that treacherous rocky length of the strait neither saw anything worth a hail. They were out of the defile now, Ben leisurely turning the boat around. Toby said, "Alex, let's trade sides. I'll search the seaward cliffs."

But even this change of viewpoint yielded nothing beyond various shades of gray and black among the stones as Ben slowly pulled them back through the Eye. It was impossible to land on either shore to pursue their investigation. The search was at an end.

"Cheer up," said Alex. "The Evil Eye ain't the devil eye of what Cap'n Noah spoke. 'Twere just an idea of mine. Ben, hand over them provisions. We'll eat now, then row a mite just for fun 'fore going back to the harbor."

They let the boat bob in the swell as they ate hard rolls, goat cheese, oranges, and bananas. Ben occasionally sculled with an oar to keep from drifting out to sea as the boat gradually floated past its owner's cottage and around a rocky point. Here the cliffs fell away to a ledge at sea level.

"Lookee!" cried Ben. "They got them a whale!"

Toby craned his neck, and saw men clustering around a huge gray mound on the shore.

Alex was already at his oars. " 'Pears to be a sperm. Let's us have a gam."

It would be a welcome change to visit with someone outside the *Rogue*'s company, Toby thought.

Soon the three were scrambling over the rocks to where the Portuguese were cutting the whale with long knives tied to poles. The lucky fishermen grinned a welcome and Alex began passing out tobacco as Ben and Toby examined the huge catch.

Walking alongside the whale, Toby counted twenty-seven paces. The creature lay on its side, light glinting from the oily water that had pooled in the slack of its blubber. The fishermen had already begun cutting a strip of blubber free just forward of the flukes, peeling it away from the flesh beneath. Toby reached out, and found that the eight-inch thick blubber was surprisingly hard. The actual skin, however, was so thin that his hand came away covered with a gray slime.

Ben said, "A big change from our dryskin, ain't it?"

"I wasn't watching too close when they cut ours open," Toby admitted. But the outside of this whale looked fuller and healthier, well-fleshed out and insulated with fat. "I don't see any marks on him, though."

"Oh, the Portugee don't whale," Ben told him. "This is a piece of luck for them. Likely the whale suffocated."

"With air all around?" Toby scoffed, knowing that whales had lungs and needed to hold their breath when diving.

But Ben was serious. "You know how light your body gets in the water so's you can swim. Same way with a whale, the water helps hold up his weight for him so's he can breathe. If he gets washed up, like sometimes happens in a storm, why, his lungs is so heavy out of the water that he can't work them at all! So he just sort of strangles under his own weight."

Toby shook his head in wonder. Now he saw that the whale was crusted here and there with barnacles like the hull of a vessel long at sea. And it bore circular scars from its fights with the giant squid that was its food. One third of this vast length was made up of the cylindrical head, yet the eye was only as big as Toby's fist. The lower jaw seemed small for such a creature, long and narrow and about the size of a full-grown man. Toby counted twenty-three curved blunt teeth, spaced like pegs in the jaw, and saw that they fitted into sockets in the head.

The Portuguese fishermen clambered back on top of the sperm with their pole knives and gaff hooks. Alex came and stood beside Toby and Ben. He pointed with his pipe. "That's a mean jawful, ain't it? Sperm's the only kind of whale what has teeth, 'cept do you count porpoise and blackfish in as whales like some do. A sperm can chaw a whaleboat or bite off a limb easy as you lads can swallow a piece of pie."

They were silent awhile, and Toby thought of the limp bloody form in the fo'c'sle that had lain moaning day and night until yesterday when the man had been discharged and rowed ashore.

Alex spoke more cheerfully. "Them teeth make a good sort of scrimshaw. I paid off many a favor in foreign ports with my carving. Bear that in mind, lads."

Toby said, "You've got a piece of ivory scrimshaw on you, Alex. How about showing your seal to Ben?"

But the boatsteerer shook his head. " 'Tis no longer in my pocket, Toby. I always keep it down in my sea chest when I'm aboard a vessel. Feared of losing it—kind of like losing my name."

Ben cocked an eye at the sun. "Time's getting on."

"Aye," the boatsteerer agreed. "We'd best get moving."

But Toby held back. "First let's bargain for two or three of those whale teeth."

Ben shook his head. "You can't get the teeth till they rot out of the jaw, Toby. But we'll have plenty of chances to fetch in our own ivory."

"Aye, right enough," said Alex. "And never mind danger as long as them sperm is big and fat, with sperm oil at a dollar a gallon! That's the whaling trade, and the men what ride the boats down is glad to take their chances." His face clouded a moment. "Though 'tis a real grief to lose a good whaleman just chasing after somebody's idea of easy wealth. Let's hoist anchor, lads."

Calling farewell to the Portuguese fishermen, they scrambled over the big boulders between them and their boat. Toby, in the lead, was just rounding a clump of thick bushes when he stopped short.

Beside the prow of their rowboat, as if expecting them at any moment, stood Captain Peter Flick.

 six

At the Masthead

CAPTAIN FLICK NODDED in greeting. "Have a good day, men?"

"Aye, sir," Alex responded dutifully.

"An unusual sport for a whaleman, isn't it, to spend his free day rowing?"

"Why, sir," said the boatsteerer in apparent amazement. "Rowing is what I can do best and it pleasures me to show these lads the way of it." He paused a moment, then added, "If'n ye come for a row, sir, I'd be glad to—"

"Nothing like that," the Captain said abruptly. He gestured toward the boulders behind which they had left the Portuguese. "I heard of a sperm here and thought it might be worth bargaining for."

Alex ducked his head respectfully. "Aye, then we'll get on and leave ye to yer business."

But Captain Flick did not move aside as Alex unbent the painter from its rock. "You rowed through the strait— what do they call it?—the Evil Eye. I suppose you saw many interesting things there."

Toby and Ben quietly clambered into the rowboat and shipped one pair of oars. They waited for Alex.

The boatsteerer grunted in reply to the Captain. "As barren a place as a land shark's heart—neither fish, feathers, nor fur."

"No wreckage there, perhaps part of a ship still above the water?" The Captain's voice quickened. "A deserted fisherman's hut? Caves?"

"Why, sir—" Alex's eyes opened in pretended interest. "Be there something worth looking for, Captain? Reckon we ought to go back and search about?"

"No, no, don't trouble." Captain Flick forced a laugh. "It's only that such things arouse the interest of young lads, and I wished to know if your outing was entirely satisfactory to these boys."

"I reckon it were." Alex pushed the boat off, climbed in and seized the second pair of oars. The three rowed in silence until the rocky shore hid Captain Flick.

Then Ben Valentine said, "He didn't find out about that sperm till he stood lookout from behind the rocks. Likely his horse is hid in some brush."

Toby recalled that Peter Flick was within hearing distance when Captain Noah spoke his dying words. "Reckon he figures to look through the Evil Eye the way we did?"

"Aye," said Alex. "Else he just come to it from following us."

"Even if I find out what my uncle meant, 'tis no business of Captain Flick's," Toby said indignantly. "Uncle Noah's message was meant for me alone. There's no call for the Captain to come trailing after me."

Alex shook his head. "Don't know 'bout the right of it, but like it or not the Cap'n's keeping a weather eye on ye, Toby." Frowning, he let his oars trail in the water. "I recollect when Cap'n Noah spoke them words for Toby, 'twas Peter Flick he was looking at."

Ben spoke eagerly. "Maybe that message was really a warning to Peter Flick, and now he fears Toby'll discover something against him."

They spoke the message again, puzzling over each word. But, however they contrived, nothing seemed to make sense. Once more Alex bent to the oars.

The sun was hull down by the time the three rode into Ponta Delgado. Returning their horses to the stable, they reached the waterfront just in time to run for the last whaleboat.

Aboard the *Rogue* the crew was drifting to the places custom reserved for abovedecks leisure: the fo'c'sle hands lounging from forehatch cover to bow railing, the boat-steerers and idlers grouping around the bench abaft the tryworks, and the officers gathering on the quarter-deck.

Cook stepped out of the galley banging on a pan, but few came forward for ship's fare. Most of the men dug fruits and sausages out of their pockets. Toby and Ben shared the remains of their tuck-out, glad now that Alex had insisted they keep the leftovers. Zachary came to sit beside them, his pannikin full from the galley. "Ain't passing up no whack due me," he explained around a mouthful. "Sweat hard 'nough for it, we do, then maybe get it took out'n our mouths." He had not forgotten those days on biscuit and water.

A shipkeeper lit the riding lights, red in the port shrouds, green in the starboard. Coming forward he hung a lamp on the foremast. Small trades sprang up—a lump of cheese for a plug of tobacco, a carved comb for a leather drawstring purse. A man stepped to the lamp and lighted his pipe. Someone hummed a port tune, "Where'd yer go, what'd yer do?" From abaft the tryworks floated the strains of a concertina. Toby wondered which of the idlers was playing.

"You lads, there. Have a good time in port?" It was a friendly invitation for Toby and Ben to join the talk.

But before either of them could answer, Jake Underhill said, "They wasn't in port much. I seen them and Alex White go off on horses."

The sailors were amazed and interested. Most of them, spending their lives at sea, were poor riders, and they distrusted the "bonebreakers." They clamored for details, and soon Toby and Ben were telling of their ride, the tuck-out in the rowboat, and the sperm that had washed ashore. Neither mentioned Captain Flick nor the message that had drawn them, fruitlessly, across the island.

The hands talked over the outing, some wishing out loud that they had had a tuck-out too instead of spending their time and money in a grog shop. "That place ye lads saw," someone said, "that'd be the Evil Eye, be'ent it? I heard tell she's a ship killer."

Zachary raised his head from his pannikin. "I recollect that name somehow."

Toby felt Ben start slightly and his own heart began pounding. Had Zachary heard Captain Noah's dying words?

Zachary snapped his fingers. " 'Twasn't no place name; she were a ship." He searched his pockets and brought out his pipe. The men, sensing a story in the offing, bided in agreeable silence while Zachary lighted up from the fore-mast lamp. " 'Twas down by the Brazil Banks. You 'n' me, Jake, we both shipped with Cap'n Noah that time. Recollect it?" His voice was cajoling, as if uncertain of Jake's response.

"Ye mean when that ship was figuring to fetch up on the shoals?" Jake Underhill was the least surly that Toby had ever known. "We was in the *Five Friends* what Cap'n Noah hired out as master. I forget the name of that ship we come up with."

"She were the *Evil Eye*—no! I recollect now she were named the *Lucifer*. Aye, the *Lucifer*—couldn't miss it. I was in one of the boats and we just passed under her counter when she lifted high up, like a pair of flukes ready to smash down on us. Same sea what lifted her was fixing to push our boat underneath of her. I tell you we rowed! We just come clear when she spanked down hard and I read her name done in gilt on the transom. *Lucifer*."

"Devil of the name," someone joked, and the men laughed.

Zachary added, "Passenger, she was, out of Baltimore. Never forget it."

"She broke up that night," Jake said. "Fine lined, couldn't take a real rough sea." He sounded smug about it.

All the foremasthands were listening intently, for though many of them had often sailed under Captain Noah, only these two had been with him in the *Five Friends*. They demanded the full story of the wreck from the very beginning.

Zachary drew on his pipe, settled back, and began. "The *Lucifer* loaded passengers and left Baltimore bound for Rio. Meanwhile, us in the *Five Friends* was six months out of New Bedford. We'd fished some in the Western Grounds where we're headed for now, stowing down 'bout 250 barrels of mixed oil."

Toby was impatient for Zachary to get on with the story of the wreck, though the other hands seemed deeply interested as he took the *Five Friends* through the Cape Verdes, then back across the Atlantic to the Brazil Banks, cruising for whales as she gradually approached the Line.

Jake Underhill broke into the tale. "The *Lucifer* didn't make enough easting in the North Atlantic to clear Brazil 'fore starting down to cross the Line. Ye know how them trades can blow you backwards!"

Zachary shook his head. " 'Twas the current she didn't mind, Jake. It fetched her just far 'nough westward so when that gale come up she was jammed behind the cape."

Toby interrupted. "But what of the *Five Friends?* Wasn't Captain Noah behind the cape, too?"

There were cries of disagreement, and Zachary explained.

Passenger ships crowded sail to drive speedily along their routes. But a whaler was built mainly for stability in all kinds of weather, and when sailing under cruising canvas such a vessel was ably handled even in sudden storms. "Howsomever, the Cap'n's always got to know what he's about," Zachary added.

" 'Twas a good gale blowing," Jake said, whistling over it. He seemed like any other fo'c'sle hand just then, pleased to be part of a good sea story. "We'd just shortened down to tops'ls and found us a nice wave to snuggle under when somebody yelled a sighting."

"And there was this passenger," added Zachary. "A-scuddin' along with sails split to rags and wrapped around her yards like ribbons. Just then a big dollop pooped her and she broached to."

"I didn't see that," Jake confessed. "We'd just shipped a

green sea ourselves and I was still tryin' to breathe it back out o' me. When I seen the *Lucifer* next she was half seas over and making broadside for the shoals."

Zachary resumed the tale. "Well, you can't make no speed on your beam ends, so Cap'n Noah figured he had time to run the *Lucifer* a line and try warping her off. That meant he had to bring the *Five Friends* up and drop a boat while running to wind'ard of her. He figured the waist boat was safest to lower. That was my station. My, that was a ride! And the wind and waves was slamming the *Lucifer* down first on the port side, then heave her up and down again on the starb'd beam ends, back and forth like a kitten batting a ball, and us in the boat like little fishes scooting out of the way of the shark's mouth!"

"To make a long story short," said Jake, who, after all, had not been in the waist boat, "they fixed the line, but the *Lucifer*'s master was fretting so over his passengers, he wanted them took off b'fore trying to save the ship. Cap'n Noah, he put the rest of the boats over—that was a tricky piece of work, let me tell you!—and we brought the passengers and crew off."

"By then," said Zachary, pulling noisily on his pipe, " 'twas so dark and wet you couldn't tell martingale from maintop. The *Five Friends* bore off and hove to under a goosewinged forecourse. And the next morning, when the gale abated some, we saw the *Lucifer* had grounded on a reef and broke up in the night."

"She was too fine lined," Jake repeated. "Else we might've saved her."

"Her master didn't much mind losing her, to hear him tell it," Zachary added. "And the passengers was so pleased with Cap'n Noah bringing them off that when we run them into Pernambuco they got up a subscription and give him a memento for the rescue—a plate or a compass or something. I forget."

Four double strokes chimed from the ship's bell, and the Mate called out, "The master's aboard. Watch and watch about, port on deck and starb'd below. Now all hands to make sail."

The *Rogue* was once more back on her sea routine. That night the bark made a long reach to the southeast, and two days later she was entering the Western Grounds.

Those two days in passage were made up of long hours of whaleboat drill. It was "Hoist and swing!" from sunup to twilight. Drop your work and run to your boat while the Mates flipped coils of line from the belaying pins for the shipkeepers to grab and haul. Aboard with the line tubs, off with the gripes! Kick in the cranes, lower away and slide down the falls! Shove off, boys, out oars and spring to! Lay on, you sons, I want to see them blades bend!

And bend they did, the good springy white ash. Toby soon felt he could do his duty in his sleep. Ben Valentine said the boat crew had to work like a machine, for when you were riding the wild white waves a maddened whale gave you no time for thinking, else it was a stove boat and six good men down.

Then one morning eight bells rang just as the work gang Toby was in finished taking in the fore-topgallantsail. Toby swung down the shrouds to fetch his breakfast, but before he could find a place to eat it on deck, Mr. Barksdale raised his voice. "Boat watches it'll be, lads! Waist boat on lookout. Lively, now, and keep a weather eye out."

Someone in the maintop shouted down. "How much t'baccy for first spout?"

But the Mate had no time to answer before Captain Flick's voice rang out. "It's oil you're working for, you clod—not tobacco! You get a part of every whale you see and take. And any man that doesn't raise up his voice proper will feel the heavy end of a belaying pin!"

When Toby carried his breakfast forward he heard the men muttering about Captain Flick's break with the traditional reward. He joined Zachary and Ben on the fore-hatch cover.

Zachary was grumbling over his porridge. "That Jake—I just can't figure him!"

"Seems like he's been friendly lately," Toby said, reaching for the port watch's breakfast molasses.

"For a couple days there, from when we tell 'bout the *Lucifer* going down, he was just like his old self, Jake was.

Now, since we got in the grounds, he starts acting up like he done in the beginning, sneering at a fellow, sassing under his breath to Mates and men alike." Zachary carefully scraped up the last of the porridge in his pannikin. "Jake Underhill, he was never like that any other voyage, and him and me sailed four, five trips together, all under Cap'n Noah one time or another, even that there last voyage when the Cap'n died. Jake was always a mite slow getting down to work, but he never riled officers nor shipmates." He shook his head. "Funny the way he changed, like maybe he took a fever in port and it turned his mind. Sure glad he's in the waist boat 'stead of with us in larboard!"

After breakfast, Toby noticed, no one in the port watch went below into the fo'c'sle. He mentioned this to Ben, adding, "I reckon everyone wants to see if we sight whales the first day."

Ben grinned. "Maybe so, Toby, but like it or not we're all of us still on duty. Didn't you hear the Mate call for boat watches? That means we can't none of us go below till the second dogwatch at suppertime."

"We've been up since four this morning!" Toby protested.

"You'll get more sleep at night now," Ben promised. "Instead of a watch turning out, just a boat crew at a time will take turns abovedecks. We'll stand watch only once a night, instead of twice like we been doing. While we was cracking it on, making passage, it took a whole watch to work ship. You know how we shortened sail before breakfast? Now we're in the grounds we won't be making speed, and we need only half a watch, or one boat crew, on deck at night. That gives us all more rest, for during the day we have to stand by, ready to lower the boats."

Toby nodded his understanding. "Do we go on lookout, too?"

"Aye, each boat crew takes its turn." Ben pointed out the stations, manned now by the waist boat crew. One hand stood at the wheel, two men were high up at the foremast truck, leaning over the lowered royal yard, and two more were higher yet at the head of the mainmast. The Second, header for the waist boat, kept a careful eye on his men. Ben added, "Lookout stations are in two-hour tricks, then you can go back painting, polishing, scrubbing, splicing, and stitching. Maybe Mr. Barksdale will let us take some scrimshaw in hand, for mainly the officers want to keep the crew busy and out of trouble."

Toby shook his head. "I doubt Captain Flick could stand seeing us do something we liked."

Ben quickly smothered a laugh. "Reminds me, you must keep your voice down and no barging about or rattling! Mind how quiet 'tis now? That's so's we can hear the lookouts when they sing out. Any noise you want to make, save for when lookouts are called down in the evening."

Toby remembered a scrap of overheard conversation.

"Mr. Barksdale says that noise gallies whales."

Ben nodded. "It don't aboard the vessel, for we'll be too far from them. But when we're close by in a boat, you almost dasn't breathe! Why, when I was sailing in the *Nancy and John,* my boat'd just run down to a pod of sperm when Stroke Oar kicked the lantern keg. The whole pod was gallied and took off in a smother of foam. That cost us maybe three hundred barrels of sperm oil. The Old Man was fit to heave Stroke overboard."

Just then Mr. Barksdale came along and, seeing their hands empty, sent Ben to tar down rigging and Toby to overhaul a jammed tackle.

That noon at the change of the watch the larboard boat was posted on tricks. Ben and Alex laid aloft to the foremast truck, Stroke and Bow went up to the main masthead, and Mr. Barksdale led Toby to the wheel under the afterhouse.

"Now, youngster," said the Mate. "Get over on the weather side and grab hold the spokes like this."

The helm was sheltered by the galley to starboard and the main companion to port, but recalling that the wind was blowing two points abaft the starboard beam, Toby stood to the right of the wheel. Gripping the spokes, he immediately felt the pulsing life of the vessel as the sea kicked against the rudder and the wind strained the masts.

The Mate showed him how to watch the sails through the opening in the afterhouse roof, moving the wheel to keep the canvas drawing full. "The wind might haul around," he warned. "So keep an eye on the compass and sing out if we get too far off course. Don't forget to strike the hours." He pointed to the ship's bell hanging within reach, then stepped through the main companion to go down to his dinner.

Toby's clutch on the wheel quickened. He glanced at the canvas above, then down at the compass suspended beneath the skylight just forward of the helm. He was not too far off course, he thought.

Then he noticed Mr. Barksdale looking up with a frown from the crowded little dining table. The compass was a telltale and could be read from below. To render a clear view of it, the bulkhead dividing saloon and main cabin stopped short of the overhead. Toby, his hands clamped relentlessly around the spokes, eased the wheel over until course and direction line coincided.

Later, when the officers came up from dinner, Mr. Barksdale muttered an encouraging, "Steady as she goes," as he passed. Then Toby remembered the time, and his eyes traveled through the skylight down the after side of the partition below, finding the chronometer hanging just above the Captain's desk. Toby could see the desk chair and a smoking stand, but the rest of the main cabin was out of sight.

At last the two-hour trick was over. Once again Toby rang the hour on the ship's bell, this time four strokes. A man from the starboard boat crew relieved him, and Toby went forward, every muscle aching from the strain.

Late that afternoon a cry rang down from the masthead.

"Blo-o-ow! He blows and whitewaters!"

Every man aboard tensed with excitement, only to be disappointed. The pod of sperm, making passage, was going too fast for the *Rogue* to down boats.

The following day, during the larboard's trick in the forenoon watch, Mr. Barksdale posted Toby on lookout. With Alex White, Toby scrambled up the main weather shrouds, around the overhanging maintop platform, up to and past the topmast crosstrees until they reached the topgallant truck. Here two planks were bolted athwartships, fore and aft the topgallant mast. Alex stood on the more hazardous lee side, and Toby balanced himself aweather, leaning forward against the royal yard which was down on its lift ever since the sail had been stowed.

Toby had been in the rigging for some days, Mr. Barksdale gradually working him higher and higher. But then he had always had some work in hand that needed all his attention. Now, at the very top of a vessel under way, he must force himself to look out on sea and sky. The slender topgallant mast seemed to bend in the wind, and when the bark nudged her port bow a mite harder into the sea, Toby was quite sure he would be pitched down into the black ocean depths. He felt Alex pounding his shoulder.

The grizzled boatsteerer grinned. "Ye looked like ye was

fixing to caulk the deck. Now hang onto that yard. Ye know what yer up here for?"

"Spouts," Toby said, wedging himself into the angle of yard and mast, glad that the wind helped hold him there.

"They's spouts and spouts, and each whale's got his own," Alex said. "A sperm spouts a single plume what slants for'ard from the tip of his square snout. He's the only one what does it that way. A right whale has a twin spout what starts from the top of his head way back from the snout and it goes straight up. They's other kinds o' whales about with double spouts, so keep in mind that the right whale has a low plume, maybe less than a boat length. That's all ye got to know for now."

"What difference do the spouts make?" Toby asked. "Can't you see from way up here the kind of whale that surfaces?"

Alex snorted his derision. "When a whale come up, his back is barely clear of the water. He looks like a shoal awash, or maybe he just gets his blowholes clear and all ye can see is his spout. Then you got to know his kind, so's the Cap'n can figure his speed, and is he worth lowering for?"

"Aren't we going after every whale we see?" Toby asked. "I mean, except for dryskins." It was the first time he had thought about that incident since the injured sailor was put off in the Azores.

Alex shook his head. "Just for sperm and right. Some

whales, like the sulphur-bottom, is so quick even ye drive a boat faster'n a horse can gallop, he'll outrun ye. Other whales sink as soon as ye lance their life. Still other kinds don't have hardly nothing in or on 'em worth the chase. And some, like the killer, ye'd be a fool to go after. That's why, way back in the shore fishery days b'fore men took to whaling from ships, folks said they was just this particular whale that was the 'right one' to take out'n the whole collection. The right whale is slow 'nough to chase in boats, ain't too concerned 'bout killing ye, and he's mighty worth the effort in whalebone and the oil he carries."

Alex spat to leeward. "Once ye start sailing in blue water looking for whales, yer going to find them. Sperm can be took, do ye keep clear o' them teeth. Humpback, too, in the islands, and likely we'll be coasting for some in the Pacific, though his oil don't be so fine. Now keep a weather eye out."

Toby scanned the seas, a monotonous plane of gray-blue broken by the wind into glassy reflections and dark shadows. The topgallant mast and the thin royal mast set into it swayed back and forth, and the *Rogue* rose and fell on the long scend of the North Atlantic.

Not entirely sure of what to watch for, Toby found his thoughts wandering. It was strange how many lives had altered after Captain Noah died. Toby was before the mast instead of sailing as cabin boy according to plan. Alex

White had been forced into a voyage he had not wanted. Peter Flick had become a tyrant. Even Jake Underhill, an ordinary hand, had changed into a sneering fo'c'sle strutter. Maybe Jake, alone, understood the secret of Captain Noah's message. "Was Jake Underhill anywhere around when my uncle was dying?" Toby blurted out.

A wry grin tugged at Alex's mouth. "It do beat all. I was just recollecting 'bout yer uncle, Toby. Seems now 'tis the first real chance we got to jaw 'bout what happened." He scratched his chin, wiry with beard. "Jake Underhill? He weren't around just then, no, but he wasn't hardly anywheres when we needed a hand. The Third—that's Cap'n Flick now, ye know—was always a-chivvying after him, and I reckon he'd of let loose with a rope's end 'cept Cap'n Noah never let his crew get beat. Did his best with Jake, the Third did. Made him pay deck seams under a boiling sun, and never mind did the hot tar burn him some. Or chip the anchor chain where it hangs overboard out'n the hawsehole. Jake weren't a bad sort, just kind o' had to be kept after. But changed some now, though. Can't figure why Cap'n Flick puts up with him, now he's top man in the vessel and no one to stay his hand.

"But about yer uncle. Toby, I'm figuring now I seen him sign the *Rogue* away to his Third Mate. I recollect it were just north of the West Indies Grounds, the *Rogue* standing in for New Bedford, a fortune in oil stowed down. Close on full to the hatches, though half a hold's a paying voyage these days. We was five, six whales short of topping off." Like all seamen, Alex took keen delight in recalling even the smallest particulars of a voyage.

"Heavy seas was making up, and the wind was freshening out of the east-southeast. The *Rogue* was all right, do we just shorten down and stand along. We was on watch and watch, and just when it rang the middle of the afternoon watch, the Second come to tell me Cap'n Noah wants to see me in the main cabin.

"I went below and there he's at his desk, talking with Mr. Flick—he were Third then, mind. 'Twere a dark day, and the lamps was lit, the one hoisted up by the compass so ye can steer, and the other hanging by the Cap'n's desk where there was a paper all wrote out. Cap'n Noah asks has I got my name seal, and I says she's always in my sea chest. Go fetch her here, he says."

Alex paused while he scanned the seas in token of his duty aloft. Toby looked around his own sector of the horizon. If spouts there were, the foremast lookouts would probably sing out first, since they were tending to their job and not jawing away.

The boatsteerer resumed his story. "There wasn't that door from steerage into the saloon then, so I had to come up on deck and go down through the booby hatch to get the seal out'n my sea chest. When I get back, 'tis like Cap'n Noah and the Third hasn't moved a quarter compass point. Then Cap'n Noah tells me to watch what he's doing. And I say, how do I know as I don't read none? Don't matter can I read or not, he says. Just to watch him. He takes up a quill, writes on the bottom of that paper on his desk, and tells me he's signed his name. Then he hands the quill to Mr. Flick, who scowls and signs it too. Then Cap'n Noah says for me to stamp my name seal, showing I watched them signing. Witnessed it, he calls it. So I do that, making a real good print of my boatsteerer 'bout to dart. Mr. Flick asks me my whole name (he didn't never know many of the crew's names) and he writes it out alongside of my stamp. Then Cap'n Noah says, 'All right, Alex.' And I go back to my duty."

"But didn't they give any kind of explanation?" Toby asked. "Can you recollect anything either one said that day?"

Alex nodded. "I can, and I just told ye the all of it. They neither says nothing, not 'bout buying nor selling the vessel, nor 'bout nothing else. Quiet as clams they both of them was, and ye'd think words was maybe costing a dollar apiece. I don't know 'bout the bark changing hands till we was fixing to drop our hook in Buzzard's Bay. The way is still on the vessel when Mr. Flick up and says he owns the *Rogue*."

"Did Mr. Flick show the paper when he claimed the *Rogue*?"

"Not to me, he didn't. But nobody else aboard witnessed nothing, else ye'd never of heard the end o' the bragging. With me, though, I maybe bring it up once or twice in steerage how Cap'n Noah asks me to give him a hand with some important paper. Later on in port it gets about that when Mr. Flick bought the *Rogue* it was all witnessed proper. 'Tain't none of my affair, but I think 'bout it now and again, and I reckon now that paper I stamped was when Cap'n Noah sold his vessel to the Third."

Toby reflected that if his uncle had trusted Alex he himself could confide something that had been bothering him. "Peter Flick told my Aunt Prudence that Captain Noah gambled his vessel away cheap. Is that the way it looked in the cabin that day, Alex? Were there cards or dice or money about—or, maybe—you think they'd been—drinking?"

"None of that!" Alex said sharply. "Yer uncle was straight 'n' sober and a fine master, he was. And that day they both of them looked right solemn, not like they'd been passing the time away gaming nor gamming. And all I ever see was just that paper on the desk. Cap'n Noah died right after that."

Toby swiveled his head around the topgallant mast. "Was it the same day?"

"Near to the same hour," Alex told him. "I didn't see it happen for I was up helping reef the main tops'l. I went right from the cabin into the rigging where my station was. It took the gang of us a good quarter hour in that stiff wind to fist down to the reef band. We was just passing the points around the yard when the *Rogue* give a lurch. We was ready, hanging on, for we'd been yawing since b'fore noon. Anyhow, of a sudden I see a scrambling on deck, and men clustering 'gainst the lee bulwarks. Trouble, looks like.

"I knotted my point and slid down a backstay. Got through the crowd to find Cap'n Noah dying. He's staring straight at Mr. Flick when he says to the First Mate, 'Mr. Hughs, tell Toby to look through the devil's eye.' And then he died. We manhandled the casks back in place—they'd broke loose from the lashrail and tumbled over Cap'n Noah."

"What were casks doing on deck?" Toby asked. "There was still room in the hold, you said."

"We'd taken a sperm in the West Indies Grounds," Alex explained. "Half the cargo'd have to to be shifted to make room for the new casks and to trim the vessel. Cap'n Noah figured not to bother, being as we're so close to home. So the casks was just made fast to the lashrail, half a dozen to a side, port and starb'd. The starb'd ones was what started free."

Toby pondered a moment. "Mr. Flick had just bought the *Rogue,* and he's got a paper to prove it. But wasn't it Mr. Hughs who took over command?"

"Sure Mr. Hughs took over. First Mate always do. He didn't linger none in any of the homeward whaling grounds, but just pressed on for New Bedford. Mr. Hughs was sure took aback when we got to port and Mr. Flick announces as he's the new owner. Standing right in the waist he is, and shouts out the glad news so's Mr. Hughs by the helm can hear him nice and clear, and the rest of the vessel, too. Mr. Hughs and the Second both looked like they could've been knocked down with the wind pennant, and later all three officers go below, I reckon maybe to jaw 'bout it and see that paper. Anyways, in the end 'twas Mr. Flick who paid us off. Not that I got anything. He made me sign up for this voyage b'fore I could even fetch my duds off the vessel." He scratched his head. "Though it beat all how I could buy and borrow up my whole lay. Vowed to Cap'n Noah I'd be thrifty that voyage."

Toby suppressed a grin, recalling how Aunt Prudence had often found Alex on the beach.

Turning his gaze seaward, Toby forced his mind on his lookout duty. Slowly the time passed. From far away came the faint chime of the ship's bell. One more hour to go at masthead.

Suddenly a silver flash marred the horizon. Toby blinked. Now came three, four, five vertical twin strokes all together. Foam streaked the sea and there was another double plume—and another!

Toby heaved in a tremendous breath. "Blo-o-o-ows!" he yelled. "Blows—he whitewaters and *blo-o-o-ows!*"

 seven

"Blo-o-ows!"

"Blows—*blows!*" Toby was yelling like a madman. The other lookouts saw the spouts, too, and joined in the shouting.

Captain Flick's voice surged up from the distant deck. "Where away?"

Toby stopped and looked wildly at Alex. But it was Ben Valentine at the fore-topgallant truck who furnished the answer. "Two points on the port bow!"

And Alex White shouted down, "Five miles off. Pod of rights, gamming."

That meant the pod was not making passage, only cruising and feeding. Breathless with excitement, Toby watched the shiny spurts on the slate-gray sea. Twin spouts all, leaning a little forward, but mainly going upward. The plumes of vapor were, he knew, twenty feet high, and now he branded the measure of their distance in his memory.

Mr. Barksdale trumpeted from the deck. "Alow, masthead! All hands, clear for lowering!"

Toby grasped the topgallant mast shrouds, but Alex shouted, "No, this way!" He looked up in time to see the boatsteerer stretch out his arms and step off into space, swinging himself aboard the weather royal backstay and sliding down out of sight. Toby glanced forward and saw the fore-topgallant truck deserted. If he was not to be left behind he would have to go down the whaleman's way.

He grasped the backstay, kicking off the crosstrees and swinging his legs to grip the line. He slid downward, conscious of speed, space, the slatting lines of the running rigging, yards swinging and blocks creaking all around him as the *Rogue* was hurriedly backed.

The deck was in an uproar as Toby's feet struck the sheerpole. He swung inboard and jumped down. Officers were bawling orders, the hands were shouting in response, and men were running to their boats. Toby leaped across to the larboard bulwarks, found his boat lowered, jumped the rail and got down the bow falls before Alex could unhook the block. As Toby tumbled to his Midship thwart, the mast was jammed in place, stays tautened, boom shipped, and the sails unfurled to bloom against the sky. Then they were off and running out to the pod, soon losing sight of the other boats but for an occasional glimpse of a sail.

Toby was momentarily dismayed to find the sea apparently empty. He understood now how the scend of the sea and the whale's habit of surfacing just enough to clear his blowholes made the creature undetectable from a boat. All hands had been required to memorize the signals on a board hanging in the fo'c'sle. The *Rogue* would use these to tell the whalemen of their quarry's whereabouts.

Mr. Barksdale, from where he stood in the stern sheets steering with the sweep, shouted over the wind, "Stroke, keep an eye on the top hamper!" They were not yet near enough for their noise to gally the whales.

Toby could hear Zachary behind him turning on his thwart to sit back to bow as he did when rowing, the handier to read the signals from the vessel they were leaving behind. They ran on swiftly, water gurgling along the bilge strakes, boom swung outboard, mainsail and jib drawing full. Ben drew a length of whaleline out of the after tub near his feet and handed a loop of it to Stroke, who reached past Mr. Barksdale to drop it around the loggerhead in the stern cuddy. Then Ben pulled more line out of the tub and around the loggerhead, tossing the slack forward to Alex. The boatsteerer carefully coiled twenty-five feet of line in the bow box, as slack for darting. He bent the end to the eye of a harpoon, then used a short warp with a loop to bend the spare iron. The job was done with accustomed speed, for sometimes they had to rig the whaleline when driving under oars, the weight of rowing falling upon the rest of the boat crew.

Twenty minutes later Alex called back from the bow, "Don't see spouts." There was a moment of silence but for the wind and water. Then Zachary shouted, "Whales to wind'ard—they's on the weather bow!"

Toby glanced back, and among the masts and rigging of the *Rogue* he saw the main-topgallantsail clewed up.

Mr. Barksdale called, "All right, douse them sails."

Tacking, with its ever-changing angles of approach, was impossible when the quarry was invisible. They would have to row.

Down came the canvas. Toby helped steady the boom as stays were started and the mast unshipped. Spars and sails were hurriedly bundled, then jammed under the Stroke thwart to jut out over the stern, a short lashing making all fast to the starboard thwart stringer. Nothing was allowed loose in the boat.

The Mate called, "Toss oars, and make a good ash breeze, boys. We've a couple miles to pull. Faster, Stroke. Mind your blade, Midship. Now hold, Three. Pull, Two!" The Mate leaned on the sweep and the boat turned into the wind. "Pull, All! Spring your backs! C'mon, lads, dollars waiting for you!"

Facing the Mate, Toby braced his feet, watching Stroke sitting directly ahead of him and pulling, feathering, and bending along with him. On Tub thwart between Toby and Zachary sat Ben Valentine at the starboard side of the boat. From the corner of his eye Toby could follow that red head as it bobbed in the rhythm of rowing, the loom of Ben's oar reaching over the after-line tub, across the boat in front of Toby and going out through the double tholepins in the larboard gunwale.

Mr. Barksdale urged them on. "Bend them blades, my bully boys! We'll cut in seventy barrels tonight, I swear. You going to let the waist boat fasten first? Pull, lads, pull!"

Toby pulled mindlessly, as if he had been a clock wound up and someone had set the weights to swinging, swinging. The oars were thrummed and made almost no noise. It was eerie, five men driving a boat through the seas nearly as soundlessly as a craft full of dead. Only the Mate's coaxing and the sough of wind across the water convinced Toby he was still alive.

Then behind him, bow on to the boat, he heard a vast deep sighing. Toby flung his head around, glimpsed a dark oval awash, and turned back to his oar. Farther ahead than he had expected, the spout was a high-flung spume whose foul odor wafted down to them on the wind. Mr. Barksdale lowered his voice. "Easy, now, lads. A long pull, a slow pull, let her glide, glide. He sounds now. Pull, pull! Let's go and meet him."

Toby heard water streaming from uplifted flukes, then the wash of waves as the whale sounded. The bull would be down less than a quarter hour. A boatheader could calculate where he would rise next. The Mate heaved on the long steering sweep and the boat curved around an oily patch. This slick left by a sounding whale must never be crossed, whalemen said, for fear of gallying him.

"Way 'nough," the Mate said.

They rested on their oars, waiting for the whale to break water, the boat rising and falling on the sea. Toby watched the play of color across the wind-broken surface—clear sky blue, murky yellow, cloudy green. As the sea bore them upward he saw far off a growing line of foam and a tiny boat sleighing behind. "Boat fast!" he called.

The Mate growled, then jerked his head. "He ripples! Give me a good long pull, lads!"

They heaved once on their oars, then sat with blades poised as the boat surged ahead.

"Once more," the Mate said, "then peak oars."

Another pull, and then it was run the oars in, wedge handles down into the cleats near the bottom and opposite the tholepins, peaking the blades up and out on either side, making V's along the boat.

Mr. Barksdale said, "Turn about and paddle. Up he comes!"

Toby swiveled around in time to see a vast dark shape, easily as big as the boat, sliding up and breaking water. Vapor plumed upward in a long rumbling exhalation, the twin jets merging into one cloud. The evil-smelling mist drizzled over the men as they pulled the boat closer.

"Eyes in the boat!" hissed the Mate from the stern sheets. "Do your duty, boys!"

With the others, Toby dug his paddle into the water,

but he could not keep from staring at the shape before them. Still exhaling, the whale kept rising, rising until, twice the length of the boat, he was surfaced from nib to flukes, and his body humped with the solidity and very nearly the outline of a boulder reef.

Different from the block-bodied, square-headed sperm Toby had seen in the Azores, the right whale had a curving mouth just under his rounded snout. Huge blubbery lower lips wrapped around the black whalebone fringe of the upper jaw which sieved his food from the sea. Close to the nib, the tip of his muzzle, was the gray horny crust called the bonnet, and no whaleman had yet guessed its purpose.

"Get set, Alex," Mr. Barksdale called softly.

Toby wrenched his eyes from the vast shape ahead. Alex boated his paddle and stood up in the bow, his left thigh wedged in the crescent-shaped clumsy cleat. Toby saw that during their final approach a double-V crotch had been set into the starboard gunwale, propping up the two live irons close to the harponier's hand. Alex took up one of the six-foot barked poles tipped with a four-foot iron, its arrow-shaped head gleaming along the razor-sharp edges. Balancing the heavy weapon in both hands, he signaled.

The Mate muttered fiercely, "Lively, lads! Run her in!"

Toby's paddle bit water and he nearly pulled his arm out of its socket. The whale was scarcely three boat lengths away and they were closing rapidly. His hands were wet and he tingled with alarm. Oil and bone were commodities, things to buy and sell and make into soap, candles, medicines, fuel, whips, and umbrellas. But to get them they had to slaughter a living creature, sharp of ear, dull of eye, and warm of blood, breather of air, bearer of young, and closer kin to man than to fish.

They came up to the right side from the blind sector in the rear, barely clearing the tip of the whale's deadly flukes. Mr. Barksdale pointed the boat in just abaft the unwitting eye. Paddling furiously, the men drove the boat nearer and nearer—

"Give it him, Alex!"

Alex pitched the harpoon. The iron drove into that huge animal up to the hitches, the pole brought up and falling free. Quickly Alex snatched up the second iron and darted that, too.

"Stern, All!" yelled the Mate.

They backed for their lives as, in a spasm of agony, the gigantic flukes lifted. Huge black triangles swung over the boat. "Back, back!" screamed the Mate. He threw himself against the sweep, the men lashed the water and they foamed clear just as the great flukes smashed down. The boat skittered broadside and shipped a sea.

"Oars, and pull for it!" Mr. Barksdale yelled. He was sculling madly.

Kicking the handles out of the cleats, the men ran their oars out and pulled. Down came the flukes again, and spray shot into their faces. But they were clear.

"B'ware line!" Alex shouted.

Hemp from the harpoons, drawn out of the tub by their retreat, looped dangerously amid the thwarts, each kink capable of wringing off a man's limb or snatching him overboard and beneath the water. Now barely clear of a thrashing whale, all hands grabbed the line, cramming it forward and out of the boat through the bow chock. The massive whale rounded his back, then dove into the sea, tossing his flukes high in the air as he plunged downward.

"Peak oars!" ordered the Mate. "Clear for running! Alex, change ends!"

They had a few bare seconds in which to brace themselves, for already the floating coils of line were squirming into the ocean after the diving whale. Stroke threw an extra turn around the loggerhead, and Ben dashed water into the tubs. This increased the friction of the line against which the whale would eventually exhaust himself.

Giving a berth to the hemp now whipping down the center of the boat, Mr. Barksdale and Alex jumped over thwarts, met and passed, each tumbling into his new place just as the boat started off with a jerk that pitched everybody to the planking. The line was pulled as taut as an oaken stave, and still it was singing around the loggerhead, humming under the kicking strap in the bow, and squealing over the roller in the chock. In the stern sheets, Alex scrambled upright and grabbed the steering oar, steadying the boat as it went creaming through the water, throwing up a bow wave. The line could not get out fast enough. It whistled and shrilled, and the boat began spanking heavily over the sea. Drenched from head to foot, Toby clutched the gunwale, half afraid, half enjoying the wild, fabled Nantucket sleighride.

Mr. Barksdale roared from the bow. "Bail! Midship, earn your keep!"

It was the only duty Toby had besides rowing. But bail at this speed? He hardly dared let go the gunwale. Crouching on the bottom in nearly a foot of sloshing water, Toby felt around for the wooden piggin, unshipped its warp, and began bailing. A furious yell came from Stroke behind him. "Not in m'face, you soger!" But Zachary had to put up with it, for every direction was windward in the whizzing boat, and Toby dared not put his arm over the gunwale for fear of the solid surface of the sea wrenching it off. He had also to be wary of the deadly crippling whale-line tearing along beside him.

At last his piggin scraped the bottom and he sat back on his haunches, braced against his thwart. Water was no longer pouring in over the bow, though spray was still drenching the men. Was the line slowing? Toby craned to look far ahead, but saw only the golden hemp slanting out and down into the slaty ocean. Bow Oar padded his hand with a quilted canvas square, then leaning past Mr. Barksdale, he grasped the running line briefly with the nipper. "Slack," he reported.

"All hands haul away," said the Mate.

Toby was afraid of burning his hands, but saw that everyone else turned to, and so with them he grabbed the line, surprised that a good heave easily brought in a bight which Stroke snubbed around the loggerhead and Ben coiled down rapidly in the after-line tub. The waist tub, between Toby and Ben, was still full, so they had not had too great a run after all compared with stories from the fo'c'sle. Every time they laid hold the line for another pull, the strain of the speeding boat went into backs and shoulders, and they braced their feet to keep from being yanked overboard.

" 'Vast hauling!" shouted the Mate. "He's coming up."

The boat slowed down even more, settling back in the water and once again taking on the scend of the ocean. But ahead Toby could see a dark shape gathering beneath the surface, growing with the rapidity of an August thunderstorm.

"Breaches!" warned the Mate.

The men were hanging on grimly.

Then the seas parted, and the great black shape burst forth, leaping high, high into the air, water streaming from the flanks. For a terrifying moment fifty tons of maddened fish-shaped animal hung motionless against the sky. Then he hurtled downward, broadside to the sea, and smashed the surface with a great echoing report. Water leaped aboard the boat. Without being told, Toby snatched his bailing piggin and set to work. Dimly he was aware that the whaleline had stilled, and an ill odor told him the whale was spouting. "All hands haul up now," said Mr. Barksdale.

Toby dropped his bailer and seized the line. Quickly they hauled the boat closer to the whale, the vast puffing of his breath throbbing in Toby's ears, the vile mist settling over them. Glancing behind, Toby saw Zachary keeping the line taut around the loggerhead, and Ben faking it down hurriedly in the tub.

Now Mr. Barksdale stood in the bow, braced firmly against the lurch of the boat as the men hauled closer to the quarry. Bow Oar pulled two lances from their rack beneath his thwart and put them on the starboard crotch where the harpoons had been. Like the irons, the six-foot leaf-bladed steel lances were mounted each to a rough-barked pole. Short warps guarded against loss.

Alex sculled with the steering oar to slacken the water-heavy line. Quickly the men fisted it aboard. As the boat drew up through the whale's blind region, Alex turned them bow on. In a low tense voice, the Mate said over his shoulder, "Out paddles. Ready to backwater." He took up one of the lances.

They paddled toward the big black flank, the light boat running easily in the water, rapidly closing the gap. The Mate reached forward with the lance, touched the tip to the whale abeam the lungs just abaft the eyefin. With both hands he shoved the lance in up to the hitches. Then he swung the pole mightily, churning that deadly tip inside the whale, feeling for the "life," cutting it.

Spume shot out of the blowholes and the whale lifted the fatal flukes. "Stern, All!" yelled the Mate. They back-watered hastily, the Mate tossing out whaleline. Down came the flukes with a smash that rocked the boat wildly. The lance, tossed, fetched up on its short warp. Bow Oar snatched it aboard. But the harpoons still held fast. "Line!" Bow yelled.

Once more the whaleline roared out, screaming around the loggerhead and racing through the chock. And again they were off in a spray of suds. But this time Toby saw the whale running on the surface, jerking the boat along in his wake. The flukes dashed up and down with tremendous speed, the horizontal blades hurtling the wounded giant through the gray sea.

Water surged in over the bow. Toby bailed steadily until the huge beast slackened speed and they were no longer shipping seas. The whale exhausted red-tinged vapor and slowed yet more.

"Chimney's afire!" Alex yelled gleefully from the stern.

"Haul up, boys," the Mate said with a grin.

They pulled in bights of line. Stroke kept snubbing the hemp taut and Ben was faking down for all he was worth. The big bull lolled to a halt, though his flukes undulated with poised danger just beneath the surface.

Before the line was shortened enough to pull against the harpoons, the crew had paddles out and Mr. Barksdale was standing ready with his lance as the boat again drew up through the blind arc. He placed the tip near the first wound, then shoved the lance in up to the socket and swung his full weight on the pole, working that wicked blade deep inside the whale's lungs.

Alex yelled, "Flukes!"

"Stern, All!" cried Mr. Barksdale, and without even a glance upward he flung himself away from the lance and down in the bow.

Toby had hardly finished the first desperate backstroke when he heard a thunderous clap. A wall of water reared at him, the boat tilted sharply to starboard, hung poised on her beam ends. "Hitch to port!" the Mate shouted. Toby felt the men on starboard pitching themselves across the slanting bottom. The boat settled back with a spank and a small sea leaped over the gunwale and sloshed in the bilges.

Toby, jarred from his thwart, saw line leaping over the bow chock. " 'Ware line!" he cried, seizing the hemp lying along the thwarts and tossing loops of it forward. Under the slack the men tumbled back to their places. The line pulled taut and ran out slowly. The whale, Toby saw now, was lurching along the surface in a curve, listing to one side.

"Oars!" said the Mate. "He's going to mill."

They ran them out, and had only to row clear of the whale as he drew a foamy agonized circle around them. With great gasps he blew gouts of blood, growing weaker, milling more slowly, his circle shrinking as life ebbed.

The men rested on their oars as the great animal halted.

Then up went that magnificent deadly tail, twin black fans high in the sky. It smote the water and reared again and again, beating the seas to a froth and the waves from it rocked and pitched the whaleboat.

"Flurry," called Bow, turning around and grinning at Toby, who felt his alarm showing on his face. "End coming."

The chunky back rounded up out of the water in a vast contraction. Then the huge whale began rolling over, spinning like a child's top. Suddenly he stopped and a long slow blast fluttered from the blowholes and died away in a spray of blood. The beast rolled on one side and floated there, waves breaking over the vast silent body.

"Fin out," the Mate said crisply.

The largest animal in the world died hard.

 eight

Watch Without End

THE AFTERNOON was half gone by the time Mr. Barksdale's boat crew had taken its second whale. They had left their first kill rolling in the ocean, marked out for the *Rogue* by the red waif fluttering the larboard boat's proud Number Two from the sharp-pointed staff driven into the blubber. "The pod's scattered some," the Mate had observed from his place back at the steering sweep as the men skimmed their oars through the sea. "But there's whales to be took for the rowing, if you don't shirk." They had not shirked, and they had rowed for hours, it had seemed, to clear beyond the horizon, stalking and maneuvering among giants now vaguely nervous of danger. And they had got a cow.

The Mate estimated her some twenty barrels smaller than the bull. She lay fin out and they rowed up to her flukes. Alex made the boat fast with a grapnel in the whale's small, where the flukes joined the narrowest part of the body.

Mr. Barksdale beckoned to Toby. "Midship, here's a job

for you."

Proud to be singled out, Toby stepped over the thwarts. The Mate handed him one end of a light chain. "Shackle this fluke chain around the small."

"Aye, aye, sir!" Toby replied smartly. He clambered over the gunwale to the whale's slippery back. Crouching in the water washing over their kill and working blindly, Toby managed to loop the chain around the small and shackle it snugly.

"Well done," grunted the Mate. "Now start the grapnel."

Toby worked the tines loose and brought the grapnel back into the boat. Once more on his thwart, he ran out his oar.

"All together, lads," said the Mate. "It'll be a long pull, but soonest back soonest we eat." Since the first spout had been seen from the masthead that morning, the boat crews had worked without eating. "Pull, All!"

Toby's first few pulls were made against all physical protest of aching muscles, but soon his body fell into the clockwork rhythm. The pulling was hard, for the cow weighed close to thirty-five tons, and occasionally a little cross sea jerked her to one side or the other. Sculling, the Mate pitched and turned his steering oar to counteract the whale's yawing.

The sun was lowering and two bells marking the first dogwatch chimed over the water by the time the Mate's boat reached the *Rogue*. The bark, impeded by two whales made fast to her starboard side, could not have run down to pick up their cow.

"The Cap'n's got hisself a kill," remarked Alex, nodding to the number One waif as they pulled around the stern of the vessel.

"We'll cut in over a hundred barrels, boys," said the Mate happily. "Greasy luck for us."

Maneuvering their cow along the larboard side beneath the forward and waist boats, the men made their kill fast with lines tossed down from the deck. Then hooking in the falls, they pulled their boat back up in davits.

While the men were cleaning and securing the boat, Ben called to Toby, "Give me a hand with the line." Together they lifted the line tubs out onto the roof of the afterhouse. Toby helped scatter the loops of line that Ben had not yet coiled from their last kill, and Ben showed him how to turn the kinks out. They were still working when the men tumbled down the short ladder to the deck and went for their dinner.

Ben grinned at Toby's face. "You can always eat, but when you get a chance to learn something, you'd best take it. Here's how to fake down a tub of line. If you know this, you're a step closer to boatsteerer."

"You're still aiming for harponier, Ben?" Carefully Toby copied the way Ben laid down a coil in a flat tight mat, then he put a second Flemish layer over that, building up the line in the tub.

Ben nodded in answer. "I figure to make it this voyage. Here, don't twist that line. Say, that's better. You'll be sitting on my thwart someday."

"Stroke goes to Tub before I do," Toby said.

"Maybe not," said Ben. "Some whalemen, like Zachary, don't care to move up, and do you wait for them to step for'ard, you'll be a-sitting still forever."

Fetching their pannikins, Toby and Ben got them filled to the brim with stew from the galley. Dodging among the hands working on deck, they joined Alex and the rest of the larboard boat crew on the fo'c'sle deck and the fore-hatch cover.

Eating slowly to spin out their rest, the larboard boat men watched the other hands rigging for cutting-in. Soon they, too, would bear a hand, for there was to be no watch below for anyone aboard until every pound of blubber was safely in the vessel. With three whales in the cut, the seamen faced a long hard job.

Alex cleared his throat. "Ye two lads ain't heard yet 'bout the Cap'n's whale."

Zachary paused briefly in his meal. "'Tain't the Cap'n's whale. The waist boat took him."

Ben looked up from his pannikin. "The Old Man's waif is in him."

Alex nodded. "So 'tis. The boats ain't hardly lowered from their davits when the Cap'n tells the Second they'll mate for a big bull. They row some and the Cap'n picks one out. Both the harpoons hook in, and off the boats go. But come time for the kill, the starb'd boat hangs back. So the Second brings his boat up and lances. The whale fins out. Cap'n Flick says he'll tow him in and for the Second to go see can he bring in another whale. Happens he don't, but when he gets back to the vessel here's the Cap'n's waif stuck in the kill and the Old Man strutting on deck and barking orders for cutting-in."

Toby spoke up. "Who's telling that story—Jake Underhill?"

Zachary nodded. "He's in the Second's boat. Stroke Oar."

By the time the larboard boat finished eating, the *Rogue* had been shortened down to topsails which barely gave her steerage way. Running lines had been pegged high in the standing rigging to clear the vessel's waist. Two sets of gigantic cutting tackles had been chained around the main masthead and guyed out so the hooks, each half as tall as a man, could drop straight down into the blubber below the opened mainhatch.

Toby and Ben were set to rigging the cutting stages overboard. Each stage was just a long oaken board, slung by ropes one fore and one aft the open gangway in the starboard bulwarks. Ben began rigging safety lines. The Third came along and handed Toby a canvas sack of wooden stoppers. "Plug up the scuppers good and tight so's the oil don't wash overboard," he ordered.

Gangs were wrestling empty casks up from the holds, ranging them along the larboard lashrail. Cooper labored over his grindstone under the boat skids, sharpening the long-poled cutting spades, while Smitty filed points on the gaffs and pikes to be used for handling the blubber. Cook was thumping bread dough while the big blackened coffee pot steamed as it would until cutting-in was done. Sails went along placing lanterns in readiness, each filled with whale oil drawn from stores.

When the bell rang the end of the first dogwatch, the Mate mustered the men in the waist around the open mainhatch. Sunset was but an hour away, and a full moon was rising in the east. Captain Flick stepped forward and stared hard at the men around him. "I won't have any hanging back, hear? You'll bend your backs till the job's done. Any man caught sogering will find himself strung up in the rigging. There's tucker aplenty, but you wait till an officer says you can eat or I'll take it out of your wages. Any questions? All right, Mr. Barksdale."

He walked toward the gangway, the men opening before him. The Mate spoke more encouragingly. "Work lively and cheerful, lads. Bear in mind them whales belong to us all, and we want 'em safe aboard, 'stead of in a shark's belly. There's coffee any time for them who ask. Now let's all turn to."

The Mate's speech raised the men's spirits, and they

went to work with a will, the starboard watch told off to the winch and the port split into gangs to help with getting the blubber aboard and stowing it below. Toby and Ben were posted at the gangway to assist the Second Mate, who was taking first turn as boarding officer.

Captain Flick, the Mate, and the Third tied safety lines around their waists and climbed overboard to the stages hanging halfway between sea and railing. The Second called for cutting spades. Toby and Ben brought them up and handed the long square-ended choppers to the officers overboard.

Captain Flick, alone on the forward stage, thrust down his 20-foot long spade and began chopping into the hard blubber beneath him. The Mates, waiting for their part in the work, watched with interest. Clear yellow light flooded across the ocean from the lowering sun, lighting the big whale beneath the stages. He was on his side, snubbed alongside the vessel by the fluke chain and a chain strap around the eyefin that turned up from the water.

Toby whispered to Ben, "Why does he list so?" He remembered how that added to the difficulty in towing their cow.

Ben murmured, " 'Tis the bleeding from being lanced. A whale strangles in his own blood, y'know. His right lung fills and weights him down to starboard, and that turns his larboard fin up out of the water."

The Second said crisply, "You, two! Fetch up that

blubber hook."

Toby and Ben unlashed one of the giant blubber hooks from the main bitt just forward the mainhatch and dragged it across the deck to the gangway. Captain Flick had chopped a big square hole through the foot-thick blubber at the corner of the huge lower lip. Toby and Ben, hanging back on the falls against the weight of the hook, carefully lowered the steel into the hole. The Second barked an order to the winch, and the gang slowly drew the tackle taut.

Once more Captain Flick methodically stabbed with his spade, chopping the lip free so it could be raised on the tackle. When he had cut to the limit of his reach, the First and Third Mates took over chopping. The Captain made a long cut up the side of the head. When he reached the blowholes, he glanced back over the railing. "Overboard man." He pointed to Toby. "Will you tumble down and reeve the head chain?"

Ben spoke up. "I'll go, sir. He wouldn't know what to do."

The orange sunset glowing across the Captain's face threw his annoyance into high relief. "He has only to reeve the chain strap through the blowholes, then toggle it so we can chop the head free. You can do that, Clayton, can't you?"

It sounded simple. "Aye, aye, sir! I reckon I can handle that job."

Ben muttered fiercely in his ear. " 'Tis a dangerous job, Toby, and always done by a volunteer. Stand aside and let me go!"

But Toby, made reckless by his success in shackling the fluke chain that afternoon, only handed him the free end of a safety line and swarmed down the falls. He clambered off the big blubber hook, his feet sliding in the blood and slime of the carcass. Bracing himself against the safety line, he worked up to the blowholes which the waves were rubbing against the timbers of the vessel. The Second called down, "Chain strap!" and paid out a line. Toby waited for it, standing ankle-deep in sea water, rising and falling with the bark and the whale, the huge dead creature hauling back and butting up against the strakes, rubbing away the thin black skin.

With the loop of chain in his hands, Toby knelt in the slosh of sea and slime. He found the first blowhole under the water and crammed the chain into it. Behind him to one side he could hear the rhythmic thud of cutting spades as the officers worked on. Suddenly the waves pitched him toward a momentary gap between whale and vessel, and only Ben's ruthless jerk on the safety line kept him from being crushed. Ignoring the pain in his waist, Toby worked the chain through the other nostril and called for the toggle.

The big wooden pin was sent down. Toby crouched again in blood and slime and rove the toggle through the chain strap. He had just signaled for the toggle line to be hauled taut when a stab of horror transfixed him.

He had forgotten about sharks, had never given them a thought, for though they had torn at the carcass of the dryskin weeks before, he had seen nothing of them until this very instant. Now a triangular fin was racing up, aiming like an arrow for the narrow slip of water between vessel and whale, toward Toby himself clinging to the edge of the bleeding head.

Suddenly steel flashed downward with a thud. Another blade plunged beside the first and withdrew. The water foamed and thrashed. A shape fell away beneath and the brief lashing turmoil was over.

Mr. Barksdale and the Third Mate, spades poised for another stab at the shark's head, now calmly returned to their work on the whale. It had happened so quickly that no one had called out, and Toby still crouched over the blowholes.

Someone touched his shoulder. It was Ben, a safety line around his waist and an ax in his hand. "Go up, Toby. I'll finish here."

Toby shook himself out of his daze. "Did you see him, Ben?"

" 'Tis the blood that drew him. He came close, but not close enough."

"I mean *him*—up there." Toby's gaze traveled up, locked with Captain Flick's intent stare, and fell away. He whispered, "Why didn't Captain Flick drop his spade on that shark? He's standing closer than the others."

"He didn't? Well, the Mates got him first. Now go up and stow away some hot coffee. The Second says you can have it."

But Toby refused to go. Shrugging, Ben positioned himself between eye and blowholes and swung the ax into the head cut that the Captain had made. Captain Flick was chopping again, carving a deep slice across the whale a yard or so abaft the first cut. Now chips of bone flew from Ben's ax. Then Toby felt the head dip sharply as the backbone was severed. Ben gestured. "C'mon. They'll start hoisting now."

They swarmed up the falls. The Second called to the winch gang. Slowly, blocks creaking, chain links squealing, the great blubber hook pulled the whale's massive head from the water. The mainmast quivered under the enormous weight. Then with a great rasping sound, the severed lower lip started tearing loose, the whale's carcass settling with a splash back in the water. The winch gang hove in the slack. Once more the whale's head was lifted. The officers reached out with their long spades, slicing under the strip of blubber, freeing it from the flesh. Foot by foot, the steel hook hauled the strip of blubber past the railing, past the sheerpole, straining toward the maintop. The *Rogue,* canting under the pull of some fifty tons of dead whale, began heeling more sharply. The Mate hurriedly slashed on the starboard side of the lower jaw, and the blanket of blubber pulled away more easily. The edge that he had cut glistened pearly white beaded with red. The smell of raw flesh was strong in Toby's nostrils.

The Second barked orders. "You, mind that fin chain! You, fetch a chain strap and toggle! You two there, bring up the other tackle!"

Toby and Ben unlashed the second blubber hook from the main bitt near the open mainhatch and brought it up to the gangway. They steadied the massive steel implement between them as the Second Mate drew the sword-shaped boarding knife from the scabbard nailed to the bulwarks. With it he cut two holes in the blanket near deck level, then motioned to a man standing by. The hand began reeving a chain strap through the holes.

As he waited, Toby craned his neck, looking around with interest. The winch gang was leaning against the brakes, for the blubber was mast-high, lifting the whale's head well out of the water. The Mate and the Third were stabbing away inside the vast open mouth with its huge comb of black whalebone hanging like a stiff fringe from the upper jaw. Captain Flick was slashing blubber on the other side of the head, cutting through the flesh as well, judging from the streams of blood washing down the carcass and staining the sides of the vessel.

The red-tinged water about the whale surged and foamed, whipped to a froth with the knife-like fins sweeping through it. Suddenly a tapered gray shape flung itself out of the water, snatching a bite of the bleeding whale carcass before falling back into the sea. Then another shark leaped out, gouging with his teeth. And yet another sprang from the ocean.

The officers paused in their cutting to drop their spades just forward a few of the triangular fins. The water lashed with life and death as the sharks turned on their wounded companions.

The voice of the Second Mate pulled Toby out of his horrified fascination. "Make that tackle fast!"

Toby and Ben dragged the hood closer, maneuvering it into the chain strap rove through the holes in the blanket of blubber. The Second waved them out of the way. The officers on the cutting stages withdrew their spades from the whale. The Second bawled out, "Board-ho!" Glancing to see that the way was clear, he quickly sliced through the blubber with his boarding knife.

Blocks squealed and the *Rogue* lurched as the whale's weight fell upon the alternate cutting tackle. The Second Mate jumped aside as the mast-high blanket of blubber swung inboard, sweeping toward the open mainhatch.

Alex and Zachary thrust out their pikes, checking the blanket. Carefully they guided the lurching strip through the hatch as the winch gang braked the hook downward.

With the first blanket received into the blubber room below, Toby sensed a quickening of rhythm. The waiting was over and there was work for all hands. He and Ben were kept busy tending the fin chain, fetching straps and toggles, and bringing up first one, then the other cutting falls. The remainder of the huge lower lip was brought aboard and steadied down the hatch, followed by the three-ton tongue. Then came the head itself with the upper jaw lined by the many long thin plates of black baleen. This was secured to the lashrail on deck, for the whalebone strips would later be separated and scraped clean.

By now lanterns were burning brightly, driving night shadows from the work areas on deck and beneath the cutting stages. The space between gangway and mainhatch was gurried with blood, sea water, and slime. The body blubber stripped off in a continuous scarf, the cutting officers making a long spiral slice as the whale's carcass, tearing free of the blubber, turned over and over in the water. Occasionally someone would drop a spade on one of the sharks milling below. The Second would slash the scarf into blankets, crying, "Board-ho!" and the *Rogue* would pitch under the sudden shift of weight.

Eight bells chimed. Toby wondered who had time to watch the chronometer, but he was glad of it when the Second called for a change of tasks. Half the winch gang came off and took the gangway jobs. Their handspikes were taken over by the men from below, and Toby's group was sent into the blubber room.

The blubber room was 'tween decks under the mainhatch. Because the blanket being lowered blocked the hatchway, the larboard boat crew had to go down into the fo'c'sle and through the after bulkhead door into the fore 'tween-decks hold. An alleyway had been left when the hold had been loaded, and now lanterns lighted the passage between barrels, bags, and boxes. When the door to the blubber room was pulled open, Toby nearly staggered from the odor reeling out.

Raw blood stung his nostrils harshly, and a thick smell of grease hung heavily over stacks of blubber pieces. The room was jammed with casks and tubs, and when the deck tilted, gurry sloshed underfoot. It was hot and stuffy, for though the whale-oil lanterns burned smokelessly, the flames had long since taken the slack out of the air. The mainhatch yawned overhead, but all cleansing breezes were shut out by the vast sheet of dripping blubber hanging down.

Alex White, as boatsteerer, took charge. "Bear a hand with that blanket, lads!"

They seized pikes and gaffs from the racks. Alex yelled up to the deck gang, and the sheet started down again. Like the others, Toby stabbed his gaff into the hard foot-thick blubber and helped haul it along the lower deck as it came down. Then he and Ben unshipped the big steel hook and sent it up. Now they took axes and knives and swarmed over the blanket to cut it up into horse pieces of about two by three feet. When Toby touched the blubber he was surprised that it was about the same heat as his own hand.

The work was well started when Alex raised his voice above the tramping of the topside men and the groaning of the winch. "Ben, you and Toby can lean."

Toby gladly laid his hatchet aside and lounged against a cask. Ben, seeing him, nearly strangled with laughter. Toby growled, "What ails you? Alex said—"

"He didn't mean to rest your backside," Ben gasped. "Leaning is a job of work. You got your sheath knife?"

Ben led him to a rough board table and heaved up a horse piece from the stack nearby, laying it skin side down. "See them strips of flesh there? That's the lean, the blubber is the fat. Got to cut the lean off or it'll burn in the trypots and spoil the oil. Pitch it into one of those lean casks. Blubber goes onto that other stack."

They set to shaving the flesh from the horse pieces. At first it seemed an easy duty, but the exactness and the monotony soon took the edge off Toby's eagerness. He was glad when Alex traded tasks around and he found himself at the mincing trough.

A plank with guide pegs along the edges rested over an open cask. Toby pitched a horse piece on the board, black side down, holding it firmly with a hand hook while Ben expertly cut thin slices to the skin. "Now that's a book," said Ben, for the blubber slices were held together by the skin like the pages of a book. Toby tossed the book into a tub and pitched up another horse piece. Alex was busy stacking up horse pieces, and the other two men were leaning. Then the boatsteerer shouted for all hands to receive the next dripping blanket.

Toby nearly forgot the smell of fresh air down in that smelly stuffy room. He was actually glad to get abovedecks for his turn at the winch, though this proved to be the most heartbreaking toil he had ever experienced. At the end of that shift he would have liked to collapse, but he was sent over to the gangway again.

The hours dragged on and on with only a few moments of relief now and then when one of the Mates sent him to the galley to down hot coffee and rolls. Toby had to drive himself to keep moving. The deck was ankle-deep in gurry. Mr. Barksdale, who was boarding officer then, set Toby to scooping up the slop of blood and oil, stowing it in save-all casks lashed to the bulwarks.

The whale's head on deck was stripped down with axes and knives. From the upper jaw the Mate carefully detached the long strips of valuable black baleen, separating the entwined fringes of each inside edge. Then he put Toby and Ben to work scraping clean all 250 blades, most of them seven feet long.

"Stinks of fish," Toby muttered to Ben.

" 'Tis the brit caught in the fringed edge," Ben replied, resting briefly before the Mate's eye fell on him. "D'you recollect how cloudy the water was when we went after the pod? That's the whalebone whale's food, little specks of plants and shrimp no bigger'n a grain of silt. He swims along with his mouth open, and when he figures he's collected enough brit he closes his jaws and his tongue squeezes the water out through the whalebone sieve. The baleen fringes keep the food back in his mouth and he swallows it."

"Sounds like hardly enough to keep him alive," Toby marveled. "The sperm gets to chew a giant squid, or at least a school of fish."

"Or a whaleman," Ben added cheerfully.

Mr. Barksdale came by and sent Toby to read the chronometer and ring the hour. Standing beside the lashed wheel, Toby peered down into the lighted cabin below. The Mate must have a good time sense, for the chronometer showed a minute to the hour. Toby waited with his hand on the clapper cord.

A movement drew his eye forward into the dining saloon. The door in the saloon's forward bulkhead had opened, and now it closed as Captain Flick came into view. The Captain stepped around the table, disappeared briefly into his stateroom and then came out, walking through the main cabin. Toby heard his step on the curving iron ladder as the hands of the chronometer met the hour. Striking the time smartly, Toby went forward to take up his work once more.

Gradually the vessel's lanterns seemed to grow dim. In

the east a line of light broadened. The men were halfway through the second whale. Boatsteerers coaxed their gangs. "C'mon, boys! Every bite a shark takes is half a barrel less oil. Money out of your pockets. Get that blubber stowed down, lads!"

They worked all day without a break. Toby felt himself pass through several stages of extreme fatigue followed by a near-miracle of freshness which more and more quickly ground down to another round of exhaustion. He stumbled from one task to another, hardly knowing who worked beside him.

Day ended and another night of unspeakable misery unwound slowly. If there was but five minutes slack between one job and the next, Toby slipped into a deep sleep, to rouse himself quickly when someone tossed an order his way.

He was topside, scooping gurry, when Mr. Barksdale, in a voice cracking with exhaustion, shouted, "Belay! All hands below."

A weak cheer straggled through the early dawn. With the other hands, Toby stumbled into the fo'c'sle and collapsed in his bunk.

He was reliving all the horror of cutting-in when someone shook him out of his dream. Half awake, Toby saw full daylight at the bull's-eyes. The fo'c'sle slumbered on.

Alex White muttered in his ear. "Toby, where is it? I vow I won't get mad at ye. Just give me back my boatsteerer's seal."

"What you talking 'bout?" Toby mumbled. "Haven't got it."

He saw Alex's eyes widen. "Then who took it, Toby? Who'd steal my scrimshaw stamp?"

 nine

A Sail From Astern

TOBY ROUSED with a start and blinked around the fo'c'sle, eternally lighted by the whale-oil lantern and, now, shafts of sunshine coming through the bull's-eyes set in the two forward bulkheads.

Alex was not there, and ringing in Toby's ears was the "Starb'd watch on deck, d'you hear?" which had awakened him this time, hours after the boatsteerer's furtive visit. Toby realized that he must have plunged immediately into sleep after drowsily answering Alex White's demand.

A voice came from the bunk next to his. "Never mind, 'tis watch and watch, and port's below." Ben's tousled red head showed above a rumpled gray blanket. "We've four hours of sleep ahead, 'less'n you're thinking of tucker?"

"'Tis Alex I'm thinking about." Toby swung his feet to the deck. He had turned in all standing and needed only to slip into his shoes. A glance showed the rest of the port watch deep asleep. "He woke me last night, claiming something was stolen from him."

Ben blinked wide awake. In spite of his surprise, caution kept his voice low. "Theft—aboard the vessel? We can't abide that!" None of the sea chests aboard had a lock. Yet all personal possessions were inviolable, for each man guaranteed the security of his belongings by respecting the ownership of others. A single theft could destroy this mutual trust which was essential for a successful voyage. "Is Alex sure of this?"

"I mean to find out," Toby said. "How can I get into steerage without answering a lot of questions?" Aboard, you lived in your alloted place, worked where you were told, and leisured in the area tradition reserved for your ranking. Any man found out of place would have to furnish the Captain with a very good excuse.

"Go through 'tween decks," said Ben. "There's a door to the sailpen aft, and steerage ought to open into that, too, for Sails to work handily belowdecks, come rain." He tumbled out of his berth. "I'll show you."

Ben led the way to a door beneath the fo'c'sle ladder and they stepped into the fore 'tween-decks alley. This was the way the work gangs had reached the blubber room, with lanterns lighting the passage that had been formed out of the boxes, bags, and barrels of supplies stowed in the 'tween-decks holds. The lamps were out now, all but one which, forgotten, flickered on. Ben took it down and carried it along. The sea washed alongside the hull, and from above came the trampling of feet and an occasional call. Ben said,

"Boiling. Hope there's nobody in the blubber room."

"Hush, Ben! What's that?" Toby stiffened, ears tingling with the echo of a shuffling sound. "Someone's got into the hold!"

"Jake Underhill, I doubt not," Ben growled. "There was times during cutting-in that he just vanished. Reckon he was catching a snooze below. Let's dig him out!"

With Ben swinging the lantern high, they began searching the side aisles which gave access to supplies. Then Toby grabbed Ben's arm. "I heard him—starb'rd."

There was someone in the last starboard aisle on hands and knees.

Alex White glanced up into the lantern's glare with a sheepish grin. "Glad it's ye two what catch me at it."

"You're looking for your seal?" Toby asked. "I recollect you said somebody stole it."

The boatsteerer rubbed his unshaven chin. "First, I figured 'twas the only way it'd get out o' my sea chest. Then I got to wondering did I maybe leave it in a pocket all this time and it tumbled out during cutting-in. I been feeling around in the dark for it. Didn't care to take the lantern—feel like a fool did somebody catch me."

Ben set the lantern on the deck and leaned back against a crate. "Toby didn't say, but I reckon you mean that carved ivory seal he's talked about?"

Alex nodded. "That's right, with a carving to the end of it." Carefully he described his seal, the picture of a harponier in the bow of a boat. "Ain't a innkeeper nor dock-side loafer on the waterside of a port what don't know that's my name, Alex White, Boatsteerer. Nobody could never use that there seal but me, even did he just pick it up innocent-like off the deck where maybe it spilled from my pocket."

Toby asked, "How did you find your seal was gone from your sea chest?" From the look and smell of Alex's clothes, Toby knew that the boatsteerer, like everyone including himself, had not changed garments for three days. And like the rest, Alex would have tumbled into his bunk all standing.

"The Mate'll likely be sharing out the jawpans of them whales for scrimshaw, y'know," Alex said. "Well, I seen no harm in collecting my piece first. So I took a chunk with me when we was sent below. I was stowing it in my sea chest when I see as my name seal is gone. That give me a jolt, all right! Then I goes through all my clothes and hunts around some on the deck—my steerage mates is all asleep then—and finally I reckon maybe Toby borrowed it to show Ben—I know, I know! 'Twas a foolish thought, but I set such store by that seal, I sure wished somebody would just hand it back to me."

"You'll find it," Ben said encouragingly. "We'll help you look in our off-watch."

Alex shook his head. "And get caught rummaging in the stores? The Old Man'd have ye both at the rope's end.

Same goes for talking about it amongst the men. The Cap'n, he'd have it that yer passing the word 'bout stealing, getting the hands roiled up, and busting up order in his vessel."

Toby nodded reluctant agreement. "Well, we'll keep a weather eye out for it anyway."

"Anybody what finds it is bound to bring it right to me," Alex said. "That there seal ain't of use to no one else, and they's sailors aboard in plenty what know it's my carven name." The boatsteerer had talked himself into a better frame of mind, and now he wanted his breakfast. "Ye'd best eat, too. Plenty of hard work ahead for all hands." Starting back to steerage, he entered the blubber room, and Toby saw through the opened door that two men of the starboard watch were working feverishly at the mincing trough. Then he and Ben went back to the fo'c'sle for their pannikins, Ben blowing out the lantern and hanging it on a nail in passing.

Abovedecks they found Zachary already on the low fo'c'sle deck, eating and watching the boiling. "Second helping," Zachary said between mouthfuls. "Double whack today for them as wants it."

Toby swallowed hard against the thick oily air and the black greasy smoke that occasionally downdrafted from the tryworks chimneys. He doubted that he could finish even a single whack. Behind him the pigs squealed a protest from their pen, but the lucky chickens had been moved from their coop abaft the tryworks to a cage near the goat's pen under the boat skids. "Can't we shift to wind'ard?" he protested when he saw Ben heartily digging into his breakfast.

Zachary barked a laugh. "You'd best pay no mind t'the stink and git on with your eatin'. Lookee!" He stabbed the air with his spoon. "With whale men workin' right 'n' left, you'd git yourself stepped on like you was a shipworm."

Toby saw the starboard watch working smartly under the eye of the Second. Two men stood on the forehatch cover directly before the square brick tryworks. One, a boatsteerer, skimmed the crisp boiled-out blubber books from the oil in the pots with a long-handled copper strainer. These cracklings he then dumped into the scrap hopper from where the fire tender fetched them to fuel the flames beneath the trypots. Wood was needed only to melt the first pot of oil. Thick black smoke rolled up from the twin brick chimneys, sooting the bunted-up fore-topsails. The men from the blubber room scrambled up with big troughs of books. Other men wrestled with empty casks, filled them from the cooling tank at the side of the tryworks, and worked them back to the lashrail.

Absently, Toby took a mouthful of food, then discovered to his astonishment that he was tremendously hungry. He went back to the galley for a second helping.

All day it was watch and watch about, mincing pieces, pitching books from tub to pots, stirring the oil, skimming scrap, feeding fires. Toby took his turn helping draw oil from the metal cooler into waiting casks and hauling them over to where Cooper beneath the boat skids was heading up, then lashing the sealed casks alongside the gunwales until they could be stowed down between more pressing tasks.

By the second dogwatch the blubber stacked 'tween decks had begun to rot. The odor was so overwhelming that the supervising Third ordered the mincing trough abovedecks. Even so, Toby had to do his shift in the blubber room, pitching the slimy and stinking horse pieces up through to main hatch with a blubber fork. When he grumbled, Ben said, "This is nothing. Wait'll the lean casks finish rotting and you have to squeeze the oil out of the meat with your bare hands."

"I can wait," Toby decided.

That night the off-watch elected to sleep on deck, for below it had grown unbearably hot from the intense fires of the tryworks. Only the brick waterpan beneath the furnaces kept the deck from springing into flames. The fo'c'sle was taken over by the rats and cockroaches the heat had driven from the 'tween-decks holds.

Ben and Toby spread their blankets on the roof of the afterhouse and to one side of the mizzen boom where the spanker flapping overhead sent down vagrant breezes. Ben Valentine fell asleep at once in true sailor fashion. But Toby's gaze was drawn to the work area in the waist, where iron baskets filled with burning scrap shed a brighter glow than the lanterns they replaced, even though the open flames sprang and guttered, making shadows leap and dance weirdly over the deck. Then Toby caught a furtive movement on the fo'c'sle deck.

The starboard watch on duty did not seem to notice, and went about its work of mincing, boiling, skimming, and drawing off, faces sooty from downdrafts and glowing ghoulishly in the leaping cresset flames. Captain Flick slowly paced up and down the deck, going from shadow to flaring brightness to shadow, occasionally stopping to speak to the Second or give an order to a hand.

Once again Toby saw movement, and then a man casually strolled aft from the fo'c'sle deck, keeping in the shadows along the larboard railing. When he came aft as far as the boat skids and turned his face in a quick searching glance, Toby recognized Alex White.

The boatsteerer climbed the ladder to the top of the skids. The two spare boats were kept here, lashed keel side up on their chocks. They both sheltered a sleeping fo'c'sle hand. Alex crouched beside each boat in turn, and, to Toby's astonishment, went through the pockets of the men. Toby wondered if he had been searching the hands on the fo'c'sle deck too.

Alex crept back down the ladder, and just then Captain Flick stepped around from behind the chest-high casks ranged along the bulwarks. "You, there, White! What are you doing there?" he demanded.

The boatsteerer jerked around, startled. He cleared his throat. "Why, sir, looks like ever' good sleeping spot is took, ain't it?"

"You can see that from below," the Captain said sharply. "What kept you up there so long—stealing from your shipmates? If I catch a thief on my vessel—"

"No, sir, Cap'n, I don't go stealing!" Alex protested. He hesitated, then went on. "Truth is, sir, someone must've picked up a little something what belongs to me, and I was fixing to get it back."

"You saying there's thievery—"

"No, sir, what I mean is maybe he don't know who it belongs to, and I didn't get to asking 'bout it yet."

"I don't believe you," Captain Flick said scornfully. "What have you got worth picking up off a clean deck?"

" 'Tis that ivory seal o'mine, that scrimshaw stamp with the boatsteerer on it. Ye recollect, sir? I put it to that paper ye and Cap'n Noah signed when ye bought the *Rogue* from him."

"Your—your stamp? Who'd want to take that?" Captain Flick's voice grew heavy with contempt. "You lost it. Sneaked a bottle aboard at Ponta Delgada, didn't you? And holed up somewhere and got drunk. That seal of yours fell out of your pocket and down a crack. Likely sloshing in the bilges."

"No, sir, I didn't never have no bottle—"

Captain Flick cut short Alex's indignant denial. "Stow

that jaw. Leave your shipmates alone or there'll be trouble. Now get below until your watch is called."

The boatsteerer slid back the booby hatch and climbed down into steerage. Captain Flick walked forward to speak with the hand at the cooling tank. And Toby, wondering over Alex's search of his watchmates, felt sleep gather heavily in his eyes. Dreamily, he saw Captain Flick pacing back along the shadowed starboard railing. The Captain paused, his arm moved, and a small pale object leaped out against the blackness of the sky to be swallowed by the sea. Toby, his eyes following the arc, at its end plunged into sleep.

A week later a clean-scrubbed *Rogue* boasted 125 barrels of oil in her hold, and there was scarcely a trace of odor to remind Toby of the weeklong labor of boiling. The bark made long and short boards through the Western Grounds without another catch. Then for six weeks they made all sail, though Captain Flick did shorten down in the whaling areas. They were lucky in the doldrums, only three days of erratic puffs of wind and they were across the Line and in the South Atlantic. The starboard boat got one right cow in the Trinidad Grounds, but they did not raise a single spout after that, though the *Rogue* stood along through the grounds down the coast of South America. Perhaps Captain Flick expected scant results here, for though the other crews lowered the few times whales were cried, after Trinidad he kept himself on the quarter-deck and the starboard boat remained in its davits.

"That crew'll get out of practice," Toby remarked to Alex one afternoon while they were once more taking the winch apart for cleaning.

"Never fear," Alex said. "He'll figure some way of using the crew without his going down with 'em."

Toby glanced at him in surprise. "Doesn't he trust the shipkeepers to tend the *Rogue* with the boats down?"

"Ain't that." Alex dipped his rag in a bucket of cleaner and scrubbed at a gear. "Seems he ain't so skillful in a boat. Last voyage, when he was Third and had the bow boat, he could scarce come on a whale without gallying the pod. Fact is he had a noisy crew, always barging about. They was slow lowering, last down and first up, I recollect. Cap'n Noah, he chided him on it, but the *Rogue* was doing so good that I reckon the Cap'n didn't much mind if the Third dragged his oar."

Toby thought about that as he daubed the clean gear with new grease and an old worry trudged across his mind. "If the *Rogue* was doing so well, Alex . . . I mean, if Captain Noah was *satisfied,* then why did he sell her before he even got home?"

The boatsteerer shook his head. " 'Tweren't like Cap'n Noah to act that way."

"The *Rogue* was—*is* a sound vessel, isn't she?" Toby persisted.

"Aye, well-found she be." Alex glanced aft to where

Captain Flick stalked the quarter-deck. "Did Cap'n Noah want to sell, he might've picked out a better master for her," he growled sourly.

Life aboard had grown increasingly harsh as the vessel pressed on. There was the ordinary labor of sailing, taking down, and hauling up canvas according to the weather, worn sails for fair with the better suits being saved for foul. All the whaleboats, including the two spares, were repeatedly overhauled. The dwindling livestock had to be tended and prepared from pen to Captain's table. There were masts to slush, rigging to tar, brightwork to polish, and wood and iron to scrub and paint.

This was not enough for Captain Flick. It seemed as if the lack of whale sightings abraded his temper so that he took to punishing his crew for the Atlantic's failure to yield up prey. The men were harassed and driven in their work, given unnecessary and disagreeable tasks, and forced often to perform the same job over and over. A man dropping a pannikin of food on his way from the galley was made to scrub the entire deck during his off-watch. Another had to stand an extra trick because the Captain found him gazing briefly at the horizon. The cooper himself had his wages logged because a sudden lurch of the vessel made him spoil the board he was shaping. The Captain's own watch, the starboard, had its molasses stopped for ten days for seeking permission to scrimshaw when there was no real work for the vessel to be done.

Then the larboard boat crew had a tremendous piece of luck. Mr. Barksdale came by as the port watch was ranged around the forehatch with pannikins full of dinner. "The Captain's calling for another boatsteerer. Any of you think you're ready to start working up to it? You, there, bow boat Midship?"

"Nawsir, ain't gonna put out any extra for Cap'n Flick. I'll make steerer in m' next vessel."

Zachary paused in his eating. "You want somebody t'bear a smart hand, sir, you git Ben Valentine."

"That's right," said the larboard Bow Oar. "Ben, he's always ready to do more'n his share."

Mr. Barksdale nodded to Ben, who sat looking down into his pannikin. "All right, Ben. Get Alex White to show you how to stop down an iron and do some darting off the jibboom. We'll lower in two days."

"Hoorah for you, Ben!" cried Toby as the First Mate left them.

"Hoorah for the larboard boat," Ben countered, grinning broadly under his freckles. "Now we get to do some real whaleman's work."

Later that day Ben contrived to share his luck with Toby. "Alex says you can pull in the harpoons after we dart," he said. "That'll save us some extra work." And Alex White, balancing on the vessel's foremost spar, managed to make his instructions carry back to Toby standing at the heel of the bowsprit with spare line looped in his hand.

When the larboard boat began lowering for practice runs, Mr. Barksdale shifted the thwarts. Alex remained on Harponier, though he often traded with Ben who sat on Bow thwart just behind. Ben had to learn two jobs at once, Bow Oar's work as well as boatsteerer's. The former Bow Oar was shifted to Midship so that Toby could move to Tub. He was glad now that he had taken Ben's advice to learn the next job ahead, for his ability in coiling and handling had already brought him two steps nearer to the Harponier thwart. Zachary kept to his favorite place on Stroke Oar, and, of course, Mr. Barksdale headed. This was exactly like the boat drill they had had before reaching the Western Grounds weeks ago, only this time it was often Ben who hove the harpoon at the floating cask and traded places with the Mate at the steering sweep.

The boat drills gradually ceased as southing brought them in with the big gray rollers sweeping from across limitless ocean. The whaling bark *Rogue* heeled far over from one side to the other. Her head pitched up and down like a bucking horse. The wind freshened and switched about, and the crew was kept jumping to haul braces and trim yards. Then Captain Flick shortened down to topsails and topgallants, taking in the two outer jibs. The *Rogue* immediately began hanging back, surging heavily in the running seas.

"Swimmin' like a knock-kneed duck," Alex White

grumbled as he and Toby rolled up the staysails for stowing in the sail pen. "Sure, 'tis blowing a bit, but the
weather's fair and we should press on round the Horn,
'stead o' waiting for a full gale."

Two days later, at 51° 38′ S., 62° W., a sail was sighted
coming up fast from astern. At noon the vessel was near
enough for the crew to identify her rigging. "She's a ship!"
cried Ben. "No wonder she's so fast!"

Square-rigged on her three masts, all canvas taut and
drawing, the ship closed rapidly with the bark until by the
middle of the afternoon watch she came abeam and spoke
the *Rogue*. Greetings were shouted back and forth through
the speaking trumpets, and then, amazingly, Captain Flick
backed his yards for a gam.

"Cape Horn fever, if you ask me," Zachary said as they
lowered the larboard boat. The port watch had won the
draw for the first visit. "Three, four vessels we meet up
t'now want to gam for a spell, but Cap'n says no, got to
rush around the Horn. 'Cept now we're here, he's of a sudden got plenty o' time for visitin'."

Mr. Barksdale glared down at Zachary from his place at
the steering sweep. "Belay that jaw, Stroke. If the Captain
figures to snug down, you haven't got any say."

"We're wallowing along like a hog on a holiday. What
would you do if you was Captain, Mr. Barksdale, sir?"
Zachary asked with seeming innocence.

"Stow your gab and row," the Mate answered shortly.

Bending their oars in the big rollers, they met and passed the two ship's boats heading for the *Rogue,* and then they pulled up alongside the ship herself. She was the whaleship *Grand Banks,* Sag Harbor, Ambrose Goodwin master, Indian Ocean bound, passaging clean. Aboard, the *Rogue's* port watch separated, each man anxious to see new faces and hear new voices.

Toby struck up a conversation with one of the *Grand Banks* men, and asked about the rigging. The man pointed upward. "You can see the mizzen rigging better aloft." They scrambled up the aftermost mast, which was crossed with yards and much different from the *Rogue's* mizzen fore-and-after.

Rigged square on three masts, this kind of vessel was designated as a ship.

Toby's new friend explained how they handled the lines. "A ship like this'n goes fastest of anything afloat," he said, standing on the topyard on the other side of the mast from Toby. "But a bark like the *Rogue* is can point up closer to the wind, and is much quicker in stays. She's a good vessel, the *Rogue.* I sailed her once 'fore Cap'n Noah bought her, and I sailed under him the time he got killed."

"I heard some talk about that," Toby said. "Did—did you see it happen?"

"Fact is, I was at the helm when he met his end." The seaman tucked a chew of tobacco into his cheek as he lowered himself to the yard. Balancing his feet on the foot-ropes, he settled himself to yarning. "Guess you heard how Cap'n Noah sold the canvas right over his head? 'Twas a jolt, let me tell you. There wasn't no way through the whole voyage that you'd reckon him to do a thing like that. Nor can we figure why Mr. Flick didn't take over command when Cap'n Noah died, seeing as he was owner then, even if Third Mate. I figure later I seen the sale of the vessel. Something must've bothered Cap'n Noah at the time, 'cause he looked fair grim."

Toby looked at him sharply. "You saw him sell the *Rogue?* What did he say—why did he do it?"

"Well, I was there only in a manner of speaking, having just took over the wheel, it being the middle of the after-noon watch. Nor did I hear nothing, for the skylight was snugged down against the half-gale making up out of the east-southeast, and dark as pitch the day was! The lanterns was lit in the cabin, and I was sneaking a look beyond the compass thinking how cozy 'twas below. Then Cap'n Noah comes in from the saloon and goes to his desk. I cast my eyes up back where they belong, 'cause he's going to glance up at the compass and maybe catch me sogering a mite. Not long after, he comes up, opens the companion door next to me and hollers for the Third. That's Mr. Flick. They both go below and I pay no mind until I couldn't help notice a lot of moving back and forth and arm-waving in the cabin. I look down past the compass and see maybe the two of them can't get to agree on something, but there's no chart on the desk, and anyhow the Captain don't argue course with nobody but the Mate."

The seaman spat tobacco juice to leeward. "Next, I sees the Third sitting at the desk, writing something while Cap'n Noah talks. Mr. Flick finishes his paper, then comes up and sends for Alex White to go down to the Old Man. Just then the wind hauls round a point or two and I had to ease the sails off a mite—them was standing orders. Anyways, Alex scrambles up and down a couple of times, I guess he had to go fetch something. Next time I look down into the cabin, Cap'n Noah and Mr. Flick both writes on that paper and then it looks like Alex is fixing his seal on it. That was when Cap'n Noah sold the *Rogue,* don't you think?"

Toby nodded. "I reckon so. There's somebody saying Captain Noah gambled his vessel away to Mr. Flick."

His friend shook his head. "Cap'n Noah was a top master. Kept his vessel, his crew, and hisself well in hand, he did. If the Old Man gambles, so does the crew. B'fore you know, there's bad blood amongst the men, and plenty of fights breaking out."

"The accident happened right after they signed the paper," Toby said. "Did you see it?"

"I did that." The *Grand Banks* hand shifted his cud to the other cheek. "Alex comes right up and goes to his job in the rigging. 'Bout a quarter hour later the Third comes up—he'd been jawing with the Captain below. The wind's freshening again, and the *Rogue* starts rolling from side to side. But that don't matter when somebody hollers, 'Blows, he blows, blows, blows!' although it won't be easy to lower with them seas running. The crew's yelling their heads off and I glance down to take a final sight of the compass in case we shift course. I see Cap'n Noah just jumping up from his desk chair. Then he turns back and snatches that paper off his desk and ducks aft out of sight. Few seconds later, he comes storming up out of the main companion, and he hollers at me, 'Hold her full for stays!' I poke the wheel down a mite. Then he starts for'ard to where Mr. Hughs is. And we're lurching so bad Cap'n Noah can't make headway without holding on with both hands. He just gets to 'midships when a sea comes over the starb'd rail. That dollop starts the casks from the lashrail there, and they tumbles smack over Cap'n Noah. The duty watch manhandles the casks off, quick as they can, but it's too late. Cap'n Noah dies a minute later with all the Mates standing by, helpless. They bury him just b'fore the storm reaches strength. We had us a good gale that night."

"Did you lower for whales?" Toby asked.

The seaman's eyes widened. "Would you, with the Captain dying? We just forgot about them."

"How was it that whaling lookouts were up if you were out of the grounds?"

"We just had our regular passaging lookouts—a man on

mainmast and another on the fo'c'sle deck. Fact is, only by chance somebody sighted whales. I recollect now the cry come from the deck, aft the waist, I think."

Toby thought about that scene, Captain Noah breathing his last in the vessel's waist made wild with seas and tumbled casks. The helmsman would not have been able to hear his last words.

"Did Peter Flick say anything when Mr. Hughs took command of the *Rogue?*"

His friend shook his head. "I sort of knew exactly when Cap'n Noah died. The Second and Third was standing by and Mr. Hughs was bending over the Captain. Then of a sudden Mr. Hughs stood up and stepped back, hopeless like. Stumbled a bit, he did, 'cause we was still pitching kind of sharp. Then while Mr. Hughs is speaking to the crew, sending most of 'em back to work, Mr. Flick hurries aft and down the main companion."

The *Grand Banks* hand jetted a brown stream toward the ocean below. "I says to myself then, '*Too bad for Missus Clayton,*' for she's a good sort, always ready to wallop up a meal for a sailor on the beach. And I look down at that painting of her what Cap'n Noah always hung on the paneling above his desk.

"And I see Mr. Flick is standing by the desk eying that picture too, maybe even glad it ain't his painful duty to tell her 'bout Cap'n Noah. Then, slow like, he stares around the cabin, and at the time I figure he's maybe thinking it's just his luck we're only three weeks away from home port, else everybody'd go up one grade and he'd get to be Second. Jealous of his rank the whole voyage, the Third was, and you got to 'Aye, sir; no, sir!' him proper smart or you'd hear 'bout it. Now, I'm thinking I was wrong, and that when he was standing down by the Captain's desk, he was likely deciding would he take over command of the vessel or not.

"Then a boatsteerer comes aft and hollers down the main companion, Mr. Hughs wants to talk to the officers. Mr. Flick, he darts through the saloon to the Captain's stateroom and comes back with a blanket which he takes up on deck. But by then Sails has already fetched a length of canvas for to shroud the body in.

"When Mr. Hughs is done speaking to the Second and Third on deck, he comes aft and tells me to up helm and keep her steady as I can. Didn't do much good, I can tell you, with that gale making up. But Mr. Hughs goes on below into the cabin. I see him through the skylight, sitting at the Captain's desk, writing in the logbook. And that's the end of it, 'cept he locks up the pearls for safe keeping."

"What pearls?" But even as he asked, Toby remembered the pearls with which Peter Flick had bought the *Rogue,* and which eventually came to Giles Thaxter's bank in New Bedford.

The man was nodding earnestly. "Aye, pearls. Maybe six

or seven of 'em. I see 'em for the first time then, rolling around on the desk top with only the desk's raised edge to keep 'em from falling off. And when Mr. Hughs is done recording in the log, he picks up a square of canvas what's lying there on the desk, wraps up the pearls, fetches a key out of a drawer and goes aft out of sight for a minute. I figure he's locking 'em up in the safe."

Toby had been sent to the cabin two or three times on errands and now he recalled the plan of its stern bulkhead. Above the horsehair sofa, a locked cuddy had been set in the paneling between the two telescopes, the ornate broken one and the unadorned glass of everyday use. In that cuddy were kept the vessel's papers and money.

The *Grand Banks* man continued. "Mr. Hughs acted as master till we run into New Bedford. It sure give us a start then when Mr. Flick claims as he's now the owner. Wonder why he backed off from taking over his vessel before?"

"It's a strange way for any man to act, let alone Captain Flick," Toby agreed.

But even as he said the words, an idea began glimmering in his mind.

 ten

Battle With the Horn

TOBY AND BEN belayed the end of the rope ladder to the starboard railing of the *Rogue,* then tossed the rest of it overboard to dangle just above the *Grand Banks* boat fending off. The two stood by as Captain Flick and Captain Goodwin came up, talking.

"Won't you change your mind, Captain Goodwin, and come around the Horn with me? We could mate for whales in the Coast of Chile Grounds."

Captain Goodwin set one foot on the lashrail and paused. "Indian Ocean for me, Captain Flick. Promised my wife I'd make a short voyage." He put a hand on a shoulder of each youth and climbed up on the railing.

Captain Flick watched his guest climbing down the rope ladder. "It's a shame to waste that big powerful ship of yours on warm water right whales. I can show you some sperm."

Captain Goodwin took his place in the whaleboat. "It's right whales I'm after, Captain Flick. My owners want baleen. I'll transship my oil from the Seychelles and come home with a load of bone."

It was Captain Flick's turn to climb the railing. His face was grave as Toby and Ben steadied him while he got his footing on the ladder. Soon the *Grand Banks* whaleboat was hauling across to the ship.

It was the second day of gamming. The vessels with yards abox scarcely moved as their officers and crews visited back and forth, each group taking turns at being hosts and guests. Now the *Rogue*'s larboard boat was keeping ship against the return of the rest of the bark's company later that afternoon.

Though the day was chill and gloomy, Toby found it pleasant to idle away the time practicing ropework, and trading around the new tales and jokes learned from the *Grand Banks*.

Late that afternoon Alex came looking for him and Ben. "Ye lads care for a bite o' fresh food, ye can come down to steerage with me."

They accepted gladly and climbed through the booby hatch beneath the boat skids. Steerage was deserted, for even the idlers were aboard the *Grand Banks*. Alex set out on his chest three apples, some slices of cold roast beef, and a half dozen rolls, gifts from the *Grand Banks* boatsteerers. "Feeds his men well, do Cap'n Goodwin," said Alex. "Tuck 'er in, lads. Ye'll not see the like for many a month t'come."

As Toby and Ben ate, the three talked about the gamming between vessels. And Toby, remembering they were alone, described his meeting with the man who had seen the signing of the sales paper and Peter Flick's actions after Captain Noah's subsequent death.

Alex listened carefully through to the end. "Ye say ye know why Cap'n Flick, as was then Third, didn't up and take charge o' his vessel?"

Toby nodded. " 'Twas because he couldn't find the sales agreement. That paper was on Captain Noah's desk when the Third had left the cabin, hardly ten minutes before. When my uncle died, I think Peter Flick hurried down to the cabin to get that paper so he could claim ownership of the vessel. How it must have stunned him to find it gone!"

Alex wrinkled his brow. "He had it when we anchored in New Bedford."

"It must have taken him nearly all that time to find it," Toby said. He thought for a moment. "The paper wasn't in the safe, because my uncle didn't take any keys from the drawer to unlock that cuddy built in the stern. Maybe Peter Flick expected Mr. Hughs to come across the paper when he checked the vessel's safe, as he would have to do when he took over command. Maybe he thought the paper was in Captain Noah's pocket. It must have taken time for him to realize my uncle had hidden it."

Ben was puzzled. "Why would your uncle hide the paper?"

"I don't know, Ben. But it must have been important for him to keep the whole thing a secret. When the whales were raised, there was just time for my uncle to hide either the paper or the pearls. And he hid the paper."

Alex scratched his grizzled head. "Pearls? They wasn't no pearls about."

"The *Grand Banks* man saw them," Toby insisted. "And so did I, in a banker's office. They're still in Mr. Thaxter's safe, for he's waiting until the price goes up before selling them for Aunt Prudence. Six pearls are what Peter Flick paid for the *Rogue* and her outfit. His half of her, I mean."

"Still a bargain for him at the price," said the boatsteerer. "But I swear I didn't see none. Desk was bare but for the paper we all signed. 'Cept they was a polishing cloth at the one corner—a square of canvas folded over all shipshape."

Toby suddenly understood. "The pearls were wrapped in the cloth! Later the vessel's motion jogged them loose. Mr. Hughs gathered them up in that same cloth when he put them in the safe."

Alex White thought about that and then sighed. "Cap'n Noah, he sure went a good cable's length to keep everything secret, not even letting his boatsteerer see a few pearls."

Ben spoke up. "Where could Toby's uncle hide the paper in a hurry? I've been down in the cabin two or three times and it's snug and shipshape with no loopholes or odd corners."

Toby shrugged. "He must have put it somewhere near the stern, for that's the direction he stepped just before coming up on deck. You could hide it under the edge of the carpet, or push it behind the sofa cushion, or even slip it between two planks of the deck, or a crack in the paneling."

"Well, I doubt Mr. Hughs, as Acting Captain, would let the Third Mate go prowling around the main cabin," Ben declared.

Alex took out a carefully hoarded sack of tobacco, tamped his pipe bowl full and lighted up. "We was three weeks coming to port after that, Ben. And Mr. Hughs had to sleep sometime whilst the Third has the watch. That there paper was just pushed out o' sight somewhere. 'Tweren't hid *permanent*. After all, Cap'n Noah didn't figure he'd get killed ten minutes later."

Ben persisted. "I said before that I figured Cap'n Noah's last words was really meant for Peter Flick. Maybe 'twas a way of telling him where the paper was hid."

"Then he would've got hold of it and took command of the vessel," Alex pointed out.

"P'raps 'twas some kind of warning for him not to take command," Ben said. "Or at least to wait till the *Rogue* made port."

The boatsteerer slowly nodded. "Makes sense in a way,

for 'twould fit in with Cap'n Noah's secrecy. What d'ye think o' that, Toby?"

But Toby scarcely heard, for, unbidden, his mind had seized Ben's earlier words and gone leaping ahead, goading a suspicion he had not known he had had. That suspicion now uncoiled fully in his brain, and he was numb at its implications. He swallowed and said shakily, "Alex, did you ever see that paper again?"

"Nor me nor any man aboard I know of," said the boat-steerer. "But ye saw it, Toby."

Toby nodded. " 'Tis in the bank of New Bedford, in an iron box. But, Alex—I wonder if 'tis the same paper you signed."

Steerage suddenly grew tense with surprised silence. Ben was the first to find his voice. "You—you mean, Peter Flick never did find that paper after all?"

"Sure he did!" cried Alex, almost angrily. "Don't ye start spinning something out o' nothing, else it'll come out the way ye act toward the Captain, and then ye'll get the rope's end, if'n he don't contrive to get ye both killed!"

"He must've found it," Toby was arguing with himself. "If he didn't have it when the *Rogue* made port, then he found it the months she was fitting for this voyage."

"Peter Flick had to find it before the *Rogue* made port, Toby," Ben pointed out. "If not, that'd mean the paper he showed at the bank wasn't real—I mean, that 'twas some kind of made-up thing he got ready."

The suspicion was out now and Toby was both relieved and disturbed. "That's the way it came to me now," he said. "I figured if Peter Flick couldn't find that paper perhaps he contrived another to take its place."

"But he's bound to've found the real one by now," Alex protested. He shook his head. "He's close on food and quick with punishments, but sure the Old Man wouldn't fix to sneak around with some kind o' false paper!"

Ben added slowly, "But if he did make a forgery, d'you think he could keep from tinkering? I mean, he might've put the price down some, or fixed it up some other way to get more'n he's got a right to."

Alex nodded reluctantly. "Aye, he might do, be he the kind t' meddle with legal things."

"It might still be there," Toby said. "If Captain Flick made a forgery and changed parts from the real sales agreement, then maybe he never bothered to look for the paper Captain Noah hid that day he got killed. Maybe 'tis still somewhere in the main cabin."

"'Twould be," Ben agreed. "'Less'n he wanted to destroy it. Worthwhile looking for, though."

Alex shook his head. "Waste o' time. Toby, was there my boatsteerer's stamp on that paper ye saw? Well, that proves 'twas the real agreement what we all signed proper."

Ben said quickly, "He could've made a copy of your seal from the articles, Alex. 'Twas three weeks' sail from Captain Noah's death to Buzzard's Bay, time enough to carve a seal like yours."

"Not 'xactly like mine!" Alex objected. "Not with every line and curve like I had it."

"But nobody compared seals, Alex!" Toby exclaimed. "Mr. Thaxter and Aunt Prudence and I never thought of it being a copy, though if we had, there were the articles to hand that we could compare it to." But not quite at hand, Toby remembered. Peter Flick had the vessel's articles for paying off the crew, and this paper, among others, was delivered to Aunt Prudence's home hours after the sales agreement had been locked in the bank's iron box. Only a strong suspicion of deception could have brought the two documents together for comparison.

Toby stood up. "I'm not sure what to look for, but now's the chance to do some searching, with most of the crew gone and the officers' quarters deserted. Alex, can I get through this new steerage door?"

Ben put his foot on the steerage ladder. "Reckon I'll go up and lounge against the taffrail, 'less somebody come around the skylight while you're still looking." He scrambled up and shut the booby hatch after him.

Toby was glad of Ben's offer. Mr. Barksdale was in the *Grand Banks* with the other officers. Zachary and Bow Oar of the larboard boat could be counted on not to give Toby away, but there were also three shipkeepers aboard, none bound by friendship to him and all anxious to earn a place in a boat with the greater share of the vessel's profits it carried.

Alex produced a strip of tin from the store of scrap in his sea chest. "This'll do handsomely." He pushed it between door and jamb and began working it against the hook.

Suddenly the booby hatch was kicked back. Ben's red head appeared in the gap. "Ahoy, there! The boats are starting back. Toby, you've got a quarter hour, no more!" His face vanished and the hatch cover rumbled back in place.

Toby's heart leaped. "Hurry, Alex!"

"Aye." His fingers strained the tin strip against the hook on the other side of the door. "Toby, search Cap'n Flick's stateroom first thing. If'n somebody sees ye in the cabin, why, that's curiosity, even if it fetches ye the rope's end. But if'n yer caught in the Cap'n's stateroom, he'll hang ye for sure." The hook flipped free. "Work smartly and keep an ear out for a warning whistle."

Toby slipped into the dining saloon. Glancing up briefly, he saw the top of Ben's head through the skylight. Then he hurried around the table and pushed aside the curtain of the Captain's stateroom.

Though the largest of the officers' quarters, the room just comfortably held the bed, a water closet, a chair, and Captain Flick's sea chest. On the bulkhead above the bed hung the harpoon gun Captain Flick had acquired in New

Bedford. So far it had gone unused. A board mounted on the bulkhead let down on a pair of chains to make a tiny table and above this was a single shelf for books. A row of hooks held changes of gear. Toby hung the curtain back on one of the hooks to let light in, for there was no port-hole.

Hardly knowing what to search for, he unhooked the folding board and let it down. Behind it, on the wall, was a rack holding a few papers. Toby hesitated only a moment, then quickly took them out and shuffled through them. Two were letters from oil shipping companies, one from a whaling company in Connecticut. There was a list of whaling grounds and a rough route worked out in pencil for a three-year cruise. He found the vessel's articles and then opened the last paper.

The India ink silhouette of a boatsteerer about to dart jumped up from the bottom of the page. Toby's hands trembled and his breath came hard as he quickly scanned the paper, then read through it more carefully. Unfolding the articles, Toby found Alex's seal and closely compared it with the paper he had just found. They matched perfectly, line for line.

A reedy whistling started up in steerage, piping "Forty Days Out of Rio." Was there real danger or was Alex just trying to hustle him?

Toby replaced the papers in the rack, hooking the folding panel up over them. He released the curtain as he stepped back into the dining saloon. A glance upward showed Ben's red head still calm against the roof of the afterhouse. Toby decided to take a risk.

He went into the main cabin, hurrying through the patch of daylight from above and into the gloom-shrouded stern half, for though the day was dull no lamps had been lit. Squeezing under the horsehair sofa, he ran his hand under the edge of the carpet. Nothing met it but dust, and the cracks between planks were stopped up tight. He backed out and thrust his hands all around and beneath the sofa cushions and found only tobacco crumbs. Above was the locked cuddy flanked by the two telescopes, though Toby could hardly make out their shapes in the cabin's gloom.

A rapid tapping came from above—Ben's fingers on the skylight. At the same time a sharp hissing sounded from the steerage door. Farther down the port side of the hull there came bumps and scrapes as of a boat.

Toby reached over the sofa briefly and brushed his hand against the paneling beneath the telescopes. The seams were as tight as those of the deck.

Then he bounded through the dining saloon and into steerage. The door slammed behind him and Alex said roughly, "Through the sail pen and tumble for'ard to the fo'c'sle—smartly!" The boatsteerer was at the door working with some kind of wire.

Toby saw that a panel had been taken away from a large

square opening. He stepped through to the sail pen. He felt his way between casks and piles of folded canvas until his fingers found the door into the fore 'tween decks and he dragged it open. He hurried forward in the dark hold, feeling his way along the alley. He went through the other compartments the same way and made it through the door under the fo'c'sle ladder just as some of the men came tumbling down. He stepped forward and mingled with them, asking after their gam with the *Grand Banks* until the cry rang down, "All hands to make sail!"

Both whaling vessels hauled their yards around and fell off on their respective tacks, the *Grand Banks* squaring in and bringing her wind over the stern quarter, stepping east toward the Falklands. The *Rogue* braced up sharp on the starboard tack to make southing, and before the watch was out she ran into cold fog.

Mr. Barksdale mustered them in the waist. "Cape Horn weather making up, lads. Dress snug, for it'll get worse before it lightens." Then he issued orders to make the *Rogue* weathertight to keep out the Cape Horn seas.

Toby, Ben, and Alex grouped together to form one of the working parties. They finished nailing tarpaulin over the forehatch, then went down into the lower forehold for planking to help Cooper roof over the skylight. There, by the light of Alex's lantern in the storeroom cold from the sea and with the timbers squealing all around them, Toby briefly told of what he had found in Captain Flick's stateroom.

" 'Twas the sales agreement I saw in the New Bedford bank," he said. "Word for word, signed and stamped with your seal, Alex. I compared the stamp with your mark on the articles. They were the same, line for line."

"If'n that's what ye saw, then yer right, Toby. But didn't ye say that paper was left in the New Bedford bank in an iron box?"

Toby nodded. "Mr. Thaxter was afraid 'twould come to harm at sea, but I reckon Captain Flick took it with him anyhow." He shrugged. "Doesn't matter now if that paper gets lost, for the *Rogue*'s all listed, insured, and registered in both our names."

Ben scratched his head. "Maybe that first paper is still in the bank, the paper we think he made himself so's he could claim the *Rogue*. This other one Toby saw might be the real sales agreement, and it took Captain Flick this long to find it."

" 'Tis of no matter, Ben," Toby said. "Both papers are written as alike as I can remember, and no one loses out by either one."

A voice rang down the hatchway. "Ahoy, down there! Cooper's chafing for them boards!"

They fell to their work, and it was all hands hammering, battening down, and stopping up for as long as daylight lasted.

That night a small but violent squall tore down from

the northwest, heeling the *Rogue* far over to larboard and blowing out the fore-topsail. It was "All hands!" into the screaming cold wind to fist in the thrashing buntlines and tattered canvas before it could jam the gear. The next day the wind backed to the south and the *Rogue* had to fight a head sea. By nightfall they ran into a hailstorm lashing from the east. Captain Flick doused the sails and they huddled, bare-poled. An early sun melted the ice from the yards, and the men took off their oilskins and sweaters as the *Rogue* ran free.

It went in that fashion, storms alternating with sunny weather and the wind boxing the compass. Foul changed to fair within the hour, and Toby did not know what to expect before the watch was out. Then, five days after parting with the *Grand Banks,* they raised the gaunt mountains of Tierra del Fuego and soon came to the strait leading to the Horn.

The wind came roaring up at them from the South Pole and the current charged through the strait toward them. The *Rogue* hesitated, shied from quarter to quarter, then plunged into those head seas like a whale reaching for the bottom of the ocean. She fought through the violent strait, then eased her pitching and once again took on the ocean's long rolling. The afternoon darkened rapidly and it began snowing.

Shortly before midnight, when Toby's watch was below, a tremendous lurch broadside tumbled the men out of their bunks. A sea leaped through the fo'c'sle companion, drenching Toby's berth. Ben laughed at his bad luck. "Now you're a real Cape Horn sailor, Toby!"

It was the last time Toby heard anyone laugh before they doubled the Horn, and the last time he was dry.

When the wind was not screaming out of the southwest, it veered to shriek down from the northwest by north. It flung hail, sleet, and snow at them, and sometimes sheets of rain as solid as the mad gray seas that slammed aboard the *Rogue*. The rigging iced up and it was usually an all-hands job just to take in a reef. The ocean raced in white crests like an endless stampede of wild horses. The *Rogue*'s timbers labored, and she groaned like a giant in pain.

They beat far, far to the south, farther, said Alex, than need be. Once, through a momentary clearing in a howling snowstorm, Toby glimpsed a distant white cliff. Ben told him, yelling in his ear above the roaring gale, that it was an iceberg.

The fo'c'sle was even worse than abovedecks. Working in the watch, Toby knew he would be cold and exhausted, but below he could not rid himself of the injustice of a fo'c'sle constantly washing in subpolar seas. His bunk was sodden and every stitch he owned soaked with brine that froze solid outside. The lantern was pitched so violently that whale oil spilled, and it had to be put out. After that they had to feel their way around. Toby never guessed how Cook managed to get up the mess, especially when the outboard port of the galley had been stove and a sea all but carried away the kettles and pots. But when their watch was called, the man who lost the draw crawled aft with the mess kit into which was dumped the entire watch's whack. This was brought below and each man dipped his pannikin into it.

The larboard bulwarks were carried away forward of the boat skids during a gale. Toby himself had been bowled from his feet and only by grabbing the mainhatch battens had he kept aboard. He expected the *Rogue* to right herself, but she stayed half seas over on her side. The Mate and Cooper scuttled past Toby and went into the fo'c'sle. They soon came up and ordered the duty watch below.

Toby managed to get down with the others, staggering against the slanting, rolling deck. At Mr. Barksdale's order they roused up the off-watch. The Mate took them all through the fore 'tween-decks hold and into the blubber room. The hatch directly beneath the sealed mainhatch yawned open and a faint glow struggled up to meet the flickering lantern Cooper carried. Bracing himself against the list of the bark, Toby followed the others down into the main hold.

They crowded around the foot of the ladder, every man staring in the light of the overhead lantern at the heartbreaking sight of tumbled casks and hurled gear that had started from lashings and fetched up in a vast chaotic pile against the lee bilges. The working timbers squealed, and beads of water dripped from the seams. Far away, in another world, the Horn wind howled. Here, no gale slashed at them, but it was as deathly cold as a tomb. Toby was acutely conscious that they were far below the waterline.

"Wrestle this gear back in place," the Mate ordered sharply. "No watch below till the deck's level."

The men, stumbling and crawling over the mountain of stowage, began pulling and heaving things free. Cooper pointed to Toby and Ben. "You two, there! Come fetch up some planks." He handed his lantern to Toby and beckoned them forward. They went through a door into the lower forehold where lumber was stored. Toby hung the lantern on a nail. Ben propped open the door. Then both of them and Cooper dragged planks back to the main hold.

The men were already having trouble keeping the barrels chocked up on the high starboard side. The motion of the *Rogue* in the heaving seas tumbled everything down to leeward. They began rigging temporary holding lines of thick harbor cable. Toby and Ben, under Cooper's direction, helped position and nail shifting boards, dividing the starboard half of the main hold into small pens into which the other hands hefted the boxes and barrels. Some of these were the great oil casks, of which, luckily, only one had split open.

Except for a little time off to eat a cold meal, all hands labored for over a day before the wave-swept *Rogue* was righted. Toby and Ben were kept at building the shifting boards higher as each layer of stowage was wrestled into place. The work grew harder, for as the bark lifted her lee bulwarks in the storm-tossed seas, she rolled more freely in the battering wind and smashing waves. Captain Flick finally had to take men out of the hold to wear ship so he could heave to under the bare poles.

As the bitter days ground past, gale came after gale, piling up monstrous seas against the *Rogue.* Captain Flick hove to so many times that Toby, dragging himself from job to soggy bunk to job again, lost count. Cook grew short-tempered and the Mate drove the men mercilessly. The days were gray, wet, and cold. The nights were black, wind-blasted, and icy. Hail scoured Toby's face and hands, and his skin reddened and chapped from his constantly sodden clothes. His arms and legs gradually turned numb and he thought he would spend the rest of his life stretched out on a yard, clawing at stiff, vicious canvas, or bracing himself on a deck, slanting and continually awash, hauling braces and slackening sheets.

There was grumbling in the dark wet fo'c'sle. "We'll be old men 'fore we get around!" Zachary declared. "Every time the Cap'n heaves to, it sets us back a week of sailing."

There was a muttering of agreement, and another voice added, "Maybe the Old Man thinks he's getting out of the worst of the Horn weather when he sticks his head under his wing. Truth is, we're sitting ducks for every storm spinning off the South Pole."

Ben Valentine spoke out in the darkness. "If 'twas me, I'd make all sail and stand northwest'ard. Double the Horn in less'n two weeks, not long enough for the wind to haul around to that quarter, 'cept maybe only once."

A spirited argument broke out among the hands. Toby did not know enough about sailing to make any suggestions, so he lay back in his damp bunk to get what rest he could in the wild yawing of the vessel.

Sleep, real sleep which refreshed body and soul, had been impossible for the three weeks they had been battering through Cape Horn seas. And even now in the black dank fo'c'sle the groan of working timbers grew louder, the yawing more violent. The gale was worsening. Toby slipped into an uneasy drowsing.

The next two weeks were as merciless as the first three had been. The winds hurtled through the top hamper in blasts up to hurricane force. Madly frothing seas brutally flogged the vessel, and solid water surged aboard. Two men were injured when the fore-topgallant yard on which they were working was wrenched off its truss. The goat and the last of the pigs were carried away. A green sea smashed the tryworks house. One of the spare boats was stove. Hull planks started, and the crewmen knew a refinement of misery when they had to keep the pumps working at all hours.

Then one night Toby saw stars in patches of clear sky above racing clouds. And though the wind varied and shifted more than ever, the gales began losing their sharp teeth. Black clouds lightened to gray and now and again weak sunlight struggled over the dark waves. The *Rogue* braced up more and more sharply on the port tack until finally, at Long. 78° W., she was standing well to the north, fetching lower latitudes as fast as her canvas could draw. And now squalls that had alarmed Toby in the South Atlantic seemed merely boisterous.

Clouds fell behind. Bright golden sun warmed the decks. The tearing seas calmed and deepened into a vivid blue. By the first dogwatch near Lat. 42° S. the grim Cape Horn memories were rapidly slipping away.

Toby, leaning over the weather rail, saw the bow wave curling back cleanly like a shaving of wood from Cooper's plane. Arches of rainbows flashed and vanished as spray dashed skyward. Gulls spiraled high over the vessel's wings of canvas.

The boatsteerers sitting on the tryworks bench began singing and soon Toby and the rest of the hands joined in.

> So blow, ye winds, in the morning,
> And blow, ye winds, heigh-ho!
> Clear away your running gear,
> And blow, ye winds, heigh-ho! *

 eleven

Close to Danger

Now THAT the weather was fine, Mr. Barksdale set all
hands to work as if they had done nothing but loaf during
those five terrible weeks around the Horn.

Sails crammed wet into the pen during gales were
brought out to dry. Storm-loosened rigging was repaired
and set up all-a-tanto. The royal sails, furled aloft these wet
cold weeks, were dried and sent below and their yards were
lowered on their lifts since the topmost canvas would not
be needed during the months-long cruising ahead.

The hatch covers were taken off and the holds opened
up to air, canvas chutes being rigged to funnel the breeze
throughout the holds. And since what shifting of stowage
had been made necessary by the storm had been haphazard, it had to be done all over again, that Cook might have
easy access to flour and salt and meat, that Cooper could
reach his casks, that gear and whalecraft would be handy.

The men grumbled, but did not really mean their
words, for they were all glad of fair weather and dry bunks.

Jake Underhill's complaints, however, were real enough, though for the past five weeks the fo'c'sle had seen and heard little enough from him.

For two weeks the *Rogue* ran north with a wind over her port quarter and the distant mountains of Chile sawing at the starboard horizon. Twice lookouts raised spouts, but they were right whales and Captain Flick let them go. He was after the more valuable sperm.

By now the galley had been repaired, the missing bulwarks replaced, the stove boat restored, and a new house sheltered the tryworks. The hands had also washed all their clothes and bedding, drying them in the sun on lines strung between the davits. The *Rogue* was back on the ordinary boat-watch routine.

For the larboard boat crew, the monotony of watching and waiting was broken by frequent practice drills for Ben Valentine. Toby, on the Tub thwart, was still handling the whaleline. The Mate seemed satisfied with their work and said they would perform their new jobs "the next time down." Impatiently, they waited for a sperm sighting.

At Lat. 30° S., the *Rogue* hauled the wind broad on her beam, took in some sail and began making westing in long reaches through the rich South Pacific Grounds.

"He blo-o-ows!" the masthead howled down one sunny morning. "Sperm, sperm! Five, six, eight—twelve! White-waters and blows!"

"Lobtailing!" screamed the foretop. "Four miles aweather! Breaches and lobtails!"

Toby heard a distant boom. Everyone was crowding into the weather shrouds. Dropping his tarbrush, he scrambled up on top of the tryhouse and found Ben there, yelling and pointing. "Look, Toby! You ever see a sight like that? Look, they're lobtailing!"

Boom, boom!

Toby squinted against the sparkling water. He saw the sudden silvery spurts of sperm vapor, each a short single plume slanting forward. Among them were the silhouettes of fanned tails thrust up above the surface, arching down, smashing the water with the flukes, first on one side and then on the other, back and forth. *Boom, boom!* They were like masts whipping in a hurricane, or the snapping recoil of a parted hawser, and they beat the water with the sound of cannon. *Boom, boom!* Among the sperm standing on their heads and lobtailing, other dark-gray bulks were breaching, leaping clear out of the sea, hurtling through the air and then falling back to the surface with a tremendous crashing.

"Why, they look to be playing!" Toby cried in amazement.

"Maybe that jumping and thrashing pleasures them some," Ben said with a grin. "But mainly a whale does it to get rid of the lice and worms that's plaguing him."

The Mate roared, "Sails to the mast! Clear to lower!"

This time when Toby tumbled to his Tub Oar thwart

he saw that Ben and Alex had traded places. Ben Valentine was going to harpoon!

They were off, sweeping their oars through the blue Pacific. Mr. Barksdale, standing at the steering oar, yelled forward. "Sperm too big to start you on, Ben?"

"No, sir!" Ben shouted aft. "I can run as fast as any man."

The crew guffawed.

"Then row, you sons!" cried the Mate. "Sperm, my bullies! Half the work and twice the dollars!"

"If'n we ain't killed," said Zachary through his teeth as he strained his Stroke oar.

"Your life's worth less'n half a barrel of fluke oil." Mr. Barksdale laughed. "Spring them oars, boys, or you'll fetch my knuckles on your heads!"

They bent their ash oars. The boat creamed over the seas. Toby hurriedly rigged the whaleline, then fell to rowing. He glimpsed the waist boat far to starboard, then she was hidden in a trough. Behind, there was a white triangle. Somebody meant to sail around the pod and come down to them with the wind. Toby could not see the boat's crew for the scend of the ocean. Even the *Rogue*'s hull was lost to sight, though he could clearly read the whaling signals she was setting in her top hamper. Zachary called them out to Mr. Barksdale and the Mate shifted course or urged them on accordingly. The booming of the lobtailing and breaching sperm sounded louder behind Toby's back.

Once he twisted around to snatch a look, and saw nothing but a vast incline of water up which they were rowing.

"Eyes in the boat, Tub!" yelled the Mate. "Try that again, I'll fetch you a boot in the jaw. Row, you clods! This isn't a pole barge. Let's see some spray!"

Stroke moved the pace up a notch, and when they were all set in it increased it again. Toby felt spray wet his back. The booming was louder, but less echoing. They were closing with the pod.

And then, as the boat rode up on a crest, the sight of a tail rising beyond the stern startled Toby out of his pace, bringing the Mate's wrath down upon him. Mr. Barksdale's tongue-lashing was interrupted by the great smashing of the flukes behind him. Water dashed into the boat. The Mate shouted and they worked their oars to keep from swamping in the leisurely lobtailing that could destroy them in one casual blow.

When they were settled back in their rhythmic pulling, the Mate said to the boat, "Now, never you mind any lobtailing, boys. You let me do all the worrying. Tub, if you're fixing to give up rowing, you can spend your time thoroughfooting the line."

Toby felt his face warming under the sarcasm. He concentrated on the stroke and tried hard to keep his eyes in the boat.

Mr. Barksdale spoke more kindly. "Them sperm are farther apart than they looked from the vessel. We got plenty of sea room to maneuver among them as long as every man does his job so I can keep a sharp watch."

There was a great bursting to starboard as a distant sperm leaped clear of the sea, hovered an instant in the air, then fell back with a crash. The whaleboat rocked in the wash. Toby glanced to larboard and saw another lobtailing whale. But Mr. Barksdale was right. By keeping eyes and ears alert, it was easy for him to steer clear of danger, for the sperm were widely scattered. Toby reckoned that the bigger you were the more room you put between yourself and the next fellow.

They rowed another quarter hour before the Mate's voice dropped to a coaxing mutter. "All right, boys, steady on. He's a-laying there, sunning himself. Big bull, maybe cut in eighty barrel. Long and strong, bend them oars nice and easy. We're close. . . ." His eyes were fixed straight ahead. Toby wished they would go in under paddles so he could watch Ben iron his first whale. But Mr. Barksdale leaned on the steering sweep, angling the boat sharply into attack. "Ready, Ben?" Then to the boat he said, "Way 'nough!"

They sat with blades poised as the boat glided in broad on to the sperm lying behind Toby's back. There was a grunt from Ben, a slight checking of the boat's run from his throw.

Mr. Barksdale hissed. "Dart th' other!"

Another grunt, a bigger push against the boat. The

Mate yelled, "Stern, All!"

Toby pushed against his oar. The crew drove the double-ended boat backward out of danger. Behind, Toby heard a thrashing, then sudden silence. "Sounds!" cried Ben.

Mr. Barksdale ordered, "Peak oars! Change, Ben!" His eyes shot to Toby. "Tub, weight that line!"

Toby cleated his oar, and as Ben and the Mate tumbled over thwarts to trade places, he dug a bailing piggin into the sea and dashed water into the line tubs.

The Mate yelled from the bow, " 'Ware line!"

The golden hemp began snaking out of the after tub, sawing around the loggerhead behind Ben in the stern sheets, and jumping down the center of the boat toward the bow. There was a jerk, and the boat was off, spray streaming in over the gunwales as the maddened sperm ran. Suddenly he vanished from the surface, tearing out nearly both tubs of line, close to three hundred fathoms of it, for sperm hugged the ocean depths.

Just when Mr. Barksdale had drogues readied for tossing the remaining line overboard, the sperm slowed and stopped. He sulked beneath the waves for an hour while the boat bobbed above, the whaleline nearly vertical between them.

Then water broke to larboard. A dark-gray mass slowly rose and a single spout of vile-smelling breath angled above it.

"Haul up, you sons!" the Mate hissed. "Get him 'fore he

has his spouts out!"

They crammed the wet line aboard, Toby coiling furiously as the boat pulled up. Mr. Barksdale plunged his lance beside Ben's harpoons, but before he could churn, the bull tossed flukes and reached for the bottom.

Throwing coils of line overboard, they backed off and waited. Sounding with lungs only partially emptied of foul air, the sperm was forced to the surface after only half an hour.

Twice more the Mate took them in, and each time his lance drove the great sperm into the depths.

At the fourth rising, the whale spouted the red flag. Mr. Barksdale said, "Back off, boys. Flurry coming."

They stood off, waiting. The sperm blasted blood-tinged vapor and the sound of his wounded lungs laboring for air was horrible in Toby's ears. The gray giant began rolling over and then suddenly slipped beneath the sea.

The Mate said sharply, "Watch for him, lads!"

They tensed over their oars, waiting for him to surface. Then Toby saw something angle up from the water. It was long, thin, gray, and spiked underneath with teeth. "Look, there! What's that?"

"Pull!" yelled the Mate.

Ben heaved mightily on the sweep. The men lashed with their oars. The Mate hollered, "Tub Oar!"

Toby, staring at the strange menace rushing toward the boat, was shocked to recognize it as the sperm's lower jaw, upside down.

"Tub!" cried the Mate.

Toby bent to his oar. Five blades whipped through the water. The boat sudsed clear.

Ben, standing in the stern sheets, shouted down, "He's jawing back, Toby! Sperm does that sometimes."

"Here he comes!" cried Alex from Bow thwart.

Ben turned the steering sweep. The men heaved with their oars. The whale, on his back with jaw poised above the water, charged the boat. He frothed past, missing narrowly, snapping his jaw in rage. The boat tossed wildly in his wake.

Once more the bull attacked, but his advance was sluggish and he wallowed to a halt. Then, rolling from side to side, he lashed out blindly with his jaw, champing wildly, fighting with all his dying strength.

Mr. Barksdale kept up a steady stream of orders as the whaleboat skittered about to stay clear. At last the great gray beast went into his flurry and finned out.

The day was spent by the time they made their bull fast alongside the *Rogue* and hoisted the boat to the davits.

"Four in the cut," said Mr. Barksdale with satisfaction. "Eat hearty, lads, there's plenty of stripping ahead of us."

"At least four days' worth," said Ben. He had meant to grumble, but could not help grinning about his first successful dart.

All hands sat around topside, eating dinner and talking

about how the boats had got their sperm. The starboard boat had to admit to a clumsy kill of a half-grown calf, for Captain Flick as header had had to pull up and lance half a dozen times before the red flag spouted. Jake Underhill, in the Second's boat crew, began deriding the starboard men, but Zachary intervened. " 'Tisn't fair to chaff them f'r what they didn't do, Jake. 'Sides, 'tis their onliest kill since that one old right cow took off Trinidad."

" 'Tis our first since the Atlantic, too," Jake muttered. "But the rest of us got a whale apiece big enough to cut into."

The boatsteerers were gathered at the bench abaft the tryworks, and Alex had invited Ben to join them during the meal. Toby could see the harponiers setting their pannikins down and going through the motions of heaving the iron as they compared experiences.

Mr. Barksdale called them to work and they set to rigging for cutting-in. Then the first sperm, a big cow, was snugged under the stage and the weary toil began.

Toby wondered, as he strained at the winch, if they would have to keep this up for four whole days. But halfway through the night, as he and Ben were standing at the open main hatch guiding a slimy, dripping blanket down to the blubber room below, Mr. Barksdale called his larboard boat crew off the job.

"Each boat crew gets a four-hour watch below once a day till the blubber's under the hatch covers," he told them. "Make the most of it."

They shuffled aft to the galley, gulped down hot coffee, filled their pockets with bread, and tumbled into their bunks.

It was still night when they were roused out near the close of the midwatch. The forward half of the vessel was brightly lighted for the men still toiling at stage and winch. The larboard boat crew edged around the work area and went aft. Alex, coming up from steerage, joined them at the galley as they got their whack doled out by Sails, who was spelling Cook.

"Best eat under the boat skids," Alex suggested. " 'Tis clean and near to quiet there." He booted shut the sliding cover of the booby hatch so they could sit down. They held their pannikins in their laps, each bracing his coffee mug between his feet against the roll of the bark as she shuddered under the pull of winch and whale. They spoke little as they wolfed down their food. Then Zachary and Midship Oar went off to fill their pannikins again.

A figure moved toward the booby hatch from the shadowed quarter-deck. Captain Flick stood before Ben, ignoring his two companions. "The Mate says you made a fine dart today, Valentine."

"I had a good boat crew backing me up, sir," replied Ben.

"There'll likely be an opening for a boatsteerer soon," Captain Flick went on. "Do you feel up to handling the job?"

"Aye, sir. That's what I've been working up to."

The Captain nodded briefly and left them.

They watched as he walked forward into the work area. Men sweated over the winch as the chains strained the blanket against the mast. The Second Mate kept his men busy bringing up hooks, gaffs, and knives, pulling and hauling and snugging down. Captain Flick strolled toward the railing to watch the Mate and the Third on the cutting stage.

" 'Twas on a night like this," mused Alex, "that I first lost my scrimshaw seal. Ye recollect, Toby?"

And, suddenly, something in the way Captain Flick was pacing along the deck recalled to Toby a good many forgotten details. "Alex, I think Captain Flick found your seal!" He forced back his rising excitement, keeping his voice low. "He found it, and then threw it overboard. I'm sure of it!"

Ben started, and Alex smothered an exclamation.

Toby rushed ahead. " 'Twas that first night we were boiling. Ben and I went to sleep on the afterhouse. You, Alex, you—" Toby hesitated only a moment. "I reckon you couldn't sleep and were walking the deck. Captain Flick spoke to you. After that, I was just dropping off when I saw him throw something overboard. Now I recollect, 'twas just the size, shape, and color of your ivory cylinder."

Alex was looking down at his empty plate. "I was a-searching out my scrimshaw, Toby, and Cap'n Flick says as he never saw it since all of us signed that there sales paper. How d'ye figure he'd lie about that?"

Ben said, "The paper!" His elbow dug into Toby's ribs. "You say you saw the paper from the bank down in the Captain's stateroom? Now, I tell you that one's a fake too! He got Alex's seal—stole it, likely—and fixed himself up a bill of sale so's even Alex would swear he stamped it himself."

Toby said slowly, "I saw him. We were cutting in, just a day or so before boiling. I was sent to ring the bell, and I saw Captain Flick below come into the dining saloon through the forward bulkhead."

Alex began to protest. "He wouldn't be coming that way—Say, there, that new door he had cut into steerage! 'Tis kept hooked, mostly, but we got Toby through it to the saloon. Guess the Cap'n could get into steerage if'n he liked, for 'twas empty then and no man the wiser."

Ben added, "Anybody'd know your sea chest, Alex, once they'd seen it. You knotted the beckets up all fancy. Captain Flick went and stole your scrimshaw seal. Suited him that you signed on again, didn't it?"

"He made Alex sign on, Ben!" Toby swiftly explained how Alex's free spending had put him in debt to the vessel.

The boatsteerer shook his head in wonder. " 'Tis a sight strange as how I ended up with no money. I promised

Cap'n Noah for sure last voyage that I'd put a little by and not spend it all b'fore pay-off day."

"I saw that last voyage account book myself," Toby said. "You kept charging chewing tobacco, razors, clothes. . . ." His voice trailed off as he realized his words did not fit the bewiskered man sitting beside him with an old pipe protruding from a torn pocket of his patched and ragged jacket.

Alex said reflectively, " 'Tis the Third Mate in a vessel what keeps the account."

Ben uttered a low whistle. "That means he'd been planning for a long time to steal Alex's carved ivory!"

Toby nodded. "Ever since he went into the main cabin after my uncle died and found the original sales agreement had vanished."

Alex added, "Peter Flick lets the First Mate take command and meanwhile fixes hisself up another sales paper. He's got to carve a copy of my seal to stamp on the bottom and that's what he shows to Mr. Hughs when we reach port."

"And to the bank and to Aunt Prudence and me," Toby said.

"But the carving ain't so good a copy," Alex went on. "Anybody puts it next to, say, the articles I'd signed that voyage, he'd see 'twas a fake on that sales paper."

Ben spoke up. "So Peter Flick made the account book read like Alex owes the vessel money and he won't let him go till he signs on for the next voyage. Then he cuts that door through to steerage. Now all he's got to do is wait till he can sneak in and steal Alex's seal. He's got a three-year voyage to do that in."

Toby remembered a rainy night in New Bedford. "He nearly had a chance to get the seal off Alex just before we sailed. He followed us for a little while through the dark streets and Alex—well, Alex didn't have his wits about him then."

The old boatsteerer grinned and stared at the deck. "So Peter Flick never did find that there paper we all of us signed. Now he's got hisself a real good fake. Come two and a half years from now, why, he'll walk into that New Bedford bank and trade the good fake for the bad fake and you can go whistle."

Ben sighed. "Seems a sight of a lot of work and planning to do. The first fake worked well enough, and, like Toby says, it don't matter much if the paper gets lost or destroyed now, what with the official registration and insurance and all. He could take the bad fake out o' the bank box and just tear it up."

"That's right," Toby agreed. "Even if we could prove that bank paper is a fake, there's the pearls paid out to show the sale of the *Rogue* really took place. But I reckon Captain Flick doesn't want to count on that and fixed up this second sales paper to be sure everything would turn out all right for him." One misplaced thought troubled him. None of this explained what Noah Clayton had meant by the devil's eye.

Mr. Barksdale's voice trumpeted the length of the bark. "Larb'd boat, bear a hand! Starb'd boat, watch below!"

They hurriedly stowed their mess kits in a rack under the boat skids and walked forward to the cutting deck. Jake Underhill met them in passing and Alex called to him. "Hey, there! Mate says starb'd boat off, not the waist. Move yer backside back t' the winch."

Jake paused to glare. "Ye ain't my boatsteerer and ye kin just shove your orders overboard."

Zachary and the larboard Midship Oar came up from the galley. Zachary said in a deceptively mild voice, "Jake, you ain't 'xactly killing yourself this voyage."

From the corner of his eye, Toby saw the Second starting toward them from the gangway. He muttered a warning. "Stow your gab!"

They froze into silence as the officer joined them. The Second took in the situation in a glance. "Underhill's wrenched his wrist and he's off for a spell. Captain's orders. Don't start parting brass rags or you'll all end up in irons."

"Jake too?" said Zachary, almost hopefully.

"Shut that jaw and lay for'ard smartly!" the Second snapped. "Underhill, fetch your coffee and keep below till called." He stayed until Jake had moved off, then assigned the larboard boat men to their work stations.

Many weary hours later, in the afternoon, Mr. Barksdale

came along as Toby and Ben were bailing the liquid out of one sperm case. This was the top of the sperm's long head, cylinder shaped and filled with the purest and most valuable oil in liquid form. Emptying the cases lashed upright against the bulwarks was a pleasant task. Mr. Barksdale watched them dip buckets and pour the contents into casks. Then he told Ben he could move his gear into steerage. "You'll dart and steer for the starboard boat, Ben. The Captain's old steerer is going to be header now and you men will lower as often as there's spouts—"

Scuffling and shouting broke out near the galley. Men hurried aft, clustering and shoving to get a view of the fight.

The Mate roared for order as he hastened toward the galley.

Toby dropped his empty bucket, but Ben pulled at his sleeve. "Stay out of it, Toby!"

"C'mon, Ben! I thought I saw Alex in the middle of it all!"

More hands came running toward the commotion. Toby and Ben joined them. Yelling advice and encouragement, the watchers crowded around the fighters. Toby circled the mass of men, trying to get a glimpse of the brawlers.

Fists flailed, curses and grunts scored the air, and feet heavily shod against cutting-in accidents lashed out. The crowd pressed close or fell back as the struggle shifted one way or the other.

The Second came up and he and the Mate roughly restored order with a few well-placed blows of their own. The fighters swayed on their feet, panting heavily and sweating freely. Alex was bleeding from a split cheek. The other man, Jake Underhill, fingered a puffed lip and a swollen eye.

Captain Flick pushed his way through the crowd. "What's this all about? Who started this?" Jake and Alex stared sullenly at the deck. The Captain's voice rose. "Speak out or I'll chain the both of you down in bilges for a week!"

And every man in hearing knew he would keep his word.

Alex spoke reluctantly. " 'Tis that Jake Underhill, Cap'n, sir. A-warming his backside in the galley whilst we's working fit to bust our hearts."

Captain Flick turned his angry gaze on Jake. His lips parted as if to speak, and then shut tightly as Jake stared back coolly, the corner of his mouth twisting up in a half-smile.

Alex saw that exchange of glances and his weathered cheeks flamed. "He was a-jawing back sassy, Cap'n. Ain't got no respect for boatsteerer nor officer, has Jake Underhill! And the rest of us is always pulling his weight for him, too. If'n he ain't caulking the deck above, he's sogering down below."

Captain Flick glared at Alex. "I know what Jake Underhill's up to, and it's my business, none of yours! As for getting into fights, Alex White, you can move into the fo'c'sle. Reckon I need you? Not any more. There's an extra boat-steerer who can take your place. All right, Mr. Barksdale, carry on." He stalked through the crowd and went down the main companionway.

The Captain's anger stayed with him, and for two weeks he drove the crew mercilessly through cutting-in and boiling out until men began to collapse at their tasks. The Mates frantically shifted jobs around, parceling out the easier ones by way of respite from the unremitting toil. At last every drop of oil was wrung from the blubber and headed up in casks, the barrels stowed down, and the whaling bark scrubbed from stem to stern.

With cruising canvas once more stretched along her yards, the *Rogue* was tacking across the sperm grounds when a line squall suddenly tore down on her, blackening out the sun and clawing the main topgallantsail to ribbons. The Mates bellowed orders and the crew jumped to the braces, easing the yards under the giant hand of the screaming wind. Lightning streaked the dark sky and thunder roared and echoed like a volley of cannon. The *Rogue* heeled far over, ponderous and steady, a dignified fat woman gliding across winter ice on one skate.

She was steady and safe and would tilt back the same way. Toby could feel that from the play of planking beneath his feet. He and Ben were ordered aft to get the thrashing spanker under control, while others sprang into the top hamper to furl canvas.

Ben and Toby fought the wild canvas between lunging boom and gaff. Painfully they inched the sail into the first, then the second reef. The yards steadied as they got the spanker down to storm size. They were just making their way off the afterhouse when Toby saw a man securing gear on the house over the trypots.

Suddenly the crewman was knocked sprawling among the poles and spades stored there. Ben's yell was swallowed up in thunder. Something, probably a broken line, was snapping in the wind over the man's still form.

They tumbled to the deck and scuttled forward, balancing against the heeling of the vessel. Scrambling up on the tryhouse, they hugged the roof and took measure of the line flailing above them.

The ruthlessly whipping cable was the halyard rigged along one of the many stays slanting forward between masts. The staysails, shaped and handled like jibs, long ago had been stowed away for cruising. Now the halyard on the main topmast forestay sloping down over the tryhouse had carried away, its forward end slashing cruelly in the tearing wind, blindly seeking victims.

The squall was roaring over them. They would have to act before the rain burst. Ben began crawling over the gear toward the unconscious sailor. Toby raised himself on hands and knees and watched the lashing halyard. Then, as the end of the cable rested briefly on the roof, he lunged.

Swiftly twining a bight of line around his arm, he leaned over the tryhouse roof and tied the end to one of the support posts. He tested the knot, and his heart gave a jump as his fingers brushed over the stumpy end of the line. He glanced around, and there looming out of the gray was a fresh white chip in the foremast.

Thunder crashed, a white wall advanced across the dark sea. Toby swung down and joined Ben under the tryhouse. The man was conscious now, dazed and sitting up. It was Jake Underhill.

Toby put his head next to Ben's. "That was no accident. The line was cut! Somebody hove a lance—it took a piece out of the mast. Just missed Jake, but parted the halyard."

Ben's face had just registered his surprise when the hard curtain of rain swept across the vessel.

 twelve

The Seventh Pearl

THE WHALING BARK *Rogue* was making a long board on the south 30° parallel, heeling under a spanking wind when Ben Valentine broke out a harpoon and bent to it a length of whaleline. Then he and Toby went up to the low fo'c'sle deck. "I know you mind how an iron is hove, Toby," said Ben. "But it seems all new when you're learning it yourself. So take care how I lay my hands on the shaft and you do it the same way."

Following Ben's instructions Toby balanced the rough-barked pole with his left hand close to where metal socketed wood and put his right hand aft across the butt. The iron was very heavy. For this reason it was never thrown freely, but always shoved or heaved at a short distance from its quarry. Toby's first dart swung the iron broadside into the sea. Ben told him where he had gone wrong and Toby tried again.

Just that morning, a few days after the line squall had roared over the vessel, Mr. Barksdale had asked Toby if he would go out for boatsteerer. "Now that Ben is to take Alex White's place in our boat, the Captain's short another steerer. He and his boatsteerer'll have to keep their regular places in the starb'd boat until a new steerer's trained," the Mate had said. "None of the other men are keen about moving up, Toby, so here's your chance if you're willing to work hard for it."

Now Toby was struggling with the ponderous dart, trying to achieve the graceful arc which would hook a line to a creature often as long as the whaling vessel herself.

A voice behind him muttered, "Watch how yer twistin' that foot off balance." It was Alex White, carefully studying the winch gear he was polishing with a bit of waste.

The rest of the practice session went much better with Alex's comments and encouragement. At last the old boatsteerer—Toby refused to think of him as anything else —tucked the polishing rag in his pocket and sat on the fo'c'sle deck. "Cap'n's gone below just now, and the Mate don't mind if'n I jaw with ye."

They sat beside him. Ben said awkwardly, "It don't suit, me taking your place in the larboard boat, Alex."

"Now, never ye give a mind," Alex replied. " 'Tain't no man's fault and ye might's well get some good out o' it, Ben. I'll be boatsteerer my next voyage."

" 'Tis Jake's fault," Toby said.

Alex nodded. "Aye, he fair started that fight with his sassy tongue and his sneerin' ways. No sailor stands for that for long. Needs a good shaking up, does Jake Underhill."

"He got a good shake during that squall," Ben said.

Toby nodded, remembering how he and Ben had crouched over a dazed Jake under the tryhouse as the pounding rain bore down upon the *Rogue*. He had felt a pull on his shoulder and had found Mr. Barksdale there, soaking wet. "Saw Ben taking him down," the Mate had yelled. "What happened?"

Ben had shouted above the rain. "Stays'l halyard parted, sir! Jake got hit with it. Toby's secured the line."

No one else had seemed to notice the incident, for crew eyes had been on the job at hand and officer eyes had been on the canvas straining in the stiff wind.

The Mate had prodded Jake here and there. The man had escaped broken ribs, but had suffered a painful welt from shoulder to waist.

Now, two days later, Alex White looked vexed at the reminder of Jake's injury. "Way he's carryin' on 'bout that bruise looks like he means the fo'c'sle to do his suffering for him." Then he turned to Ben and grinned. "Got yer bedding dry yet, young fellow?"

"Still sleeping on the boards," Ben admitted. Someone had left the booby hatch open during the squall and the hard short rain had pelted down into steerage slanting directly over Ben's bunk, soaking everything. His mattress was still secured on top of the boat skids, drying under the sun. Then Ben's face grew serious. "We've been wanting to talk this over with you, Alex. Toby says he found the halyard that parted to hit Jake was cut off square, not wore through."

"And there was a new chip out of the foremast," Toby added. "Somebody was out after Jake. Threw a lance, likely, and missed."

"A try for Jake?" mused Alex. " 'Tain't no wonder, way he's been acting and no punishment coming like on other vessels. But a lance now—why not a sheath knife? Some o' these hands are fairly smart tossing a blade."

And every hand wore a sheath knife. A sailor needed it continually in his work, to clear fouled gear, to trim frayed line, to help in splicing.

" 'Twas a stiff wind," Ben recalled. "That'd throw a knife off it's mark."

"And it did miss," Alex said. "Reckon Jake didn't notice anything like that or we'd all of us be in irons this minute. Ye didn't let on to the Old Man either, did ye?"

"Didn't dare," said Ben. "You know how he lights out after the men when Jake's in any kind of a fix."

"Jake's a bad shipmate," Toby said. "But who'd do a thing like that, Alex? This was attempted murder!"

"Now, quit kicking up a froth, Toby," the old boat-steerer said calmly. "Murder's all sneaky and deliberate and no sailor'd stoop to it. But brawlin's different, ashore or aboard, and sometimes a seaman gets his head kicked in for keeps, accidental-like. I reckon somebody just tried to put a scare into Jake, and it didn't come off the right way."

"But who?"

"Ye notice we got a fairly good collection o' men in the fo'c'sle," Alex went on. "Still, one or two of the hands, well-meaning fellows, are kind o' simple, sort o' weak in the head. They don't figure things out, just go from one thing to the next, doing the job and no complaints and even liking everything about life."

Toby grinned, recalling the two or three hands who asked nothing more than a meal, a place to sleep, and perhaps a jaw and a pipe after the hard day's work.

"Take a man like that and roil him some," said Alex. "And it'd take a lot to do that. Well, he don't think, but just goes right ahead, not meaning to really hurt Jake, but put a scare into him. Reckon whoever went for Jake is proper scared now, so let's let the whole thing be. Who spliced that halyard?"

"I did," said Ben. "Offered to do it before the Mate could order it."

The bell rang out the change of the watch. Alex got up and stretched. "Boat tricks. You and me on masthead, Ben."

Toby practiced hard for the next week and at last the heavy dart began to fit naturally into his hands. Now he could concentrate on developing the powerful thrust needed to drive the point through several inches of hard blubber. He was just stowing away the harpoon late one morning when the masthead raised spouts.

"Blo-o-ows! He blows and flukes!"

The men sprang for their boats. Toby made for the Bow thwart, since he was learning to be a boatsteerer. Alex was on Tub and the other men kept their usual places. The larboard boat spanked into the sea. The Mate turned the boat across the whaling bark's wake. They rowed behind the vessel's stern just as the starboard boat was lowering. The Captain, standing in the stern sheets, shouted impatiently at the men handling the falls.

Suddenly a heave of the sea shouldered the *Rogue* to port. The starboard boat smashed against the hull. There was the cracking of planks and yells from the men. The bow falls slipped free and spilled the crew into the waves. The boat dangled from the stern fall, dashing itself into splinters against the hull.

Mr. Barksdale shoved on the steering oar. "Pull, Two! Back, Three! Pull, All! Lay on, boys, and get 'em out quick!"

They swept up, boated oars, and began hauling the men in. Captain Flick grimaced with pain when someone pulled at his arm, so two hands together carefully hoisted him over the gunwale. Above, at the bark's railing, the shipkeepers worked to get the stove boat up to its davits. "Take 'em around to our quarter, boys," said the Mate.

Captain Flick was cursing savagely by the time they got the larboard boat hoisted back into place. The Mate gestured to Ben and Toby. "Here, now, boys, take him down gently to his stateroom." He paused to give orders about the rest of the starboard crew, then hurried to catch up and open the main companion for Toby and Ben with the Captain between them. Carefully they eased Captain Flick down the curving iron steps, through cabin and saloon and, finally, laid him down in the bed of his stateroom. The Mate unlaced the Captain's shoes. "Soaking wet. Let's get these duds off. Ben, fetch some dry clothes down from those pegs."

Though not unconscious, Captain Flick was in the grip of a consuming pain. He groaned through clenched teeth as the Mate probed his chest. The Mate said, "He's cracked a rib or two. Toby, get me the surgical plaster from the kit so's I can strap him up." He began unbuttoning the Captain's shirt.

When Toby returned with the medical kit from the cabin desk, they had got Captain Flick's wet shirt off and dry pants on. The Mate ordered Ben to the galley for bags of hot sand, as the Captain's teeth were beginning to chatter from shock.

And as Ben moved out of the cramped stateroom, Toby saw the bruise.

It was a big purple mark on Captain Flick's right shoulder, beginning to yellow around the edge.

Mr. Barksdale frowned. "Something wrong, Toby?"

"That's a bad bruise he's got, sir."

The Mate glanced at it. "An old one. Probably got it when that squall hit us. Cut me five or six strips of tape, will you?"

Obediently, Toby cut lengths of sticking plaster. But Captain Flick's bruise was exactly like the kind suffered by novice musketmen. And on the bulkhead above the bed hung that strange new device, the harpoon gun from New Bedford.

Toby was not able to voice his thoughts for three days. After strapping up the Captain's ribs, the Mate rode the larboard boat down and they got a big cow sperm. The waist boat struck a smaller cow, and the bow boat fetched in a nearly grown male calf. Lacking a header, the starboard boat had stayed behind. Then came cutting-in, a few hours' rest from that exhausting task, and finally the boiling.

Now the larboard boat crew was enjoying its first respite since the trypots were fired up. Toby lounged on top of the boat skids with Ben and Alex, enjoying both the waning sunset and the waxing glow of the tryworks chimneys while the other hands sweated away. "I reckon I know who tried to scare Jake Underhill," he said. "Though it didn't work, for the halyard parted and Jake never knew what hit him." Toby described the bruise on Captain Flick's shoulder and the harpoon gun whose recoil might have inflicted it.

Alex shook his head. "Don't make sense. Cap'n wants to

square a man up, he don't a-fright him secret-like. He'd just tell him to shut his jaw and buckle down to work. Jake, he's had a right restful time this last week." In fact, Jake was at the moment spelling Cook in the galley.

Ben had an idea. "Up to now the Old Man's swallowed Jakes's excuses like they was hooks baited with crab. If he turned around now and showed he's caught on, 'twould make him look a fool to the crew."

"He's a strange fish when it comes to how he wants to be thought of," Alex admitted. " 'Fraid of losing his dignity. But lookee here, a harpoon ain't no fine-tuned weapon, be it hand hove or fired from a gun. And the *Rogue* was shifting pretty lively there in that squall. Don't know how a man'd brace hisself on deck and take aim."

"The booby hatch!" exclaimed Ben. " 'Twas open, remember?" Ben's mattress, soaked by the driving rain, had finished drying only two or three days ago. "He could stand on the steps and rest the harpoon gun on the coaming."

"He got through the saloon door into steerage before," Toby added, "the time he stole Alex's seal."

"More'n that, I mean," said Alex. "Ye don't aim a harpoon to hit a point as small as a nail head, do ye, Ben? Ye got to figure on it striking somewheres inside a big circle, eh?"

Ben's face fell. "Right you are, Alex. You need a target as big as a water butt. The Old Man couldn't figure on aiming it so's the iron would just miss Jake."

"He aimed at the foremast," Toby argued. "There was a chip there like the point of a dart."

"A knife could do the same," Alex said. "Now if'n the Old Man aims at the foremast, how can he figure Jake even notices the harpoon bolt shooting past him in all that windy racket? Nor did Jake, for the bolt or knife struck before the line could swing free and hit him. So if'n the Cap'n's going to do anything like that, to have it count he'd have to aim at Jake hisself. Right?"

They were silent a few moments. Then Toby whispered, "But, Alex . . . that would be . . . murder!"

Now the old boatsteerer dropped his voice even lower. "And d'ye think the Cap'n would set out to murder Jake Underhill? What for? You sit there a spell and think me up a good reason."

Ben nodded slowly. "Reckon you're right, Alex. The Captain's got no call to kill Jake. Say, Toby, was there a dart in that harpoon gun down below?"

"Aye," Toby admitted. " 'Twas mounted along the barrel the way I saw it in New Bedford. But there were two or three spare irons to go with the gun. You could shoot one and load up with another." He was quiet a moment. "Still, I reckon if Captain Flick wanted to get rid of Jake, he'd plan to discharge him at New Zealand."

"A pleasure of a place to get paid off in," Alex said. "One of our hands from the last voyage took his share in

Bay of Islands. Figured to settle down into some sort of business. We'll be raising New Zealand in a few weeks now." The boatsteerer grinned. "Get us a run ashore, likely. If'n we run into some of Cap'n Noah's Maoris, we'll get the royal treatment, lads!"

Toby and Ben were quick with their questions and Alex settled back against a spare boat and began telling them of that last voyage.

Many of the places the boatsteerer mentioned had been listed in the *Rogue*'s log for that cruise. Since the names had been unfamiliar, Toby had not been able to follow clearly his uncle's laconic daily entries.

Now Alex explained that, as the natives of New Zealand were easily trained into good whalemen, it had been Captain Noah's practice to ship enough Maoris to man an extra whaleboat for several weeks. "Fetched us men from the same tribe, 'cause they was a good bunch o' workers," Alex said. "Come from a village a little down the coast from Bay of Islands. This last voyage, Cap'n Noah's first in the *Rogue,* he just 'bout shipped the whole tribe, men, women, and children. They wanted to visit 'mongst their kin b'tween New Zealand and the Line. We did a lot of island hopping, whaling from boats out o' the lagoons. Cap'n Noah, he don't mind the extra time out for all that passaging and gamming, for the Maoris give us a good tuck-out where we goes and we has greasy luck aplenty. We brung us a mighty well-fed and happy crew back to Bay of

Islands. Say, Toby!" Alex snapped his fingers. "I recollect now that after them Maoris go off home, Cap'n Noah went along to see a Yankee shipping agent. I figure at the time he means to transship his oil, but, no, we stand right out for New Bedford and don't stop once, 'cept half a day at Talcahuano for whack and water."

"P'rhaps Toby's uncle was carrying letters back with him from the shipping agent," Ben suggested.

"Maybe so," Alex replied. "But they's fortunes being made in New Zealand, lads, do a man dredge up enough cash for a good start. They's the timberlands, and the kauri gum what they use to make varnish, and all kinds of trade connected with ships and whaling. And likely the shipping agents got their fingers in more'n one pie. Tell ye what. Let's us go along to see that agent when we get our run shore at Bay of Islands. P'rhaps Cap'n Noah got the chance to get into a good thing and figured then to sell his vessel and send the money to New Zealand."

Toby nodded slowly. "Aunt Prudence would like to hear that instead of talk of Uncle Noah gambling away the *Rogue*." But he was not entirely satisfied. Why did Captain Noah fail to make clear that only his half of the vessel was for sale? And for what reason would he, dying, command his nephew to look through the devil's eye?

The *Rogue* continued to raise spouts as she made westing in long boards. They struck two cows and a calf off Easter Island, ironed a lone bull south of Pitcairn, and brought in two more out of a pod a hundred miles north of Maria Theresa Reef. They would have done better except that the starboard boat, after Captain Flick's accident, never once lowered.

In the slack time between boiling and sighting new spouts, the Mate lowered to run up to a floating cask, letting Toby toss the dart, change ends with him, and steer for a while. Standing up at the steering sweep, balancing against the spank of waves as the boat surged through the seas, Toby felt like king of the world.

Crossing the 160° W. meridian into the vast New Zealand sperm grounds, the bark captured and cut in three more bulls before raising the hills rimming Bay of Islands.

The *Rogue* swept grandly into the mouth of the bay, then under bunted-up courses she cautiously threaded her way among the many ships moored between the innumerable islands and peninsulas to drop her hook off the whaling port Kororareka. From this colorful and haphazard jumble of native huts, traders' shacks, a slap-together hotel, and a few well-built European houses streamed outriggers and double canoes filled with laughing tan-skinned Maoris.

The seamen leaned over the railing, calling out to them, ready to bargain. Suddenly the word was passed down from Captain Flick. There was to be no trading and no gamming. The Mate would assign tasks, and no run ashore until the vessel was well-stowed and shipshape.

"Eight months at sea, seven without a run ashore, three

without no gamming," muttered Alex, heaving at the winch. The larboard crew was bringing down the heavy foretop yard which had warped and needed replacing.

Toby nodded, strained on the handspike until the pawls clicked, then during this brief respite said, "Is the Old Man going to let us ashore at all?"

The Mate's voice came from behind. "Work smartly and cheerily, lads, and I'll see you get your run ashore. That's a promise."

Zachary lifted his head from the other end of the winch. "I'll hold you to that one, sir!" and he pushed so eagerly that Toby nearly lost his own grip.

For a week they labored at all speed, knowing Mr. Barksdale was as good as his word. Captain Flick spent most of his time ashore, sending out supplies and orders. Since it was May and the start of the local whaling season, vessels continued to arrive for supplies and recruiting until everywhere Toby looked a forest of masts and spars nearly hid the real forest surrounding the hill-rimmed bay.

Then early one morning Mr. Barksdale announced they could all have the day ashore, but every man had to be back aboard by sundown. With a dollar advanced from wages in every pocket, and trade goods charged from the *Rogue*'s slop chest, the men headed for the boats.

Ashore, Toby, Ben, and Alex gathered together while the other seamen spread out among the shacks and huts, pleasure bent.

"Alex, do you remember the name of that purchasing agent my uncle saw when he was here?" Toby asked.

"Aye. Name's Salter. We can ask our way."

The purchasing agent's office was in a white clapboard building which looked strangely out of place in a subtropical land, but Mr. Salter was not there. His clerk, a polite Chinese in European clothes, told them the agent was off in the mountains inspecting a stand of timber for purchase. He would be back late that afternoon.

As they went away, Alex said to Toby, "Ye look like ye've swallowed vinegar. Don't ye fret none. I done my share o' waiting around and the sun always drops over the foreyard sooner or later."

"Let's get some tucker and then go trading," Ben suggested.

The native marketplace offered tempting odors from fruits, cooked eel, and steamed *toheroa* wrapped in leaves. They made a full meal of these, topping off with fresh coconut milk. Then, followed by a troop of friendly children, the three shipmates roamed among the thatched huts of the settlement, bargaining in trade English with smiling Maoris clad in colorful garments of woven hemp. They bought combs, napkin rings, and paper knives carved from hardened amber-colored kauri gum, warrior figures of wood, and greenstone talismans. The hours drifted by pleasantly and at last it was time to return to Mr. Salter's office.

"I'll wait for you near the larboard boat," said Ben. " 'Tis said you can pick up some good shells along the beach."

Alex and Toby went ahead without him.

When Mr. Salter heard Toby was Noah Clayton's nephew, he welcomed them warmly into his light and airy office. He was distressed to learn of Captain Noah's death. "A high hook Captain like Noah Clayton should not have got caught in a pinch like that," he said, shaking his head. "Well, I suppose when the debt is paid I must send it on to his wife."

Toby leaned forward in his chair. "What debt is that, Mr. Salter?"

"Why, close on one thousand dollars that he let a hand of his have whom he discharged here in Kororareka his last voyage."

Alex spoke up. "That'd be Oliver Jones, sir. I didn't know the Cap'n give him extra cash."

Mr. Salter nodded. "Mr. Jones saw me last month. He's saved up three hundred dollars toward the debt." The purchasing agent tilted back in his swivel chair. "Yes, he borrowed the money and bought a trading schooner. He's been doing well, I understand, plying between the various islands and whaling stations. Ought to have the rest of the debt paid up within another year. I'll send it on then. Do you think your aunt would want it in cash, Master Toby, or shall I replace the original pearl? A pearl would probably fetch more in the States than its cash equivalent here."

Alex said in a strangled voice, "Pearls."

Toby's thoughts spun. Pearls. Money. Debts. Payments. He opened his mouth and closed it again.

Mr. Salter frowned, then smiled again. "I see. Captain Noah didn't say anything about pearls, did he? He must have sold the others in some port before he was killed in that storm. However, I'm sure your aunt has attorneys looking out for her interests, and no doubt everything is in good order."

Toby swallowed a knot in his throat. There was nothing to be gained by explaining the entire complex situation. "Aye, sir. Do you know where my uncle got the pearls?"

"Think to get yourself some more?" Mr. Salter chuckled. "Captain Noah got them from some Maori chief down the coast. He gave the tribe passage among the islands, and when they returned to New Zealand the chief gave Captain Noah seven pearls as a gift of thanks. The Captain showed them to me and asked my advice. I said they would bring more money where they were rare, rather than by selling them locally through merchants. Six were fine gems. The seventh, though, was a small one of lesser value."

"That'd be the one he give Oliver Jones for to buy his schooner," Alex said.

Mr. Salter nodded. "Captain Noah wanted to invest in something here, just to try his hand at it, I suppose. When

Oliver Jones asked to be discharged here, meaning to go into some kind of business, it was Captain Noah who suggested a small trading company. I converted the seventh pearl into cash so Jones could buy his vessel and a cargo."

Alex nodded. "Aye, 'twas like Cap'n Noah to give a man a helping hand."

Toby spoke through stiff lips. "And now Oliver Jones is saving up to pay back the loan?"

"With a modest interest," Mr. Salter said. The slight frown came again. "You needn't fear, young man. It will be paid; you may depend on it."

Toby's breath was so tight it nearly pained him as he rose from his chair and said, "Thank you, sir. My aunt will be glad to know you're taking care of things."

Toby could hardly wait until they were clear of the white clapboard office building to burst out with, "Alex, that sales agreement! 'Tis a fake. 'Twas always a fake. Uncle Noah couldn't get six pearls for the *Rogue* because the pearls belonged to him in the first place."

"Aye." Alex squinted over the hilltops. "Sun's behind them hills. Best make it back to the vessel." He seized Toby's elbow and piloted him through the crooked streets toward the beach.

Words tumbled from Toby's lips. "But there was a paper, Alex. You stamped some kind of paper. It wasn't a sales agreement at all. What was it? What kind of paper did the Captain and the Third Mate sign, and get you to witness?"

Alex stopped short and faced Toby. "That ain't the half of it, Toby Clayton. If'n Cap'n Noah didn't sign away his vessel, that means Peter Flick stole her. Or Noah's half of her."

"And that's why Peter Flick was surprised to find out the *Rogue* had two owners!" Toby added. "Captain Noah never told him about the partnership because he never sold the vessel at all!"

They met Ben Valentine coming through the market-place. He held up a net bag filled with beautiful and unusual shells. But Alex cut short his cheerful greeting and told Ben what they had learned in the purchasing agent's office.

Ben was all for immediate action. "Let's hurry aboard, burn that fake sales paper the Old Man's got below, and hide out ashore till the *Rogue's* sailed."

Alex gestured impatiently. "Are ye daft? If'n Toby don't show up come sundown, Cap'n Flick'll think 'bout that paper first thing and go looking for it. And it'd be gone and that'd blow the gaff for certain sure. All the Old Man would have to do is post a reward for us and he'd have men combing the forests and hills and prowling along the coast. We'd never even get as far as that Maori tribe Cap'n Noah knew, even s'posing they'd want to hide us. Cap'n Flick can tell any kind of story 'bout us he's got a mind to so's nobody'd want to help us out. And they's plenty of men on the beach what ain't fussy what they does to collect a little coin, like tossing a knife first and claiming the reward later on."

Toby was thinking furiously. "We can forget about the forgery Captain Flick has on board, if we can just get to New Bedford first and challenge the paper that's in the bank there. All we'd have to do to prove that one's a fake is to compare it with Alex's real stamping on the articles of the *Rogue's* last voyage. My aunt still has all the vessel's papers."

"Ye mean to ship out in a vessel leaving now before Cap'n Flick finds ye've gone?" Alex asked. "Ye can't buy passage without no cash. And I doubt Mr. Salter's going to hand your aunt's three hundred dollars over to a couple o' deserters. Ye'd have to work yer way home, maybe not get there for months or even years. Why, Toby Clayton, once he finds ye're gone, Cap'n Flick'd lay a straight wake for New Bedford so's he can put the good forgery in that iron box and tear up that first paper what can't stand muster. Then ye can go whistle with yer charges."

Ben shifted his feet impatiently. "Let's get aboard now, before Cap'n Flick. All of us looking through the main cabin can maybe find that real paper that Alex witnessed, whatever it be. Then we could go to the authorities—"

The boatsteerer was shaking his grizzled head. "Living down there all this time, Cap'n Flick's found that paper by now and got rid of it. And if'n he didn't find it, neither can we."

Toby picked up a stone and hurled it aside in exasperation. "Then what can we do, Alex?"

"Go back aboard and stick with the vessel till she's hove her anchor in Buzzard's Bay," Alex replied. "Then it don't matter do we jump in a boat and get to the bank b'fore Cap'n Flick does. Ye can tell yer story to that banker, and he'd see the paper was showed up for a fake, and never mind Cap'n Flick walking in with another copy, for then 'tis too late. Ye'd get yer *Rogue* back all proper and Peter Flick'd find himself in irons."

"Two years to wait," Toby muttered, kicking the dust.

"Maybe only one, do ye get to be a boatsteerer," Alex said encouragingly. "Then the Old Man'll be lowering that starboard boat again. Come along, lads. 'Tis close on sundown."

Zachary, Midship Oar, and the Cooper were waiting near the larboard boat. They pushed off and rowed back to the vessel. Captain Flick was standing beside the afterhouse ladder by the time they finished securing the boat's gripes. "Is Jake Underhill among you? Did any of you men see him in port?"

But none of them had seen Jake since that morning. "Nor much o' him the whole voyage, come to that," muttered Alex, as they all went toward their casting-off posts.

The seamen stood by their various lines and winch stations, waiting for orders. Mr. Barksdale glanced around ceaselessly, checking with his eye every piece of rigging. The

Second and Third moodily leaned over the railing, staring shoreward, scanning every moving boat in the harbor. Captain Flick stalked up and down the deck, visibly becoming angrier as the sun lowered and the tide began to run out.

Finally, when the sun had gone and its last rays flattened themselves redly along the horizon, the Third called out that Jake was coming in a native boat. Ben threw down a line, and after some arguing and pushing and pulling, Jake was at last on deck, weaving noticeably, a silly smirk on his face.

Captain Flick strode up to him. "What do you mean coming an hour late? I've near lost this tide and with the wind hauling to box us in for another night! Where've you been, you good-for-nothing?"

Jake hooked his elbows over the railing behind him. "Come back when I take a mind ta," he slurred. "Jus' bear in mind who ya talking ta, Cap'n."

Toby saw Captain Flick's face bleach with shock and anger. The master whirled. "Mr. Barksdale—"

But Jake only raised his sodden voice. "Ne'er mind the Mate. And ne'er mind no rope's ends 'r irons 'r what. 'M Jake Underhill, thass who, 'n I comes and goes as I likes. Know why?" He pushed himself away from the railing, floundered with his feet, and fetched up, facing the Captain with a sneer. "Same reason ya din't sail 'thout me, ain't it?" He raised a hand and derisively flicked at the Captain's lapel.

The Captain looked around at the men waiting by their stations, and he smiled a tight, strained smile. "Why, Jake," he said in a voice meant to sound amused, but which vibrated with tension. "Jake's drunk, aren't you, Jake? Go below and sleep it off. No harm done."

Jake grinned a broad, unpleasant grin. "Thas's my nice Cap'n. He don't harm me none. Y'know—he ain't even got th' guts ta face a whale." He laughed brokenly until he began to hiccup.

The strained smile on Captain Flick's face froze there, a horrible grimace. "Mr. Barksdale, you can have the anchor hove. Carry on." He turned woodenly and marched toward the main companion.

The Mate's voice boomed the length of the vessel. "Break out the anchor. Starb'd the helm." He paused in front of Jake Underhill. "You. Lay below. I'll take care of you tomorrow."

 thirteen

Terror in Hemp

BRACED UP SHARP on the starboard tack, the *Rogue* stood northeast, shaping course for Tonga, and Samoa beyond, for a month or so of leisurely humpbacking among the tropical islands before cruising the Line for sperm.

During those days in passage, Toby worked under Ben and Alex's direction, darting from the bow of the vessel. And even off-watch, they kept him busy sharpening irons and stopping them down with line.

"Ye're 'bout ready to dart," Alex said during one watch below as they lounged over the starboard bow railing. "I says as much to the Mate, and likely he'll have ye iron a few humpbacks in the islands. They's easy to get."

"How do they spout?" Toby asked.

Ben described the humpback spout, low and busy, three or four puffs in quick succession between shallow dives. "They sink when the header cuts the 'life,' but the carcass gases up quick and surfaces again."

"They've been saying that the oil isn't worth as much as

whale and sperm oil," Toby remarked. "And humpback baleen is shorter than the size bone of the rights. I can't see why Captain Flick bothers with humpbacks at all."

Alex nodded. " 'Tis true they ain't worth quite so much as t'other whales, only a few hundred dollars each carcass. But humpback is plentiful and easy to kill. 'Sides, maybe the Cap'n figures to load up his casks so he can rush home and plunk that good forged sales paper in his bank box."

" 'Twas learning that Captain Noah really owned the pearls all along that jolted me so," Toby said. "Else I'd likely have thought to ask Mr. Salter to write to Giles Thaxter and ask him to compare the seal of the bad forgery still in the bank with the stamp on the *Rogue*'s articles my aunt has from the last voyage. The letter would somehow reach New Bedford, even if it took months to get there."

"Maybe so," said Alex. "But by the time ye'd finished explaining everything to Mr. Salter's satisfaction, the sun'd been gone and the moon'd been up. We'd of had to come creeping aboard the vessel well past the deadline to face Cap'n Flick. Jake Underhill can get away with that kind of thing, but not us!"

The night Jake had come aboard drunk the *Rogue* had canted her head around and pointed out of Bay of Islands, going on the last of the tide. The next morning the Captain had recovered some of his poise, though his hands had been trembling. When he had found Jake Underhill tarring down rigging under the stern eye of the Mate, he had ordered the seaman to some easier task. And later that day Captain Flick had exchanged Stroke Oars between the larboard and waist boats, Zachary to row for the Second, and Jake Underhill to set the pace for the Mate. That had been an open affront to Mr. Barksdale's authority.

Now Toby, leaning over the railing and watching the bark cut a feather with her bow, reflected that Alex was right about their own course of action. All they could do was stay in the vessel until Captain Flick docked her at New Bedford. Then would come the time for action. He thought of something. "Alex, now that we know my uncle never sold Peter Flick the *Rogue*, what did he really mean with his dying words, 'Tell Toby to look through the devil's eye'?"

The boatsteerer—and Toby still thought of him as that though he bunked in the fo'c'sle—rubbed his stubby chin. "I been turning that over, and the best I can figure is what come to me when we was done rowing through the Evil Eye in the Azores. I reckon it for sure now that with the wind howling and Cap'n Noah dying, his words got all twisted up somehow. He must've been saying something else, and we all mistook it."

"Suppose he was saying something about the real paper," Ben suggested. "Likely telling what it was about."

Toby shook his head. "He went through a lot of trouble to keep it all secret. He got Alex to witness it, and he knew

Alex couldn't read. Then when he was alone in the cabin and whales were raised, he stepped back to the stern out of sight of the skylight, and when he came up on deck his hands were empty, showing that he put the paper away. Peter Flick couldn't find that paper either when he went below after my uncle died. And there wasn't any out of the ordinary paper in the vessel's safe or in my uncle's pockets. That means Captain Noah deliberately hid it, even though he left those six pearls of his lying on the desk."

Alex nodded. "They was wrapped in that square of canvas on the desk what I took for a polishing cloth. Cap'n Noah likely figured they'd lie safe a few minutes till he got back."

Ben went on. "But he never got back. The pearls was joggled loose. That's how Peter Flick knew Captain Noah had them, so later he wrote out he gave them in trade for the *Rogue*."

Toby sighed. "I still wish I knew what that real paper was all about."

"Ye'll likely never know," Alex said.

Balmy tropical days sped by. Raising the Tongatabu group, the *Rogue* moored in the spacious lagoon of one of the islands. A small and friendly tribe of Polynesians lived in thatched huts along the palm-edged shore. Half a bolt of cloth and a keg of nails from ship's stores quickly brought from the chief permission to use the harbor. The larboard boat was put on duty watch. It seemed strange to stand masthead with the bark at anchor and land an easy swim away.

Ben raised the first spout. "He blows, blows, *blows!*"

Toby, with him at the foremast truck, glimpsed three spouts darting up from the sparkling sea, three humps rounding out, then three more spouts, another dive. "Pod of three, broad on the starboard beam!" he hollered. "Two miles off. Blo-ows!"

From the deck rang the Mate's answering roar. "Alow from aloft! Clear to lower!"

Toby and Ben slid down a backstay and ran to the larboard boat. The men snatched off the tub covers, lifted the tubs aboard, cast off gripes, kicked in the cranes, and lowered away in the space of a breath. But this time it was Jake Underhill who tumbled to the Stroke thwart.

Mr. Barksdale levered them away from the anchored vessel with a heave on the steering sweep. "Toby, Captain says you're to dart. Get up there!"

Ben crowded back to Bow thwart and Toby, confused and excited, stumbled forward to Harponier. He seized the oar and ran it out. Then they were driving out of the lagoon, bending the long white ash, whipping suds into the air.

The Mate scanned the sea, and Toby risked a glance around too. Here in the tropics the ocean did not have as great a swell as in higher latitudes, and Toby could see one or two of the other boats frothing through the seas.

Mr. Barksdale growled. "The Captain's lowered, lads! That makes four boats after three whales. You going to leave us out of the hunt? Pull, my bullies, pull your guts out! Heave, you wind-broke boardinghouse crimps!"

Alex, as Tub Oar, hurriedly rigged the whaleline, and a bow box length of it was fisted forward. Ben, taking the end, bent two irons. Toby turned on his thwart and quickly faked down the slack in the bow box, conscious of three distant whales rapidly humping toward the boat. Finished with the line, he took up his oar again, vaguely aware of other boats not far behind theirs. Looming large in his mind was the task of pitting his tiny man's strength against the greatest creature on earth.

The anchored *Rogue* grew small in the distance, and it seemed to Toby that the two miles were quickly paced. All too soon the Mate dropped his voice and 'vasted oars. "Get up there, Toby, and set yourself."

He rose shakily. Before him, diving in unison, spouting at whitewater, rounding out again, rising and blowing, three humpback whales came toward him with the easy stride of giants.

Ben tugged at his sleeve, and Toby looked down to find the crotch set up, the two live harpoons resting within easy reach. He hefted the first iron in his hands, balancing against the ocean's roll. Humpbacks, smaller than sperm, were less than twice the length of the boat. Toby singled out the bull, slightly larger than the other two. Half an

inch of planking and a rapidly diminishing stretch of water were all that separated Toby from his monstrous
quarry.

And monstrous he was. Though the back was fairly flat
and the snout tapered, the creature was warted and
scabbed with white fleshy knobs and scaly patches of barnacles on the black skin, disfiguring the head and the im-
mensely long, powerful flippers. Forward of the small, a
dorsal fin hugged the tail, humplike, as the whale, arching
and blowing with his cow and nearly grown calf, ran down
to Toby.

Wedging his left thigh in the half-circle clumsy cleat,
Toby poised his heavy harpoon. He could not see the other
boats. They must be behind, waiting as he was waiting.

The black lumpy heads rose and fell, spouting as they
neared, looming larger and uglier. The Mate, shifting the
boat with the steering sweep, said sharply, "Next rising!"

One moment the sea was quiet, and the next instant water foamed and roiled as a great black flank rose before
Toby like a wall, moving past, hunching up—

The Mate yelled, "Give it him!"

The long dangerous flipper glided past. Toby hove the
iron. It stabbed in just abaft that long fin, buried up to the
hitches. He grabbed the spare iron and darted that beside
the first. The whale was harpooned! Toby could hardly believe that he had really done it.

"Stern, All!"

The boat lashed backward, Toby crouching against the lurching.

And then the water seemed to explode as the humpback's great flukes smashed the surface. The boat skittered broadside, but the oars steadied it.

The humpback started to run, whipping line out of the bow box. But when Toby shook the water out of his eyes he saw a second line leaping out of another whaleboat. Captain Flick stood at the starboard boat's steering oar. He must have swept up on the other side just as the whale passed the larboard boat.

Mr. Barksdale hollered, "Peak oars—change ends!"

Toby skipped over the thwarts and nearly fell into his place at the steering oar just as the boat jerked and began sudsing through the seas. Bracing himself upright, he wedged the sweep under his arm, working it to keep the speeding boat from yawing too sharply, both to prevent an upset and to keep from fouling with the starboard boat's line.

He snatched a glance over his shoulder at the other boat. It was trailing far behind, though Captain Flick should be leading the chase, as the ranking officer does when two boats hook on to the same whale. Even more surprising, the Captain was still at the sweep. His boatsteerer huddled in the bow, a puzzled expression on his face.

" 'Ware line!" Mr. Barksdale roared from where he stood in the bow. He meant the starboard boat's line, for Toby had let his own boat stray too near it. He pushed on the big oar, setting the larboard boat well to the right of the running whale.

Yet again his boat crept near the taut, murderous line. Once more Toby shoved the sweep, edging his boat clear.

Incredibly, the speeding line moved closer. The men were shouting. Toby turned his boat as far to the side as their own whaleline, whipping around the loggerhead, would permit. He glanced back to find the other boat almost directly behind his, and waved an arm to signal Captain Flick to steer clear. He saw the other sweep turn, and the Captain's boat began nudging to one side—the wrong side!

Toby shouted, "Mr. Barksdale—the line!"

The Mate took one look at the tearing whaleline closing with their boat, and turned pale. He motioned as if to fend off. Toby shook his head. They were as far over as they could get behind the racing whale. The Mate raised his hands to his face and shouted back to the starboard boat, but the wind of their racing snatched his words away.

The killer line was brushing the larboard strakes with a low growl which quickly grew into a nerve-racking whine as the speeding rope pressed tighter.

"Down!" yelled the Mate. "Hit the bilges!"

The crewmen scrambled off their thwarts and huddled on the bottom. Still Toby stood at the steering sweep. Without it, the boat would soon capsize in the frothing wake of the running whale.

The ripping line moved upward, jumped off the gunwale and caught under the blades of the peaked oars with the scream of a saw tearing at a pine knot.

Jake Underhill cowered in the stern sheets against Toby's legs, a look of terror frozen on his face. Both bow and stern of the whaleboat were built high, and in the scant space allotted to the boatsteerer and Stroke Oar, Jake could not escape the murderously whipping line.

Toby yelled to him, "Move for'ard!" There was plenty of room among the 'midship thwarts, and Toby planned to tumble forward himself at the last moment, if it came to that.

Jake stared beyond Toby. Suddenly he raised his arms and screamed. "Don't—no—no! I won't—I swear I won't!"

"Down!" Toby roared.

But panic was in Jake now. He seized Toby around the waist. "Make him stop—make him—"

Thrown off balance, Toby's hold on the steering sweep loosened. The handle flailed out of control. Something rammed into his head. Sky and sea tilted from their places. Then everything was spinning like a windmill and Toby was falling, falling. . . .

Salt water drove into his mouth and ears, stung his nose and eyes. Breath burning in his lungs, Toby thrashed wildly. Solid water poured over his head. Fighting to control his limbs, Toby forced them through remembered swimming strokes. He planed upward, broke through to air!

Hauling breath into his lungs, he looked around at the silent sea and open sky. There was a muffled shout, and then Toby caught sight of the long steering oar floating a good distance away. Someone was clinging to it.

Paddling deliberately to conserve his strength, Toby swam toward him, then paused, treading water.

It was Jake Underhill.

"If it weren't for you—" Toby began angrily, then broke off. He might have ended up in the ocean regardless of Jake. The man was a victim of his own fright, and now he was clutching the steering sweep desperately. When a wave washed over his head, he choked and sputtered. His eyes rolled fearfully, like those of a horse caught in a barn fire. Most whalemen could not swim, and Jake was no exception. Toby counted his own days in the country swimming hole as lucky ones. "Move your legs as if you're walking," he ordered sharply.

But Jake's efforts only drove him deeper. With a yell, he disappeared under the waves. Toby shoved the steering oar at the hands clawing above water, and Jake reappeared. He coughed for a long time. Finally he managed a question. "Boat stove?"

Toby had not thought of that. "Let's find out." He hauled a big breath into his lungs and loosed a long shout. He yelled again and again, listening carefully between shouts. But only the lap of waves and the gentle sigh of wind broke the vast silence.

Jake gasped, "Boats hull down—now. Just ye 'n' me in water."

"They'll find us," Toby said encouragingly. "Just hang on for an hour or two." The hollows between the waves began gathering shadow. Toby noticed the sun was quite low in the west. They had raised spouts in midafternoon. It would be night before the boats carried word of their accident to the *Rogue* and the whaling bark broke out her hook to begin searching for them.

Jake must have been thinking the same thing. "No telling what zigzag that whale took them boats on. Time one o' them cuts loose, they's Davy-knows-where from us. Reckon they'd try sighting a couple o' heads what's awash?"

Toby found that if he just rested his hands on the steering sweep, it would still float under Jake's weight and he himself could ease up somewhat in his constant treading. "We'll see the *Rogue*'s lights when she comes searching. Then we can yell our heads off."

"Not likely. He—" Jake must have relaxed his hold a moment for he abruptly slipped below the surface. Coming up gasping, he tightened his grip on the oar.

Toby said, "Move your legs."

Jake shook his head wearily. "Can't get the knack." He rested his cheek a moment on the loom of the oar, but a tiny dollop of water drove into his nose and he had to jerk his head upright. "They ain't going to be no search. Cap'n Flick means to kill me." His breathing was harsh, and his eyes were red-rimmed from salt water.

" 'Twas an accident," Toby said, half-afraid the man's mind was going. "He didn't get to change places with his steerer. And he hasn't lowered his boat in months, so he—"

"Nor he don't haul in close like ranking officer's got to," Jake said, his voice hoarse with salt and accusation. "I seen his boat comin' up when ye was fixing to dart. I seen how he worked it so's both boats'd get hooked, then he hangs back, tossing out line, so's our boat's leading. Get it? All he's got to do now is cross over back of us with his line. I can't hardly scrooch down out'n the way, and he means to saw my head off."

Toby turned on his back and floated, keeping one hand on the oar so he would not drift away from Jake, since two men are more easily found than one. He spoke soothingly, trying to calm the man. "Jake, I reckon the Captain treated you fairly fine this voyage. He wouldn't kill you."

"Fancy lot you know," Jake muttered darkly. "Reckon I pushed him a mite too far, though. But he ain't gonna get away with it." He choked and sputtered for several moments, and Toby guessed Jake had let his head fall forward into the water again. "Toby, listen! I tell ye I seen him do it. He was Third Mate then—"

Toby turned his head and saw Jake's eyes burning like

coals. Panic was gone now, and revenge was etched in his face.

"Ye didn't know I seen how yer uncle died, did ye?" Jake said between his teeth. "I was sogering that day, lying up on the afterhouse 'neath the mizzen boom. Don't matter do she gust a bit, sailors take their rest when they can. The Third, Peter Flick, he come up from below and goes to the starb'd bulwarks, next to the full oil casks at the lashrail. The *Rogue*'s rolling heavy then." Sea water lapped into Jake's face. Doggedly he shook it away, driving himself to continue his story. "Of a sudden, Mr. Flick jumps up on the railing, catching at the shrouds, and he yells, 'Blow—he blows!' and points to starb'd. I stand up to look. Higher than him, I was. And they *ain't no whales!*"

Toby remembered the *Grand Banks* hand who was at the wheel then. He had said the cry for whales had come from the deck, not from the lookout posted during the *Rogue*'s passage.

Jake was panting after his long speech. The wave shadows deepened. The broad empty sky was washed with gold from the lowering sun.

Jake had to pause between phrases, but he kept to the thread of his story. "So Cap'n Noah, he come a-storming up on deck. 'Where away?' he yells, and is making his way for'ard. The vessel pitches steep then, but just that 'xact same time as she heels to larboard, Mr. Flick jumps down from the rail beside the casks and I see the flash of a knife blade. That flash darts out, then back, and then the casks is loose, rolling over to the lee side, crushing Cap'n Noah."

Toby's grip on the oar tightened in anger and fear. "Are you certain? Maybe you only thought you saw the knife."

"Certain sure!" Jake barked a laugh. "I taxed him with it. When we was paid off in port, I hung about till I got him alone. Then I told him how I seen him do Cap'n Noah in. Reckon if'n we wasn't abovedecks, he'd of laid me out, too. Scared he was. Tried to put me off but I knows what I seen." Jake's grin at the recollection faded into bitterness. "Pushed him too far, maybe. Now he's turned the tables and 'tis me for Davy Jones."

"He admitted it—Peter Flick said he killed Captain Noah?" Toby's senses were spinning. "But why—why'd he do it?"

"Sure he did it, and he said so!" Jake insisted. "He never told me why he done it, though, and it never mattered to me. The long and short is I had an easy berth there for a spell—plenty o' money on leaves ashore, extra food when I liked, sogering half the time. There I am—me, from the fo'c'sle!—and every time I snicker at him or say something sly, Cap'n Flick, he turns scaredy white o' me! Aye, 'twas a grand time I had, the best voyage ever!"

"You crowed some in the fo'c'sle too," Toby could not resist adding. He had never liked Jake Underhill, and now, while the man told his wretched story, Toby's feelings were dragged from shock to pity to disgust. "Peter Flick is a murderer. You should have gone to the authorities!"

But Jake was dreaming of his lost glory. From time to time he mumbled an account of some infinitesimal victory which even now loomed large in his small life. He began to forget where he was, and to let go of the steering sweep, dropping briefly below the waves, to come up choking, and begin dreaming once more.

"Don't talk," Toby said. "Save your strength. Move your legs!"

It was useless. Night swept down upon them. There was no moon. The waves, breaking, made chevrons of cold white light. Jake was letting go of the sweep more frequently, swallowing a lot of water, getting sick on it. Toby tried holding him up, but soon his own strength began ebbing.

Once more floating on his back, one hand on the steering oar, Toby's thoughts were in a turmoil. Would the *Rogue* never come? Was Jake right in thinking Captain Flick had deliberately plotted his death? Did the plan include the death of Toby Clayton?

The black hours walked with measured stride.

The moon, when it finally edged up out of the east, shone on a floating oar that was empty but for Toby's hand.

He stared. He had not even known when Jake had gone down for the last time.

Then there were thumps and creaking. Voices called in blunt, foreign syllables. Light sprang into Toby's eyes and hands pulled him up out of the sea.

Just as Toby slipped into exhausted sleep in the bottom of the boat, he heard Ben and Alex's voices.

But he knew that was impossible.

 fourteen

An Answer in Glass

WHEN TOBY opened his eyes he saw a ship's lantern swinging gently on a hook overhead. Then Ben Valentine's features came into view, with Alex White's worried face hovering over his shoulder.

"Where—?"

Ben grinned. "You're aboard a Dutch trader, the barkentine *Kaatje Van Zandt*. It was one of her boats picked you up. Alex and me were along. Mr. Barksdale was in her other boat."

Toby levered himself up on one elbow and looked around. He was in a clean comfortable lower berth, one of several against the bulkheads. Half the bunks were neatly made, the others had tousled bedclothes, as if the watch below had been roused out.

Alex said, "This's 'prentice quarters 'midships. Lives fancy, these merchantmen, don't they? The Mate's in the main cabin, talking with Cap'n Van Zandt. Speaks English fair good, he do."

Toby looked out the deckhouse's lee porthole. A black sky was pricked with stars and the water was sousing along the *Kaatje*'s hull. "How'd the *Kaatje* come into this—and where's the *Rogue?*"

"The *Rogue*'s still back in her lagoon, cutting in and brightly lighted." Ben's voice was harsh. " 'Twas the lights that fetched up the *Kaatje Van Zandt*. She'd just been coming from trading in the Cook Islands, and knowing a whaler usually needs something, she hove to and sent a boat over. Captain Flick wasn't of a mind to buy stores. But Alex and me and the Mate saw our chance. Mr. Barksdale got that boat to carry us over, and then he talked Captain Van Zandt into cruising around for you and Jake Underhill. The Captain even put both his boats down. Right now I reckon we're beating back to the *Rogue*."

Alex added. "Ye're a sight lucky, Toby. Jake never made it. Mr. Barksdale's boat fished his body out'n the sea. Cap'n Van Zandt buried him proper 'neath the waves."

"He drowned." Toby swung his legs to the deck, sitting up. "He couldn't keep his head out of the water. I tried to help—" He looked at his friends. "Captain Flick meant for him to die. He planned the whole thing."

Ben's face darkened. " 'Twas you he tried to kill, Toby. The minute you was in the sea, Captain Flick sheered his boat off to port, taking his whaleline with him. At the same time Alex scrambled aft and shipped Stroke's oar for steering—we was still running, mind. Then Mr. Barksdale chopped our line."

Alex took up the tale. "By then we'd run maybe two, three mile since ye and Jake got tossed out the boat. But we rowed back and made a good search about till it started getting dark. Then we had to pull for the *Rogue*."

Ben spoke angrily. "Captain Flick's boat'd been in for some time, likely got towed near by the whale circling. He had them rigging for cutting-in. Mr. Barksdale was so mad he could hardly talk. He figured the *Rogue* should've run down to pick us up and look around for you and Jake."

Toby nodded. "I kept hoping to see her lights."

Alex snorted in contempt. "Cap'n Flick, he says it ain't worth hoisting sail over. Likely ye and Jake was dead when ye hit the water, and if ye ain't, ye're both drowned by now with nothing to hang onto. That's how 'twas when the *Kaatje* sent her boat over."

"There's something else, Toby." Ben seemed a little embarrassed. "On the way over to the *Kaatje* we told Mr. Barksdale about how you was half owner of the *Rogue*, and that's why Captain Flick wanted to kill you."

"Ben! That's to be kept secret!"

"Don't blame him none," said Alex. "We was so roiled up it kind of come out of itself. 'Sides, 'tis best Mr. Barksdale know what he's up against if'n he's going to have to stand 'tween the Old Man and one of the crew. We could do with a friend on the quarter-deck."

"We didn't say anything about the papers that Captain

Flick fixed up," Ben assured him. "Nor about the pearls. Say, Toby, I reckon now you're partners with your Aunt Prudence, ain't you?"

Toby nodded. "That's the way 'twill be when everything gets straightened out. Now let's not say anything more to Mr. Barksdale. We know Captain Flick stole my uncle's vessel, or at least half of her, but it'd be heavy weather trying to convince anybody without proof right to hand."

The door swung open and Mr. Barksdale came into the midship quarters. "Glad to see you awake, Toby." He sat down on a biscuit keg. "Boys, I've arranged to take passage on the *Kaatje* to Honolulu in the Sandwich Islands. Captain Van Zandt said he would let you three work your way there. We can all of us readily find berths, for this time of year there's upward of a hundred whalers in port. What d'you say?"

Toby glanced at his companions, and saw that they were thinking the same thing as he was, that the moment they left the *Rogue* Captain Flick would break out his hook and stand for New Bedford. "Thanks, Mr. Barksdale, but I reckon we're staying in the *Rogue.*"

The Mate frowned. "You're partners with Captain Flick, Toby. If you die, he owns the vessel entire. You'd be safer in a different whaler."

" 'Twas Jake Underhill he meant to die, sir," said Toby. "Jake saw him kill my uncle." He told them of those hours in the water, of Jake's spiteful tale, his bragging, and his final delirium.

The Mate's hands stiffened into fists as Toby finished. "If Jake had lived—I reckon there's no way now to prove murder. But maybe if you could show there'd been bad blood between Captain Noah and his Third Mate. . . ."

"Aye, sir, I'm on to something like that now," Toby said. "There's a banker in New Bedford who sees to my half of the vessel's business. When I get back to talk with him, everything will work out all right. But till then I've got to stick with the *Rogue* and keep Captain Flick in sight all the way back to Buzzard's Bay."

Alex White cleared his throat. "That's why we ain't fixing to go to Honolulu, thanking ye just the same, Mr. Barksdale."

Ben Valentine nodded in agreement.

The Mate rubbed his jaw. "It still seems to me that Captain Flick might be after you too, Toby. Way back in the Atlantic he had me put you in a whaleboat before you were really ready for that kind of work."

Ben added, "He got Toby to go down and reeve the head chain on the first whale we cut in."

Mr. Barksdale nodded. "Both were dangerous jobs for a green hand and Captain Flick had every right to expect a fatal accident. But none came, and when Jake Underhill went too far our last night in Bay of Islands, he likely figured to get rid of both of you at the same time. He ordered

Jake into my boat on Stroke Oar, and he said Toby was to dart that lowering. The Captain lowered, too, for the first time in months. Well, Toby, Jake's finned out, but you're still as spry as baleen. Captain Flick won't like that very much." He walked toward the 'midship companionway. Reaching the door, he paused. "I'll ask Captain Van Zandt to make for the *Rogue*. Reckon I'm staying in her, too."

During the hour of passaging it took to reach the *Rogue*, Toby, Ben, and Alex ate hugely of the meal sent them from the galley. Then by signs and gestures Toby asked for and received from one of the young midshipmen a pen and paper. He wrote to Mr. Giles Thaxter, explaining everything as clearly as possible, asking that the seal on the paper in the iron box be compared with the genuine ivory impression on the *Rogue*'s articles for Captain Noah's last voyage. This letter was given to Captain Van Zandt, with the hope that after a year or so of being handed on from vessel to port to traveler, it would ultimately reach New Bedford.

The Dutch barkentine stood off outside the lagoon. As they waited while the hands lowered one of her boats, Mr. Barksdale turned to Toby. "I'll keep my eye on you the best I can to see you come to no harm, lad. But I've got to mind Captain Flick's orders, and I can't treat you any different from before."

"If you did, sir, we'd both be worse off," Toby replied.

The *Rogue*'s deck was brightly lighted and slimy from

the cutting as Toby and his companions clambered aboard over the gunwale. Captain Flick, boarding knife in hand, stared aghast at them. Then, stiffly, he walked up to Toby. "Where's th' other one? W—where's Jake?" His hands clutched the swordlike knife, white against the gray steel.

The Mate spoke crisply, as if reporting from a mission. "Jake Underhill drowned, sir. The Dutchman committed his body to the sea all proper. I'm sending Toby below for a spell." He gestured to Alex and Ben. "You two, lay aft to your cutting stations."

"Aye, aye, sir."

The three moved off, but Toby felt pinned to the deck by Captain Flick's sunken staring eyes. The Captain licked his lips, and his voice seemed to come from a long way off. "You saw Jake drown? Were you with him—what'd he say?"

Toby felt clammy fingers closing about his spine and it seemed that once again he heard the high-pitched whine of the murderous towrope. When he answered, it was with absolute truth. "I didn't see Jake drown, sir." Forcing himself to move, he turned his back on the man holding the boarding knife. With legs that shook, he walked toward the fo'c'sle companion and the rest Mr. Barksdale had ordered for him.

During that week of cutting-in and boiling, Captain Flick hardly ever appeared on deck. And when all the oil was headed up in casks and the staves of baleen scraped and bundled, he broke out his anchor and put about for Samoa, though even as the *Rogue* reached north by a quarter east a pod of humpbacks came diving and blowing through the seas.

Captain Flick did not lower with the starboard boat again. Instead, he appointed his former harponier as header. When Toby, now the starboard boat's steerer, moved into steerage, he asked his new superior, "Do I have to call you Mister?"

A pleased light sprang into the header's eyes, but Cooper spoke up. "A header is a sort of betwixt and between. He's top man in steerage and in his boat, but he's no officer, seeing as he'd have trouble navigating a duck across a rain puddle. I wouldn't Mister him none 'less he gets to move into one o' the officers' staterooms aft."

"You can call me header for now," said the top man grandly. " 'Fore the voyage's out, I'll make Fourth Mate, you'll see."

They ran into flawing winds just off Pago Pago, but Captain Flick kept all canvas on, though they lost the fore-topgallant sail and fouled the gear of the flying jib. They fished sporadically through the Samoas, hoisting anchor and moving on for seemingly no reason. There were times when the Captain came up on deck to shout at any busy seaman whose pace did not suit him, and yet in slack times when there was not enough to keep the hands occupied, he would still not permit the traditional scrimshawing.

The Captain put about for the Cook Islands far to the southeast, and the rumor spread that they were on their way home with casks less than half filled. But days later, when they had nearly reached the islands, he canted the bark's head around once more, standing west for the Tongas.

Back where they had started humpbacking, Captain Flick drove the crew mercilessly, vowing not to hoist a sail until they were full up to the hatch covers with oil. Zachary's mild temper was rumpled. "And with sperm likely running 'long the Line by now. Drive us into th' Sailor's Rest, he do, with not 'nough dollars coming in to pay the slop chest by voyage's end."

There were two humpback calves left to cut in when Captain Flick ordered them towed out of the lagoon and turned loose. "It's sperm we're after," he declared from the quarter-deck. "No watch below until we finish boiling, then we're heading for the Line."

Sometime through the nightmare of boiling the Mate managed to secure a break for the men. Toby, Ben, and Alex made their way to the afterhouse, the coolest place in the vessel, since the Captain did not permit anyone to sleep ashore. Ben said with contempt, "Captain Flick's been losing his nerve ever since Toby come back from the dead."

Toby nodded in the dark. "He asked me again today if I saw Jake drown. I could say no, but I'm worried he might ask if we were together in the water."

"He ain't got the guts," Alex said with relish. "He figures Jake might've told Toby ever'thing 'fore he drowned, but if'n he was *certain* sure, Toby'd be dead this minute. As 'tis, Cap'n's just plain scared, fluking like a gallied whale. They say we're hoisting anchor for Buzzard's Bay tomorrow."

"It can't be soon enough to suit me," Toby muttered.

But the next day, as soon as the trypots were empty, the *Rogue* trimmed her yards, not for home but west for Fiji. Captain Flick ordered royals set for a fast passage, though the distance was fairly short and the wind was making up.

Toby, working with his gang in the top hamper, fought against the freshening wind. Far down the horizon clouds were massing into leaden sheets. Conscious of the rhythmic pounding of rising waves against the hull and driving up through the mast, Toby was glad when the royal was set and the gang made its way down the shrouds.

He had hardly followed Ben to the deck when a tremendous wind struck the vessel. Shivering, the *Rogue* laid far over. Toby and Ben grabbed the lashrail and hung on while all around yards slammed, lines thrashed, and sails thundered. The newly set royal tore with a shriek and Toby, glancing up, was startled at how quickly black clouds had driven over the vessel. Now spray dashed over the high starboard gunwale, wetting him and Ben to the bone. The *Rogue* tried to fight back to even keel but, though her masts rose a little higher to point toward the stormy sky, she still sloped sharply leeward.

The screaming wind mounted and solid seas began pouring over the starboard bulwarks, streaming over the deck to the lee scuppers where the water from time to time flooded back when the racing swell buried the larboard washports.

The storm had pounced so suddenly that men were just hanging on to keep from being washed about the deck. A man, Cooper it was, struggled here and there, shouting. He reached Toby and Ben and hung on beside them, water tugging at his legs as it crashed over the gunwale. "We're caught aback!" he yelled. "Mainmast is sprung and half the braces tore loose. Cap'n says we can't work ship." The vessel, her yards violently flung around and sails slanting against the masts, was driving her larboard quarter into the leaping seas.

Mr. Barksdale worked his way through the deepening gloom and driving spray, shouting orders. "Lay aloft! Get that canvas in! Clear that gear. You, there, tail onto that weather brace!" Reluctantly the hands fought their way to their stations. Toby caught the Mate's sleeve. "Sir, they say the vessel's given up to the sea!"

Mr. Barksdale shook his head. "Not that bad. We'll save her, but it needs work. Now get those braces in!"

Toby and Ben had hardly conquered a thrashing weather brace when the rain burst upon them. Slashing, stabbing, cutting, it drove down in such a torrent that nothing was visible beyond the reach of a hand. The two clung to the pinrail, washed by surging seas, beaten by the shrieking wind, lashed by the terrible rain.

After a while the downpour slackened. But then through a howling gale came a cry of terror. "Land! Land alee!"

Stunned, Toby and Ben stared across the deck over the lower lee railing at a long distant mound, rising black and horrible from the dark running seas. It was one of the Fijian out islands, and the *Rogue* was driving broadside for it.

Captain Flick bellowed through the storm. "Abandon ship!"

Toby's cry of protest was swallowed by the wind. He stared at the mizzenmast where the Captain and his Mates were clinging to the encircling fife rail. Mr. Barksdale raised his voice. "Captain Flick, we can club haul off that lee shore and wear ship around the island."

"The sails have gone, Mr. Barksdale!" In the gray storm light, the Captain's face was as white as the tattered canvas above.

The Second yelled, "I can double-reef the spanker. With that and a goose-winged fores'l—"

"Not a chance!" cried Captain Flick. "Swing the boats."

Toby saw the Third turn away to pass the word, and then suddenly the rain increased, charging down on men and vessel. Biting and slashing, the torrent shut out nearly all sight and sound. A sea leaped over Toby and Ben, sweeping them across the deck where they fetched up against the skylight. Before he could rise, Toby felt a foot drive into his side. "Out of my way!" cried Captain Flick, making his way aft along the skylight.

Toby fought to his feet and the Captain's eyes narrowed as he recognized him. Toby shouted against the wind, "Please, sir, you can't let the vessel go down like this!"

A vicious smile twisted the Captain's mouth. "Never fear, Clayton. We'll all make shore safely. As for the vessel, she's fully insured. Now stand aside!"

He thrust Toby back against the skylight and passed on to shelter inside the galley. Seamen scuttled through the scouring rain to the starboard boat falls. Toby knew he should join them. To be cast adrift in the same boat as Captain Peter Flick!

Another green sea thundered across the deck. Toby and Ben shielded their faces against the grill of the skylight. The lantern beneath the glass was dancing like a maniac, shooting its light around the empty cabin. Go Toby must, but not without finishing the task which had so far kept him aboard the *Rogue*.

Ben was yelling in his ear. "Come with the larboard boat! You're not safe in the Captain's."

"You go ahead, Ben, and never mind me! I have to get below!"

"Wh—what? Are you daft?" Then Ben's eyes showed comprehension. "Let that paper go down with the vessel!"

"Captain Flick might dash below the last minute and fetch it up. Leave me be, Ben!" Toby pulled out of his friend's grasp.

On hands and knees, pausing to crouch against the sweeping seas, Toby crawled across the wet slanting deck to the booby hatch. A sudden lift of the vessel helped him slide back the cover and he quickly scrambled below. The lantern had been dashed from its hook. In the dark he felt his way to the after bulwark, then thudded with his shoulder against the hooked door.

When it gave way, he crashed to the saloon deck. Quickly scrambling to his feet, Toby made his way around the dining table and into the Captain's stateroom. The crazily swinging lantern under the skylight clawed the room's darkness with a nervous finger of light. Toby seized the hinged panel and swung it down, rapidly sorting through the papers in the rack behind. His heart jumped in fear, and once again he went through the papers. But the second forgery, the perfect one Toby had seen months before, was missing!

The desk, then!

Staggering against the larboard list of the vessel, Toby went through the saloon and into the cabin. The wildly swinging lantern hurtled its rays from bulkhead to bulkhead. The desk chair was bolted in place, but the other had tumbled down the slanting deck. Navigational instruments were scattered from their places, and a framed chart of New Bedford harbor lay on the water-stained carpet, its glass broken.

Kneeling before the Captain's desk, Toby jerked open drawer after drawer, recklessly capsizing charts, pens, blotters, carved whale stamps, and other items over the desk. There was no sign of the paper he sought.

Then his hands closed over a ring of keys.

The vessel's safe—it would be in there!

As he rose to his feet, the bark lurched to larboard. The main companion door burst open under a sea that roared down the iron ladder. Deep in the hold timbers groaned and squealed and there was a distant snapping as some remote plank split under the twisting hands of the savage storm.

Toby crossed to the horsehair sofa against the stern bulkhead. The metal bindings of the two telescopes on the paneling above it glimmered as the lantern rays swept over them. The smooth brass bands of one and the elaborate fittings of the other glowed and vanished as the light came and went, came and went. . . .

He poised the first key before the safe's lock. Suddenly there seemed to leap to his eye the brass rectangle of a presentation plate. He stared at the ornately bound telescope, and words roared through his mind. "I read her name on the transom. The *Lucifer*. They give him a memento f'r saving them—a plate or something."

Toby wrenched the telescope from its hooks and in the vaulting lantern light he read the inscription. "The grateful passengers and crew of the ship *Lucifer.* . . ."

Lucifer—the devil! And this glass, this *eye*—

Toby raised the glass and *looked through the devil's eye.*

 fifteen

Between Wind and Water

THE LEAPING LANTERN cast a segment of yellow light through the lenses. A sharp-edged shadow cut off the rest of the circle. Something inside—

Quickly unscrewing the larger of the telescope's two lenses, Toby drew out a scroll of stiff paper. It crackled as he unrolled it.

There was Alex White's stamp on the bottom, the silhouette of a boatsteerer about to dart. And there Peter Flick's name, and Captain Noah Clayton's own signature. . . .

I, Peter Flick, Third Mate, acknowledge my guilt. . . .

The paper was a confession! Peter Flick had stolen six pearls from Captain Noah. The gems were again in their owner's possession and the thief was writing out a statement of his crime.

When Toby finished reading the confession, he again looked through the presentation glass. One of the lenses was badly cracked, distorting the image. His finger traced the dust down the barrel. The telescope, known to be broken, was never used. Captain Noah had kept it as a memento of the shipwreck.

No one could say whether Noah Clayton had intended to hand his Third Mate over to the authorities or use the written confession as a guarantee of Peter Flick's future good behavior. It was likely Captain Noah still had need of a Third Mate during the remaining weeks of the homeward passage, offering as it did a final chance of taking the last few whales which would bring the oil up to the hatches, thus greatly enhancing his reputation as a whaleman. But any hint of villainy spreading among crew or officers would utterly destroy the Third's authority. His crime had to be kept secret for a while.

And so for witness to the confession's signing, Captain Noah had chosen a man he knew could not read. And when the cry of whales sighted impelled him abovedecks, the Captain had first stepped to the stern bulkhead and had quickly hidden the confession in the telescope no one used. Then Noah Clayton had gone up to meet his death.

As the Captain's life ebbed, had he seen revenge in Peter Flick's face? Or the prospect of his once more seizing the pearls for himself? Toby would soon arrive in New Bedford to join the *Rogue*. If the confession could be got into his hands— "Tell Toby. . . ." But Peter Flick was listening keenly. "Tell Toby to—look through the devil's eye."

Noah Clayton could not know that Peter Flick would

fashion a document which, in effect, stole the pearls in order to make himself master of the *Rogue*. Nor that this would bar Toby from access to the "devil's eye."

The whaling bark slewed sharply. Toby lurched against the pull of the water dashing up from the lee. Quickly he rolled up the confession and began replacing it in the telescope.

"So that's where he hid it!"

Jamming the lens cap in place, Toby whirled, his grip on the telescope tightening.

Captain Flick was on the iron ladder, clutching the railing against the tilt of the vessel. "It was there all the time. Too bad I couldn't fix it for him to die before he passed the secret on to you." His hand moved like a snake and suddenly a sheath knife glinted in it. "You'll die for knowing about me, the way Jake Underhill had to die. This time I won't need to manufacture an accident. Your body'll go down with the vessel." Captain Flick made his way down the iron ladder, pausing in the sea water pooling at the bottom. "Hand over that glass!"

Toby thrust the telescope into his waistband. Captain Flick braced against the slanting deck as he started toward him. Toby measured the scant space between the murderer and the saloon doorway. "Sir, someone's bound to come down and fetch you up to your boat! He'll see—"

The Captain chuckled harshly. "They know I've gone below to fetch a few things—and will be up directly."

Toby's hand closed protectively over the telescope as, helpless, he watched Captain Flick advance toward him through the gloom. With his other hand Toby fumbled for his own sheath knife and his fingers brushed over the bunch of keys he had unwittingly dropped in his pocket.

There was a sharp crack, as of a pistol shot. The vessel quailed.

Toby cried, "That sounded like the mainmast split!"

Even in the gloom Captain Flick's face showed the white of fear. "She's going—going fast!"

"That forgery, sir," Toby said. "Still in the safe. Here're the keys!" He whipped them out of his pocket and tossed them in the forward larboard corner where they vanished in over a foot of water. "Hurry, before we sink!"

With a frenzied cry, the Captain turned and scuttled down the tilting deck.

Toby leaped across the main cabin, through the dining saloon, and into the dark steerage. Someone abovedecks had closed the booby hatch. He stumbled over a sea chest, dragged himself erect through the agony of a bruised leg, and made for the steerage ladder. Finding it, he clawed his way upward. His hands scraped on the hatch cover.

It was jammed shut.

His frantic fingers felt a piece of torn canvas caught between one runner and the cover. Tearing out his sheath knife, Toby hacked away, prying the runner loose. He was sliding the hatch cover open to the wind and rain when a yell and a rush of steps warned him of danger.

Captain Flick did not need the forgery. All he needed was for Toby Clayton to be dead.

Toby flung himself over the coaming and suddenly a wall of water reared over him. It thundered across the deck, dragging him along until he fetched up in the lee scuppers.

The rain charged down in torrents and the wild wind hurtled sea spray so that it bit into flesh like shot. Overhead, rigging whined, blocks rattled, and canvas boomed threateningly. Half choking, Toby saw Captain Flick coming out of the booby hatch. Beyond, he could dimly make out two or three men working the forward starboard boat falls. Toby recalled the "abandon ship" order. His old boat, the larboard, must be ready for launching.

He dragged himself aft along the larboard lashrail, turning his face down from the storm. Reaching the afterhouse ladder, he stumbled up to the roof. The wind moderated, the rain and spray lessened, and he found himself partly sheltered by a spanker which, surprisingly, was double-reefed into a neatly snugged triangle, its boom braced in trimly by taut lines. Shielding his face from the storm, Toby made out dark figures swarming in the rigging aloft. To leeward lay the rocky island, but the *Rogue*'s sternway toward it had slowed. The larboard boat was empty, still in her davits, her gripes keeping her fast. Was someone attempting to work ship?

An officer scrambled up the afterhouse ladder.

"Mr. Barks—"

But it was Captain Flick. He had lost his cap, his hair and beard streamed water, his eyes were red from salt spray. Yet he still loomed menacingly. He stroked the naked blade of his knife. "The telescope, Clayton. Give it to me and I'll let you live."

"D'you fear it'll get washed overboard with me?" Once more Toby drew his own knife, his feet seeking balance for the coming attack. Suddenly the wind flawed, the vessel shuddered, and he fell to his knees.

The Captain was on him in an instant. Toby felt the grate of the knife blade scoring the length of the telescope. He twisted free, rolling down the slant of the afterhouse roof, fetching up against the larboard boat's stern davit.

Captain Flick scuttled down the slope after him. But caution slowed him, and Toby was up, ready to face him. Captain Flick lunged. Toby flung up his arm, locking it with his enemy's. For several seconds they struggled, their blades whetting each other.

Then Toby turned his knife hand downward, deliberately accepting a cut on his forearm in order to drive his own blade into the Captain's shoulder.

His cry hard in Toby's ear, the wounded Captain sagged forward. Toby thrust him aside and stepped free, letting the man slide down against the davit to the planking. He lay without moving, his body rocking in the vessel's motion. Toby moved closer.

Suddenly a hand whipped out, snatched his ankle and tripped him to the roof. Toby had only a glimpse of a knife, and summoning all his strength, wriggled aside as the blade plunged into the planking only a handspan from his throat.

Blood welling from the Captain's shoulder mingled with the rain dropping into Toby's face as the man leaned over him to wrench his knife free.

Levering with his knees, Toby shot himself backward several feet, but the Captain dropped on his legs, imprisoning him once more.

Close beside them reached the spanker boom, straining under the wind. If Toby could just drag himself underneath it, the taut canvas would shield him from that deadly blade. He stretched his arms overhead, seeking a handhold.

Captain Flick now had his knife free. His grimace of pain had changed to a grin of victory.

Searching desperately, Toby's left hand found the edge of the afterhouse roof, and his knife hand felt a cable. The spanker sheet!

The Captain, still weighing down Toby's legs, raised his arm high, the knife shiny with death.

Blindly, Toby slashed the spanker sheet.

The line shrieked through the tackle blocks, and the boom roared out of control overhead, inches from Toby's face. Whipping leeward, it smashed into Captain Flick. The storm-swollen spanker hid him from view, but Toby heard the smash as the boom struck the larboard boat davits. He thought he heard a scream, but he could not be certain.

He turned over, still keeping flat against the afterhouse roof, and stared at the raging ocean. Black waves, crested with white, were working over something long and dark. It could have been a log. Or a man. It soon dipped and swirled out of sight.

Toby started as a hand dropped on his shoulder, but it was Mr. Barksdale's voice in his ear. "You all right? Boom strike you?"

"I'm all right, sir. Captain's washed overboard. I—" He watched a gang of men at the larboard boat davits. They had secured the boom and were now reeving a new tackle. Toby took a breath. "Mr. Barksdale, the Captain came after me—he meant to kill me, sir! I cut the spanker sheet, and the boom knocked him overboard." He found he was still clutching his knife. He dropped it.

The Mate picked it up and handed it back. "You'll need this if we're going to save the vessel, Toby. I've got a lot of hands volunteered to stay with the *Rogue*. Rigging still needs work, though. And—" His eyebrows rose in surprise. "Well, sir, you're my owner and superior now! What do you say?"

Toby started up to his feet. "I say break out the kedge

anchor and let's claw off that lee shoal, Mr. Barksdale!"

The Mate grinned. "Aye, sir! Now lay aloft and make yourself useful."

There was very little time for all that had to be done. The *Rogue* could not maneuver to save herself until the jammed gear had been overhauled. Toby, in the top hamper, saw that Acting Captain Barksdale had sent the starboard boat crew and some others ready to abandon ship back to work in spite of the driving rain and the wind that threatened to tear them all from their shaking perches aloft.

They slashed at fouled line and pieces of canvas. They coiled up loose and useless rigging. They freed blocks and tackles and cleared fair-leads and deadeyes. Not everything had to work, just four or five critical sails. But nothing must be allowed loose to jam the working gear at the vital moment. Toby labored frantically, forgetting the pain of his cut arm, one eye on the shoal stretching out its rocky arms toward the vessel.

At last Mr. Barksdale had Toby, Alex, and Ben break out a kedge anchor and make it fast to a warp in the port bow. The men took their stations. The reef was very close and the wind ever fought to drive them up on it.

"Down helm!"

Up swung the *Rogue,* directly into the mad wind! Already pounding waves were sending her sternmost for the shoal.

"Kedge overboard!"

Alex pushed it overboard, Toby and Ben tossing out bights of line. They felt the kedge hit bottom, drag and scrape, and then the anchor bit in and held!

The *Rogue's* sternway was checked against the warp, and she swung her bow starboard across the eye of the wind. Canvas thundered as, timed exactly right, sails hauled around on the port tack, free to do their work for the first time since the storm struck.

At the instant the vessel tugged under her drawing canvas, the Mate bellowed, "Part the line!" Toby snatched up the hatchet he had laid by. A single blow severed the warp, the overside section whipping down into the waves toward the anchor. The *Rogue,* cut loose, sprang ahead eagerly.

Rigging whined and stretched as Mr. Barksdale held the vessel close on the wind until the bark was well clear of the shoal. Then he paid off to run free around the rocks. He gave himself plenty of sea room against a change of the wind, and then hove to in safety for the night.

The port watch was sent below, and Toby did not even mind that his bunk was soaked from the booby hatch having been left open. The last thing he did before he lay down was to take the telescope from his waistband and put it in his sea chest.

Morning brought a flat sea and gentle winds. Mr. Barksdale assessed the damage to the *Rogue,* set the men to work, and then took Toby, Ben, and Alex down into the main cabin. Air drafted down through the broken skylight. The cabin's deck was bare, for the carpet had been taken up to dry in the sun. But the framed charts and navigational instruments had been hung back in place. And the ring of keys that had bought Toby precious moments the day before had been recovered and now lay on the desk.

Toby had brought along the presentation telescope. He went over the entire story of how Peter Flick had stolen, murdered, and deceived. He showed them the written confession, and from the safe took the second forgery Captain Flick had prepared.

"Aye, that's my true seal, that is," said Alex.

"We'll keep that paper to help prove the lengths he went to," said Mr. Barksdale. "Lock both documents in the safe, Toby. Well, lad, this is your vessel, and I'd be glad to know what plans you have for her."

Toby looked around the main cabin, and though it was storm battered, he felt the thrill of ownership. "Reckon there's no need to go back to New Bedford, sir. That letter of mine to Mr. Thaxter will reach him inside of a year or two. I can write him another, to tell him the end of it. As for the *Rogue*, she'll go whaling!"

Alex cleared his throat. "Can't go whaling without we got us a Captain, Toby."

Toby grinned. "Will you take on the job, Mr.—I mean, Captain Barksdale? That'll mean promotions all around.

The starboard boat header'll make a good Third."

Captain Barksdale nodded. "Glad to have the job, Toby. There's good sperm to be had up on the Line just now. I want Alex back in steerage—you can stay on as a preventer steerer and take a dart now and again. Mostly—" he reached for a sextant "—mostly I'll be pounding facts into your head. Ben, too, if he's a mind to learn navigation. Let's go above."

The *Rogue*'s bow lifted gently under the even pull of her head sails. The rigging was swarming with hands bending new canvas. Sails and a couple of helpers were cutting and stitching as fast as they could. The split main topgallant mast was being sent down. Toby and Ben watched, glad of the calm warmth of the Pacific sun, the friendly breeze, the sturdiness of the vessel they called home.

Captain Barksdale's voice roared from behind them. "Lay aft, you clods, or I'll fetch my knuckles to your heads!"

"Aye, aye, sir!"

They scampered to the roof of the afterhouse to find him with the sextant at his eye. "Now, lads, here's the trick of shooting the sun—"

There was adventure and danger to be had in the world between wind and water. And fortunes to be made and lost in whaling. Sometimes the sky would rage and the ocean storm. But there were to be times, too, like today, when rainbows arched in the spray of a bow wave under a tropical sun. And still to come, for as long as Toby followed the sea, was that tense, spine-tingling moment when the lookout brought every man to his feet with his hail:

"Blows—he blows, blows, *blo-o-ows!*"

Bibliography

ADAMS, HARRIET CHALMERS. "European Outpost: The Azores," *The National Geographic Magazine,* Vol. LXVII, No. 1, pp. 34–66, January, 1935.

ASHLEY, CLIFFORD W. *The Yankee Whaler,* Houghton Mifflin, Boston and New York, 1926.

BOSTELMANN, ELSE. "Whales, Porpoises, and Dolphins," *The National Geographic Magazine,* Vol. LXXVII, No. 1, pp. 41–80, January, 1940.

BRADFORD, GERSHOM. *A Glossary of Sea Terms,* 2nd edition, Dodd, Mead, New York, 1942.

BRADY, WILLIAM. *The Kedge Anchor; or Young Sailors' Assistant,* 3rd edition, privately published by the author, New York, 1848.

CHURCH, ALBERT COOK. *Whale Ships and Whaling,* W. W. Norton, New York, 1938, reissued in 1960.

COGGESHALL, GEORGE. "Voyage in the Pilot-boat Schooner Sea-Serpent, 1821–1822," pp. 309–351, in *Five Sea Captains: Their Own Accounts of Voyages Under Sail,* edited by Walter Teller, Atheneum, New York, 1960.

DELANO, AMASA. "Voyage in the Ship Perseverance, 1799–1802," pp. 23–101, in *Five Sea Captains: Their Own Accounts of Voyages Under Sail,* edited by Walter Teller, Atheneum, New York, 1960.

DULLES, FOSTER RHEA. *Lowered Boats, a Chronicle of American Whaling,* Harcourt, Brace, New York, 1933.

KELLOGG, REMINGTON. "Whales, Giants of the Sea," *The National Geographic Magazine,* Vol. LXXVII, No. 1, pp. 35–

90, January, 1940.

MITCHELL, CARLETON. "To Europe with a Racing Start," *The National Geographic Magazine,* Vol. CXIII, No. 6, pp. 758–791, June, 1958.

MOORE, W. ROBERT. "New Zealand 'Down Under,'" *The National Geographic Magazine,* Vol. LXIX, No. 2, pp. 165–218, February, 1936.

RICKETSON, DANIEL. *The History of New Bedford,* privately published by the author, New Bedford, 1858.

SCHOFIELD, JOHN, and SISSON, ROBERT F. "A New Volcano Bursts from the Atlantic," *The National Geographic Magazine,* Vol. CXIII, No. 6, pp. 735–757, June, 1958.

Sea Explorer Manual, seventh edition, Boy Scouts of America, New York, 1950.

STEVERS, MARTIN D., and PENDLEBURY, JONAS. *Sea Lanes: Man's Conquest of the Ocean,* Minton, Balch, New York, 1935.

TOBIEN, WILHELM. "Communications Hub of the Atlantic," *The National Geographic Magazine,* Vol. LXVII, No. 1, pp. 41–48, January, 1935.

VERRILL, A. HYATT. *The Real Story of the Whaler,* Appleton, New York and London, 1916.

VILLIERS, ALAN. *The Cruise of the Conrad,* Scribners, New York, 1937.

VILLIERS, ALAN. *The Way of a Ship,* Scribners, New York, 1953.

WALKER, HOWELL. "New Zealand, Pocket Wonder World," *The National Geographic Magazine,* Vol. CI, No. 4, pp. 419–460, April, 1952.

WHITING, E. M., and HOUGH, H. B. *Whaling Wives,* Houghton Mifflin, Boston, 1952.

The Author

Rita Ritchie, the author of five successful books for young people, says, "I cannot remember a time when I was not scribbling something." Born in Milwaukee, she majored in zoology at the University of Wisconsin and went on to work as a chemical technician and a research associate for a pharmaceutical company. Throughout high school and college, however, she continued to write, and before her high-school graduation had already had several feature articles published in a suburban newspaper. She also wrote short plays for a children's radio program on a Milwaukee station.

After college, Mrs. Ritchie began to write science-fiction stories, all of which had children in them. The children in these stories were so successful that Mrs. Ritchie soon turned to writing for and about young people. Her historical adventure tales include *The Year of the Horse, The Golden Hawks of Genghis Khan* and *Secret Beyond the Mountains,* all of which concern the Mongols at the time of Genghis Khan, *The Enemy at the Gate,* about the Turkish siege of Vienna in 1529, and *Ice Falcon,* an exciting story set in Iceland at the time of the Vikings.

Rita Ritchie lives with her husband, Jack, a free-lance writer, in an old farmhouse on Washington Island, Wisconsin. The couple has three young children.